THE RED HELL OF JUPITER

AND OTHER TALES FROM THE PULPS

THE RED HELL OF JUPITER

AND OTHER TALES FROM THE PULPS

PAUL ERNST

WILDSIDE PRESS

THE RED HELL OF JUPITER AND OTHER TALES FROM THE PULPS

Published in 2009 by *Wildside* Press LLC.

"The Raid on the Termites" originally appeared in *Astounding Stories*, June 1932. "The Planetoid of Peril" originally appeared in *Astounding Stories*, November 1931. "The Radiant Shell" originally appeared in *Astounding Stories*, January 1932. "Marooned Under the Sea" originally appeared in *Astounding Stories*, September 1930. "Death Ray" originally appeared in *Popular Detective*, September 1936. "The Red Hell of Jupiter" originally appeared in *Astounding Stories*, October 1931

CONTENTS

THE RAID ON THE TERMITES

CHAPTER I

The Challenge of the Mound

IT was a curious, somehow weird-looking thing, that mound. About a yard in height and three and a half in diameter, it squatted in the grassy grove next the clump of trees like an enormous, inverted soup plate. Here and there tufts of grass waved on it, of a richer, deeper color, testifying to the unwholesome fertility of the crumbling outer stuff that had flaked from the solid mound walls.

Like an excrescence on the flank of Mother Earth herself, the mound loomed; like an unhealthy, cancerous growth. And inside the enigmatic thing was another world. A dark world, mysterious, horrible, peopled by blind and terrible demons — a world like a Dante's dream of a second Inferno.

Such, at least, were the thoughts of Dennis Braymer as he worked with delicate care at the task of sawing into the hard cement of a portion of the wall near the rounded top.

His eyes, dark brown and rimmed with thick black lashes, flashed earnestly behind his glasses as they concentrated on his difficult job. His face, lean and tanned, was a mask of seriousness. To him, obviously, this was a task of vital importance; a task worthy of all a man's ability of brain and logic.

Obviously also, his companion thought of the work as just something with which to fill an idle afternoon. He puffed at a pipe, and regarded the entomologist with a smile.

To Jim Holden, Denny was simply fussing fruitlessly and absurdly with an ordinary "ant-hill," as he persisted in miscalling a termitary. Playing with bugs, that was all. Wasting his time poking into the affairs of termites — and acting, by George, as though those affairs were of supreme significance!

He grinned, and tamped and relit the tobacco in his pipe. He refrained from putting his thoughts into words, however. He knew, of old, that Denny was apt to explode if his beloved work were interrupted by a careless layman. Besides, Dennis had brought him here rather under protest, simply feeling that it was up to a host to do a little something or other by way of trying to amuse an old college mate who had come for a week's visit. Since he was there on sufferance, so to speak, it was up to him to keep still and not interrupt Denny's play.

The saw rasped softly another time or two, then moved, handled with surgeon's care, more gently — till at last a section about as big as the palm of a man's hand was loose on the mound-top.

Denny's eyes snapped. His whole wiry, tough body quivered. He visibly held his breath as he prepared to flip back that sawed section of curious, strong mound wall.

He snatched up his glass, overturned the section.

Jim drew near to watch, too, seized in spite of himself by some of the scientist's almost uncontrollable excitement.

Under the raised section turmoil reigned for a moment. Jim saw a horde of brownish-white insects, looking something like ants, dashing frenziedly this way and that as the unaccustomed light of sun and exposure of outer air impinged upon them. But the turmoil lasted only a little while.

Quickly, in perfect order, the termites retreated. The exposed honeycomb of cells and runways was deserted. A slight heaving of earth told how the insects were blocking off the entrances to the exposed floor, and making that floor their new roof to replace the roof this invading giant had stripped from over them.

In three minutes there wasn't a sign of life in the hole. The observation — if one could call so short a glimpse at so abnormally acting a colony an observation — was over.

Denny rose to his feet, and dashed his glass to the ground. His face was twisted in lines of utter despair, and through his clenched teeth the breath whistled in uneven gasps.

"My God!" he groaned. "My God — if only I could see them! If only I could get in there, and watch them at their normal living. But it's always like this. The only glance we're permitted is at a stampede following the wrecking of a termitary. And that tells us no more about the real natures of the things than you could tell about the nature of normal men by watching their behavior after an earthquake!"

Jim Holden tapped out his pipe. On his face the impatiently humorous look gave place to a measure of sympathy. Good old Denny. How he took these trivial disappointments to heart. But, how odd that any man could get so worked up over such small affairs! These bugologists were queer people.

"Oh, well," he said, half really to soothe Denny, half deliberately to draw him out, "why get all boiled up about the contrariness of ordinary little bugs?"

Denny rose to the bait at once. "Ordinary little bugs? If you knew what you were talking about, you wouldn't dismiss the termite so casually! These 'ordinary little bugs' are the most intelligent, the most significant and highly organized of all the insect world.

"Highly organized?" he repeated himself, his voice deepening. "They're like a race of intelligent beings from another planet — superior even to Man, in some ways. They have a king and queen. They have 'soldiers,' developed from helpless, squashy things into nightmare creations with lobster-claw mandibles longer than the rest of their bodies put together. They have workers, who bore the tunnels and build the mounds. And they have winged ones from among which are picked new kings and queens to replace the original when they get old and useless. And all these varied forms, Jim, they hatch at will, through some marvelous power of selection, from the same, identical kind of eggs. Now, I ask you, could you take the unborn child and make it into a man with four arms or a woman with six legs and wings, at will, as these insects, in effect, do with theirs?"

"I never tried," said Jim.

"Just a soft, helpless, squashy little bug, to begin with," Denny went on, ignoring his friend's levity. "Able to live only in warm countries — yet dying when exposed directly to the sun. Requiring a very moist atmosphere, yet exiled to places where it doesn't rain for months at a time. And still, under circumstances harsher even than those Man has had to struggle against, they have survived and multiplied."

"Bah, bugs," murmured Jim maddeningly.

But again Denny ignored him, and went on with speculations concerning the subject that was his life passion. He was really thinking aloud, now; the irreverent Holden was for the moment nonexistent.

"And the something, the unknown intelligence, that seems to rule each termitary! The something that seems able to combine oxygen from the air with hydrogen from the wood they eat and make necessary moisture; the something that directs all the blind subjects in their marvelous underground architecture; the something that, at will, hatches a dozen different kinds of beings from the common stock of eggs — what can it be? A sort of super-termite? A super-intellect set in the minute head of an insect, yet equal to the best brains of mankind? We'll probably never know, for, whatever the unknown intelligence is, it lurks in the foundations of the termitaries, yards beneath the surface, where we cannot penetrate without blowing up the whole mound — and at the same time destroying all the inhabitants."

Jim helped Denny gather up his scientific apparatus. They started across the fields toward Denny's roadster, several hundred yards away —

Jim, blond and bulking, a hundred and ninety pounds of hardy muscle and bone; Denny wiry and slender, dark-eyed and dark-haired. The sledge-hammer and the rapier; the human bull, and the human panther; the one a student kept fit by outdoor studies, and the other a careless, rich young time-killer groomed to the pink by the big-game hunting and South Sea sailing and other adventurous ways of living he preferred.

"This stuff is all very interesting," he said perfunctorily, "but what has it to do with practical living? How will the study of bugs, no matter how remarkable the bug, be of benefit to the average man? What I mean is, your burning zeal — your really bitter disappointment a minute ago — seem a bit out of place. A bit — well, exaggerated don't you know."

Denny halted; and Jim, perforce, stopped, too. Denny's dark eyes burned into Jim's blue ones.

"How does it affect practical living? You, who have been in the tropics many times on your lion-spearing and snake-hunting jaunts, ask such a thing? Haven't you ever seen the damage these infernal things can do?"

Jim shook his head. "I've never happened to be in termite country, though I've heard tales about them."

"If you've heard stories, you have at least in idea of their deadliness when they're allowed to multiply. You must have heard how they literally eat up houses and the furnishings within, how they consume telegraph poles, railroad ties, anything wooden within reach. The termite is a ghastly menace. When they move in — men eventually move out! And their appearance here in California has got many a nationally famous man half crazy. That's what they mean to the average person!"

Jim, scratched his head. "I didn't think of that angle of it," he admitted.

"Well, it's time you thought of something besides fantastic ways of risking your life. The termite has been kept in place, till now, by only two things: ants, which are its bitterest enemies, and constantly attack and hamper its development; and climatic conditions, which bar it from the temperate zones. Now suppose, with all their intelligence and force of organization — not to mention that mysterious and terrible unknown intelligence that leads them — they find a way to whip the ants once for all, and to immunize themselves to climatic changes? Mankind will probably be doomed."

"Gosh," said Jim, with exaggerated terror.

"Laugh if you want to," said Dennis, "but I tell you the termite is a very real menace. Even in its present stage of development. And the maddening thing is that we can't observe them and so discover how best to fight them.

"To get away from the light that is fatal to them, they build mounds like that behind us, of silicated, half-digested wood, which hardens into a sort of cement that will turn the cutting edge of steel. If you pry away some of the wall to spy on them, you get the fiasco I was just rewarded with. If you try to penetrate to the depths of the mystery, yards underground, by blowing up the termitary with gun powder, the only way of getting to the heart of things — you destroy the termites. Strays are seldom seen; in order, again, to avoid light and air-exposure, they tunnel underground or build tubes above ground to every destination. Always they keep hidden and secret. Always they work from within, which is why walls and boards they have devoured look whole: the outer shell has been left untouched and all the core consumed."

"Can't you get at the beasts in the laboratory?" asked Jim.

"No. If you put them into glass boxes to watch them, they manage to corrode the glass so it ceases to be transparent. And they can bore their way out of any wood, or even metal, containers you try to keep them in. The termite seems destined to remain a gruesome, marvelous, possibly deadly mystery."

He laughed abruptly, shrugged his shoulders, and started toward the car again.

"When I get off on my subject, there's no telling when I'll stop. But, Jim, I tell you, I'd give years of my life to be able to do what all entomologists are wild to do — study the depths of a termite mound. God! What wouldn't I give for the privilege of shrinking to ant-size, and roaming loose in that secretive-looking mound behind us!"

He laughed again, and slapped Holden's broad back.

"*There* would be a thrill for you, you bored adventurer! There would be exploration work! A trip to Mars wouldn't be in it. The nightmare monsters you would see, the hideous creations, the cannibalism, the horrible but efficient slave system carried on by these blind, intelligent things in the dark depths of the subterranean cells! Lions? Suppose you were suddenly confronted by a thing as big as a horse, with fifteen-foot jaws of steely horn that could slice you in two and hardly know it! How would you like that?"

And now in the other man's eyes there was a glint, while his face expressed aroused interest.

Every man to his own game, thought Denny curiously, watching the transformation. He lived for scientific experiments and observations having to do with termites. Holden existed, apparently, only for the thrill of pitting his brain and brawn against dangerous beasts, wild surroundings, or tempestuous elements. If only their two supreme interests in life could be combined. . . .

"How would I like it?" said Jim. "Denny, old boy, when you can introduce me to an adventure like that . . ." He waved his arm violently to complete the sentence. "What a book of travel it would make! 'The Raid on the Termites. Exploring an Insect Hell. Death in an Ant-hill. . . .'"

"Termitary! Termitary!" corrected Denny irritably.

"Whatever you want to call it," Jim conceded airily. He dumped the apparatus he was carrying into the rear compartment of the roadster. "But why speak of miracles? Even if we were sent to a modern hand laundry, we could hardly be shrunk to ant-size. Shall we ramble along home?"

CHAPTER II

The Pact

"WHAT are we going to do to-night?" asked Jim.

Dennis looked quizzically at his big friend. Jim was pacing restlessly up and down the living room of the bachelor apartment, puffing jerkily at his eternal pipe. Dennis knew the symptoms. Though he hadn't seen Jim for over a year, he remembered his characteristics well enough.

Some men seem designed only for action. They are out of step with the modern era. They should have lived centuries ago when the world was more a place of physical, and less of purely mental, rivalry.

Jim was of this sort. Each time he returned from some trip — to Siberia, the Congo, the mountainous wilderness of the Caucasus — he was going to settle down and stop hopping about the globe from one little-known and dangerous spot to another. Each time, in a matter of weeks, he grew restless again, spoiling for action. Then came another impulsive journey.

He was spoiling for action now. He didn't really care what happened that evening, what was planned. His question was simply a bored protest at a too tame existence — a wistful hope that Denny might lighten his boredom, somehow.

"What are we going to do to-night?"

"Well," said Denny solemnly, "Mrs. Van Raggan is giving a reception this evening. We might go there and meet all the Best People. There is a lecture on the esthetics of modern art at Philamo Hall. Or we can see a talkie —"

"My Lord!" fumed Jim. Then: "Kidding aside, can't you dig up something interesting?"

"Kidding aside," said Dennis, in a different tone, "I have dug up something interesting. We're going to visit a friend of mine, Matthew Breen. A young man, still unknown, who, in my opinion, is one of our greatest physicists. Matt is a kind of savage, so he may take to you. If he does — and if he's feeling in a good humor — he may show you some laboratory stunts that will afford you plenty of distraction. Come along — you're wearing out my rugs with your infernal pacing up and down!"

MATT Breen's place was in a ratty part of the poorer outskirts of town; and his laboratory was housed by what had once been a barn. But place and surroundings were forgotten at sight of the owner's face.

Huge and gaunt, with unblinking, frosty gray eyes, looking more like an arctic explorer than a man of science, Matt towered over the average man and carelessly dominated any assembly by sheer force of mentality. He even towered a little over big Jim Holden now, as he absently shook hands with him.

"Come in, come in," he said, his voice vague. And to Denny: "I'm busy as the devil, but you can watch over my shoulder if you want to. Got something new on. Great thing — though I don't think it'll have any practical meaning."

The two padded after him along a dusty hallway, up a flight of stairs that was little more than a ladder, and into the cavernous loft of the old barn which had been transformed into a laboratory.

Jim drew Denny aside a pace or two. "He says he's got something new. Isn't he afraid to show it to a stranger like me?"

"Afraid? Why should he be?"

"Well, ideas do get stolen now and then, you know."

Denny smiled. "When Matt gets hold of something new, you can be sure the discovery isn't a new kind of can-opener or patent towel-rack that can be 'stolen.' His ideas are safe for the simple reason that there probably aren't more than four other scientists on earth capable of even dimly comprehending them. All you and I can do — whatever this may turn out to be — is to watch and marvel."

* * * *

MATT, meanwhile, had lumbered with awkward grace to a great wooden pedestal. Cupping down over this was a glass bell, about eight feet high, suspended from the roof.

Around the base of the pedestal was a ring of big lamp-affairs, that looked like a bank of flood-lights. The only difference was that where flood-lights would have had regular glass lenses to transmit light beams, these had thin plates of lead across the openings. Thick copper conduits branched to each from a big dynamo.

Matt reached into a welter of odds and ends on a bench, and picked up a tube. Rather like an ordinary electric light bulb, it looked, save that there were no filaments in the thin glass shell. Where filaments should have been there was a thin cylinder of bluish-gray metal.

"Element number eighty-five," said Matt in his deep, abstracted voice, pointing at the bluish cylinder. "Located it about a year ago. Last of the missing elements. Does strange tricks when subjected to heavy electric current. In each of those things that look like searchlights is one of these bulbs."

He laid down the extra tube, turned toward a door in the near wall, then turned back to his silent guests again. Apparently he felt they were due a little more enlightenment.

"Eighty-five isn't nearly as radioactive as the elements akin to it," he said. Satisfied that he had now explained everything, he started again toward the door.

As he neared it, Dennis and Jim heard a throaty growling, and a vicious scratching on the wooden panels. And as Matt opened the door, a big mongrel dog leaped savagely at him!

Calmly, Matt caught the brute by the throat and held it away from him at arm's length, seeming hardly to be aware of its eighty-odd pounds of struggling weight. Into Jim's eyes crept a glint of admiration. It was a feat of strength as well as of animal management; and, himself proficient in both, Jim could accord tribute where it was due.

"You came just as I was about to try an experiment on the highest form of life I've yet exposed to my new rays," he said, striding easily toward the glass bell with the savage hound. "It's worked all right with frogs and snakes — but will it work with more complex creatures? Mammalian creatures? That's a question."

Denny forbore to ask him what It did, how It worked, what the devil It was, anyway. From his own experience he knew that the abstraction of an experimenter insulates him from every outside contact. Matt, he realized, was probably making a great effort to remain aware that they were there in the laboratory at all; probably thought he had explained in great detail his new device and its powers.

Vaguely wrapped in his fog of concentration, Matt thrust the snarling dog under the bell, which he lowered quickly till it rested on the pedestal-floor and ringed the dog with a wall of glass behind which it barked and growled soundlessly.

Completely preoccupied again, Matt went to a big switch and threw it. The dynamo hummed, raised its pitch to a high, almost intolerable keening note. The ring of pseudo-searchlights seemed in an ominous sort of way to spring into life. The impression must have been entirely imaginary; actually the projectors didn't move in the slightest, didn't even vibrate. Yet the conviction persisted in the minds of both Jim and Dennis that some black, invisible force was pouring down those conduits, to be sifted, diffused, and hurled through the lead lenses at the dog in the bell.

Thrilled to the core, not having the faintest idea what it was they were about to see, but convinced that it must surely be of stupendous import, the two stared unwinkingly at the furious hound. Matt was staring, too; but his glance was almost casual, and was concentrated more on the glass of the bell than on the experimental object.

The reason for the direction of his gaze almost immediately became apparent. And as the reason was disclosed, Dennis and Jim exclaimed aloud in disappointment — at the same time, so intense was their nameless suspense, not knowing they had opened their mouths. It appeared that for yet a little while they were to remain in ignorance of the precise meaning of the experiment.

The glass of the bell was clouding. A swirling, milky vapor, not unlike fog, was filling the bell from top to bottom.

The dog, rapidly being hidden from sight by the gathering mist, suddenly stopped its antics and stood still in the center of the bell as though overcome by surprise and indecision. Motionless, staring vacantly, it stood there for an instant — then was concealed completely by the rolling vapor.

But just before it disappeared, Jim turned to Denny in astonishment, to see if Denny had observed what he had; namely, that the fog seemed not to be gathering from the air penned up in the bell, but in some strange and rather awful way to be exuding *from the body of the dog itself!*

The two stared back at the bell again, neither one sure he had been right in his impression. But now the glass was entirely opaque. So thick was the vapor within that it seemed on the point of turning to a liquid. Inside, swathed in the secrecy of the fleecy folds of mist — what was happening to the dog? The two men could only guess.

Matt glanced up at an electric clock with an oversized second hand. His fingers moved nervously on the switch, then threw it to cut contact. The dynamo keened its dying note. A silence so tense that it hurt filled the great laboratory.

All eyes were glued on the bell.

The thick vapor that had been swirling and crowding as if to force itself through the glass, grew less restive in motion. Then it began to rise, ever more slowly, toward the top.

More and more compactly it packed itself into the arched glass dome, the top layers finally resembling nothing so much as cloudy beef gelatin. And now these top layers were solidifying, clinging to the glass.

Meanwhile, the bottom line of the vapor was slowly rising, an inch at a time, like a shimmering curtain being raised from a stage floor. At last ten inches showed between the pedestal and the swaying bottom of the almost liquid vapor. Jim and Denny stooped to peer under the blanket of cloud. The dog! In what way had it been affected?

Again they exclaimed aloud, involuntarily, unconsciously.

There was no dog to be seen.

WITH about fourteen clear inches now exposed, they looked a second time, more intently. But their first glance had been right. The dog was gone from the bell. Utterly and completely vanished! Or so, at least, they thought at the moment.

The rising and solidifying process of the vapor went on, while Dennis and Jim stood, almost incapable of movement, and watched to see what Breen was going to do next.

His next move came in about four minutes, when the crowding vapor had at last completely come to rest at the top of the dome like a deposit of opaque jelly. He stepped to the windlass that raised the bell, and turned the handle.

Immediately the two watchers strode impulsively toward the exposed pedestal floor.

"Wait a minute," commanded the scientist, his eyes sparkling with almost ferocious intensity. The two stopped. "You might step on it," he added, amazingly.

He caught up a common glass water tumbler, and cautiously moved to the edge of the platform. "It may be dead, of course," he muttered. "But I might as well be prepared."

Wonderingly, Jim and Dennis saw that he was intently searching every square inch of the pedestal flooring. Then they saw him crawl, like a stalking cat, toward a portion near the center — saw him clap the tumbler, upside down, over some unseen thing. . . .

"Got him!" came Matt's deep, fuzzy voice. "And he isn't dead, either. Not by a long way! Now we'll get a magnifying glass and study him."

Feeling like figures in a dream, Jim and Dennis looked through the lens with their absorbed host.

Capering about under the inverted tumbler, like a four-legged bug — and not a very large bug, either — was an incredible thing. A thing with a soft, furry coat such as no true insect possesses. A thing with tiny, canine jaws, from which hung a panting speck of a tongue like no bug ever had.

"Yes," rumbled Matt, "the specimen is far indeed from being dead. I don't know how long it might exist in so microscopic a state, nor whether it has been seriously deranged, body or brain, by the diminishing process. But at least — it's alive."

"My God!" whispered Dennis. And, his first coherent sentence since the physicist had thrown the switch: "So this — *this* — is the overgrown brute you put under the bell a few minutes ago! This eighth-of-an-inch thing that is a miniature cartoon of a dog!"

Jim could merely stare from the tumbler and the marvel it walled in, to the man who had worked the miracle, and back to the tumbler again.

Denny sighed. "That thick, jellylike substance in the top of the bell," he said, "what is it?"

"Oh, that." The miracle worker didn't lift his eyes from the tumbler and the very much alive and protesting bit of life it housed. "That's the dog. Rather, it's practically all of the dog save for this small residue of substance that clothes the vital life-spark."

Jim dabbed at his forehead and found it moist with sweat. "But how is it done?" he said shakily.

"With element eighty-five, as I told you," said Breen, most of whose attention was occupied by a new stunt he was trying: he had cut a microscopic sliver of meat off a gnawed bone, and was sliding it under the glass. Would the dog eat? Could it . . . ?

It could, and would! With a mighty bound, that covered all of a quarter of an inch, the tiny thing leaped on the meat and began to gnaw wolfishly at it. The effect was doubly shocking — to see this perfect little creature acting like any regular, full-sized dog, although as tiny as a woman's beauty spot!

"Marvelous stuff, eighty-five," Matt went on. "Any living thing, exposed to the lead-filtered emanations it gives off when disintegrated electrically to precisely the right degree, is reduced indefinitely in size. I could have made that dog as small as a microbe, even sub-visible perhaps, if I chose. Curious. . . . Maybe the presence of eighty-five in minute quantities on earth is all that has kept every living thing from growing indefinitely, expanding gigantically right off the face of the globe. . . ."

But now Dennis was hardly listening to him. A notion so fantastic, so bizarre that he could not at once grasp it fully, had just struck him.

"Listen," he said at last, his voice so hoarse as to be almost unrecognizable, "listen — can you reverse that process?"

Matt nodded, and pointed to the viscous deposit in the dome of the bell. "The protoplasmic substance is still there. It can be rebuilt, remolded to its original form any time I put the dog back in the bell and let the particles of eighty-five, which are suspended in the vacuum tubes, settle back into their original, inert mass. You see, there is such a close affinity —"

Dennis cut him short almost rudely. It wasn't causes, marvelous though they might be, that he was interested in; it was results.

"Would you dare . . . that is . . . would you like to try that experiment on a human being?"

Now for once the inventor's entire interest was seized by something outside his immediate work. He stared open-mouthed at Dennis.

"Would I?" he breathed. "Would I like . . ." He grunted. "Such a question! No experiment is complete till man, the highest form of all life, has been subjected to it. I'd give anything for the chance!" He sighed explosively. "But of course that's impossible. I could never get anyone to be a subject. And I can't have it tried on myself because I'm the only one able to handle my apparatus in the event that anything goes wrong."

"But — would you try it on a human being if you had a chance?" persisted Denny.

"Hah!"

"And could you reduce a human being in stature as radically as you did the dog? For example, could you make a man . . . ant-size?"

Matt nodded vigorously, eyes fairly flaming. "I could make him even smaller."

Dennis stared at Jim. His face was transfigured. He shook with nervous eagerness. And Jim gazed back at Dennis as breathlessly and as tensely.

"Well?" said Dennis at last.

Jim nodded slowly.

"Yes," he said. "Of course."

And in those few words two men were committed to what was perhaps the strangest, most deadly, and surely the most unique, adventure the world has yet known. The improbable had happened. A man who lived but for dangers and extraordinary action, and a man who would have gambled his soul for the scientist's ecstasy of at last learning all about a hidden study — both had seen suddenly open up to them a broad avenue leading to the very pinnacle of their dreams.

CHAPTER III

Ant-Sized Men

NEXT morning, at scarcely more than daybreak, Jim and Denny stood, stripped and ready for the dread experiment, beside Matthew Breen's glass bell. The night, of course, had been sleepless. Sleep? How could slumber combat the fierce anticipations, the exotic imaginings, the clanging apprehensions of the two?

Most of the night had been spent by Denny in dutifully arguing with Jim about the advisability of his giving up the adventure, in soothing his conscience by presenting in all the angles he could think of the risks they would run.

"You'll be entering a different world, Jim," Denny had said. "An unimaginably different world. A terrible world, in which you'll be a naked, soft, defenseless thing. I'd hate to bet that we'd live even to reach the termitary. And once inside that — it's odds of seven to one that we'll never get out again."

"Stow it," Jim had urged, puffing at his pipe.

"I won't stow it. You may think you've run up against dangers before, but let me tell you that your most perilous jungle is safe as a church compared to the jungle an ordinary grass plot will present to us, if, as we plan, we get reduced to a quarter of an inch. I'm going in this with a mission. To me it's a heaven-sent opportunity — one I'm sure any entomologist would grab at. But you, frankly, are just a fool —"

"All right," Jim had cut in, "let it go at that. I'm confirmed in my folly. You can't argue me out of it, so don't try any more. Now, to be practical — have you thought of any way we could arm ourselves?"

"Arm ourselves?" repeated Dennis vaguely.

"Yes. It's a difficult problem. The finest watch-maker couldn't turn out a working model of a gun that could be handled by a man a quarter of an inch tall. At the same time I have no desire to go into this thing bare-handed. And I think I know something we can use."

"What?"

"Spears," said Jim with a grin. "Steel spears. They make steel wire, you know, down to two-thousandths of an inch and finer. Probably our friend has some in his laboratory. Now, if we grind two pieces about a quarter of an inch long off such a wire, and sharpen the ends as well as we can, we'll have short spears we could swing very well.

"Then, there's the matter of clothes." He grinned again. "We'll want a breech clout, at least. I propose that we get the sheerest silk gauze we can find, and cut an eighth-inch square apiece to tie about our middles after the transformation."

He slapped his fist into his palm. "By George! Such talk really begins to bring it home. Two men, clad in eighth-inch squares of silk gauze, using bits of almost invisibly fine steel wire as weapons, junketing forth into a world in which they'll be about the smallest and puniest things in sight! No more lords of creation, Denny. We'll have nothing but our wits to carry us through. But they, of course, will be supreme in the insect world as they are in the animal world."

"Will they be supreme?" Denny said softly. That unknown intelligence — that mysterious intellect (super-termite?) that seemed to rule each termite tribe, and which appeared so marvelously profound! "I wonder. . . ."

Then he, in his turn, had descended to the practical.

"You've solved the problem of weapons and clothing, Jim," he said, "and now for my contribution." He left the room and came back in a few minutes with something in his hands. "Here are some shields for us.

"Oh, not pieces of steel armor. Shields in a figurative more than a literal sense."

He set down a small porcelain pot, and opened it. Within was a repulsive-looking, whitish-brown paste.

"Ground-up termites," he explained. "If we're to go wandering around in a termitary, we've got to persuade the inmates that we're friends, not foes. So we'll smear ourselves all over with this termite-paste before ever we enter the mound."

"Clever, these supposedly impractical scientists," murmured Jim, with a lightness that did not quite succeed in covering his real admiration of the shrewdness of the thought.

And now they stood in front of Breen's glass bell, with Breen beside them all eagerness to begin the experiment.

"What am I supposed to do after I've reduced you to the proper size?" he asked.

"Take us out to Morton's Grove, to the big termitary you'll find about a quarter of a mile off the road," said Denny. "Set us down near the opening to one of the larger termite tunnels. Then wait till we come out again. You may have to wait quite a while — but that isn't much to ask in return for our submission to your rays."

"I'll wait a week, if you wish. Let's see, what had I better carry you in?"

It was decided — with a lack of forethought later to be bitterly regretted — that an ordinary patty-dish of the kind in which restaurants serve butter, would make as good a conveyance as anything else.

Matt got the patty-dish and placed it on the pedestal floor, tipping it on edge so Jim and Denny would be able to climb into it unaided (he wouldn't dare attempt to lift bodies so small for fear of mortally injuring them between thumb and forefinger). Into the patty-dish, so they could be readily located, were placed the bits of wire, the tiny fragments of silk gauze to serve as breech clouts, and a generous dab of termite-paste; and the two men stepped inside the glass dome to share the fate that, the night before, had been the dog's.

The bell was lowered around them. They watched the inventor step to the switch and pull it down. . . .

At first there was no sensation whatever. Almost with incredulity, they watched the glass walls cloud, realized that the fogging vapor was formed of exudations from their own substance. Then physical reaction set in.

The first symptom was paralysis. With the vapor wreathing their heads in dense clouds, they found themselves unable to move a muscle. The paralysis spread partially to the involuntary muscles. Heart action was retarded enormously; and they ceased almost entirely to breathe. In spite of the cessation of muscular functioning, however, they were still conscious in a vague way. Conscious enough, at all events, to go through a hell of agony when — second and last stage — every nerve in their bodies seemed of a sudden to be rasped with files, and every tiny particle of their flesh jerked and twitched as if to break loose from the ever-shrinking skin.

TIME, of course, was completely lost sight of. It might have been ten hours, or five minutes later when they realized they were still alive, still standing on their own feet, and now able to breathe and move. The spell of rigidity had been broken; nerves and muscles functioned smoothly and painlessly again. Also they were in clear air.

"I guess the experiment didn't work," Dennis began unsteadily. But then, as his eyes began to get accustomed to his fantastically new, though intrinsically unchanged surroundings, he cried aloud.

The experiment *had* worked. No doubt of that! And they were in a world where all the old familiar things were new and incredible marvels.

"What can be the nature of this stuff we're standing on?" wondered Jim, looking down.

Following his gaze, Denny too wondered for an instant, till realization came to him. "Why, it's ordinary wood! Just the wood of the pedestal platform!"

But it didn't seem like wood. The grain stood out in knee-high ridges in all directions to the limit of visibility. It was like a nightmare picture of a frozen bad-lands, split here and there by six-feet-broad, unfathomable chasms — which were the cracks in the flooring.

"Where's the patty-dish?" queried Jim.

Dennis gazed about. "We were standing right over it when the reducing process started. . . . Oh, there it is!"

Far off to the right an enormous, shallowly hollowed plateau caught their eyes. They started toward it, hurdling the irregular ridges, leaping across the dizzy chasms.

The tiny dish had been tipped on edge — but when they reached it they found its thickness alone a daunting thing.

"It's a pity Matt didn't select a thinner kind of china," grumbled Dennis; gazing at the head-high wall that was the edge of the plate. "Here — I'll stand on your shoulders, and then give you an arm up. Look out — it's slippery!"

It was. Their feet slid out from under them on the glazed surface repeatedly. It was with the utmost effort that they finally made their way to the center of the shallow plateau.

There, lying beside two heaps of coarse cloth and a mound of horrible-smelling stuff that he recognized as the dab of termite-paste, they saw two glistening steel bars. About five feet long, they seemed to be, and half an inch in diameter. The wire-ends which, a few moments ago, they had been forced to handle with tweezers for fear of losing!

Jim picked one up and drew it back for a pretended spear-thrust. He laughed, vibrantly, eagerly.

"I'm just beginning to realize it's really happened, and that the hunt has started. Bring on your bugs!"

Dennis stooped and picked up his spear. It was unwieldy, ponderous, the weight of that long, not-too-thin steel bar. Jim's great shoulders and heavy arms were suited well enough to such a weapon; but Dennis could have wished that his were some pounds lighter.

They turned their attention to the evil-smelling hill of termite-ointment. With many grimaces, they took turns in smearing each other from head to feet with the repulsive stuff. Then they knotted about them the yard-square pieces of fabric — once sheer silk gauze, now cloth as stiff and cumbersome as sail-cloth. They faced each other, ready for their trip.

The heavens above them, trailing up and up into mysterious darknesses, suddenly became closer and sparkled with a diamond sheen. Stretching off and up out of sight was a mountainous column that might conceivably be a wrist.

"Matt's looking at us through a magnifying glass," concluded Denny.

Abruptly the ridged bad-lands about them began to vibrate. Thunder crashed and roared around their ears.

"He's trying to say something to us," said Denny, when the awful din had ceased. "Oh, Matt — we're ready to go!"

Jim echoed his shout. Then Denny snorted. "Fools! Our voices are probably pitched way above the limit of audibility. He can't hear us any more than we can understand him!"

They gazed at each other. More than anything else that had happened, this showed them how entirely they were cut off from their old world. Truly, in discarding their normal size, they might as well have been marooned on another planet!

A tremendous, pinkish-gray wall lowered near them, split into segments, and surrounded their plateau. The plateau was lifted — with a dizzy swiftness that made their stomachs turn.

With sickening speed the plateau moved forward. The texture of the heavens above them changed. The sun — the one thing in their new universe that seemed unchanged in size and aspect — shone down on them. The plateau came jarringly to rest. Great cliffs of what seemed black basalt gleamed high over them.

Matt had carried them out of the building, and had set the patty-dish on the black leather seat of his automobile.

There was a distant thundering, as though all the worlds in the universe but Earth were being dashed to pieces. That was the motor starting. And then, as the car moved off, Jim and Dennis realized their mistake in choosing a patty-dish to ride in!

In spite of the yielding leather cushion on which their dish was set, the two quarter-inch men were hurled this way and that, jounced horribly up and down, and slid headlong from one end of the plateau to the other as the automobile passed over the city streets. Impossible to stand. They could only crouch low on the hard glazed surface, and try to keep from breaking legs and arms in the worst earthquake it is possible to imagine. Anyone who has ever seen two bugs ill-advisedly try to walk across the vibrating hood of an automobile while the motor is running, will have some idea of the troubles that now beset Dennis and Jim.

"The ass!" groaned Jim, in a comparatively quiet spell. "Why doesn't he drive more carefully?"

"Probably," groaned Denny, "he's doing the best he can."

Probably! All that was left them was conjecture. They could only guest at what was happening in the world about them!

Matthew Breen's face and body were lost in sheer immensity above them. They knew they were riding in a car; but they couldn't see the car. All they could see was the black cliff that was the seat-cushion behind them. The world had disappeared — hidden in its bigness; the world, indeed, was just at present a patty-dish.

Somehow they endured the ride. Somehow they avoided broken bones, and were only shaken up and bruised when the distant roar of the motor ceased and the wind stopped howling about their ears.

"Well, we're here," said Dennis unsteadily. "Now for the real —"

His words were stopped by the sudden rising of the plateau. Again they felt the poignantly exaggerated, express-elevator feeling, till the plateau finally came to rest.

The crashing thunder of Matt's voice came to them, words utterly indistinguishable. The saucer was tipped sideways. . . .

Doubtless Matt thought he was acting with extreme gentleness; but in fact the dish was tilted so quickly and so without warning that Jim and Dennis slid from its center, head over heels, to fall over the edge and land with a bump on the ground. Their spears, sliding after, narrowly missed impaling them.

Once more came the distant crashing of Matt's voice. Then there was silence. Their gigantic protector, having dumped them unceremoniously into the grass of Morton's Grove, had ushered them squarely into the start of their insane adventure. From now on their fate belonged to them alone.

CHAPTER IV
The Raid

BEWILDEREDLY, they looked around them.

Ahead of them, barely to be seen for the trunks of giant trees intervening, was a smoothly-rounded mountain. Majestic and aloof it soared, dwarfing all near it — the termitary which, yesterday, had been but waist-high. There was their eventual goal; but meanwhile their immediate surroundings roused their greater interest — and all their alertness!

When Dennis had said they would find a common grass plot a wild and exotic jungle, he had spoken perhaps more truly than he knew. At any rate, the jungle they now found themselves in was something to exceed man's wildest dreams.

Far over their heads towered a wilderness of trees. But such trees! Without branches, shooting up and over in graceful, tangling curves, their trunks oddly flat and ribbonlike and yellow-green. It was impossible to look on them as grass stems.

Here and there the trees had fallen, presenting a tangled wilderness of leathery, five-foot-wide strips. Webs of roots, tough and gnarled, whitish in color, curled in all directions to catch the feet and baffle the eye. It was an appalling underbrush. And it was an underbrush, moreover, in which there was plenty of wild life!

A hairy, pulpy thing, reddish in color, with gauzy wings and a myriad flashing eyes scuttled close to them as though drawn by curiosity to inspect them. As big as an eagle it appeared to them; both grasped their spears; but soon, with a wild whistle of its wings, it rose up through the tangle of underbrush and hummed off. A fruit fly.

And now a monstrous thing appeared far off, to stalk like a balloon on twenty-foot legs in their direction. With incredible quickness it loomed over them. Six feet through, its body was roughly spherical, and carried on those amazingly long, jointed legs. It stared at them with beady, cruel eyes, but finally teetered on its way again, leaving them untouched.

"I'll never again be able to see a daddy longlegs without shivering," said Jim. His voice was unconsciously sunk to little more than a whisper. This was a world of titanic dangers and fierce alarms. Instinct cautioned both of them to make no more noise than necessary. "We had better make for your termitary at once."

Dennis had been thinking that for some time. But he had been unable to locate a termite tunnel anywhere. Matt had been supposed to set them down near one. No doubt, to his own mind, he *had* placed them near one of the termite highways. But his ideas of distance were now so radically different from theirs that Dennis, at least, was unable to see a tunnel opening anywhere.

He spoke his thoughts to Jim. "There must be a tunnel opening somewhere very near us," he concluded. "But I — Good heavens!"

Both crouched in wary alarm, spears held for a thrust, if necessary, at the frightful thing approaching them from the near jungle.

Thirty feet long, it was, and six feet through, a blunt-ended, untapered serpent that glistened a moist crimson color in the rays of the sun. The trees quaked and rocked as it brushed against them in its deliberate advance. Dead leaves many feet across and too heavy for the combined efforts of both men to have budged, were pushed lightly this way and that as the monster moved. The very ground seemed to shake under its appalling weight.

"If *that* comes after us," breathed Jim, "we're through!"

But now Denny drew a long breath of relief.

"Be still," he said. "Make no sound, and no move, and it will probably pass us by. It's blind, and couldn't harm us in any way — unless it rolled on us."

The two stood motionless while the nightmare serpent crashed by. Then, with the earthworm fading into the distance, they resumed their hunt for the near tunnel entrance.

Jim, whose eyes were more accustomed to searching jungle depths, finally saw it — a black hole leading down into a small hill about two hundred yards ahead of them. He pointed.

"There we are. Come on."

Laboriously they set out toward it. Laboriously because at every step some almost insuperable hurdle barred their way. A fallen grass stalk was a problem; sometimes they had to curve back on their tracks for sixty or eighty feet in order to get around it. A dead leaf, drifted there from the trees near at hand, was almost a calamity, necessitating more circuitous maneuvering.

With every yard the realization of the stark peril that was now theirs increased.

A grasshopper, blundering to the ground within a rod of them, nearly crushed them with its several tons of weight. A bumblebee, as big as a flying elephant and twice as deadly, roared around them for several minutes as though debating whether or not to attack them, and finally roared off leaving them shaken and pale. But the most startling and narrow of their narrow escapes occurred an instant after that.

They had paused for an instant, alert but undecided, to stare at a coldly glaring spider that was barring their path. It was a small spider, barely more than waist-high. But something in its malevolent eyes made the two men hesitate about attacking it. At the same time it was squatting in the only clear path in sight, with tangles of stalks and leaves on either side. A journey around the ferocious brute might be a complicated, long-drawn-out affair.

Their problem was decided for them.

Overhead, suddenly roared out a sound such as might have been made by a tri-motored Fokker. There was a flash of yellow. The roar increased to an ear-shattering scream. Something swooped so breathlessly and at the same time so ponderously that the men were knocked flat by the hurricane of disturbed air.

A fleeting struggle ensued between some vast yellow body and the unfortunate spider. Then the spider, suddenly as immobile as a lump of stone, was drawn up into the heavens by the roaring yellow thing, and disappeared. A wasp had struck, and had obtained another meal.

"Thank God that thing had a one-track mind, and was concentrating on the spider," said Jim, with a rather humorless laugh.

Dennis was silent. He was beginning to realize that he knew too much about insects for his peace of mind. To Jim, insects had always heretofore been something to brush away or step on, as the circumstance might indicate. He had no idea, for example, of exactly what fate it was he had just missed. But Denny knew all about it.

He knew that if the wasp had chosen either of them, the chosen one would have felt a stabbing thing like a red-hot sword penetrate to his vitals. He knew that swift paralysis would have followed the thrust. He knew that then the victim would have been taken back, helpless and motionless as the spider was, to be laid side by side with other helpless but still conscious victims in the fetid depths of the wasp's nest. And he knew that finally an egg would have been laid on the victim's chest; an egg that would eventually hatch and deliver a bit of life that would calmly and leisurely devour the paralyzed food supply alive.

"Let's hurry," he suggested, glancing up to see if any more wasps were hovering about.

The lowering tunnel mouth was very near now. Barely twenty yards away. What with the crowding monsters around them, the tunnel began to look like a haven. Almost at a run, they continued toward it.

Then a commotion like that which might be made by a mighty army sounded in the underbrush behind them. Dennis looked back over his shoulder.

"Hurry!" he gasped, suddenly accelerating his pace into frank flight. "Ants. . . ."

Jim glanced back, too — and joined Denny in his flight. Pouring toward them at express train speed, flinging aside fallen stalks, climbing over obstructions as though no obstructions were there, was coming a grim and armored horde. Far in the lead, probably the one that had seen the men first and started the deadly chase, was a single ant.

The solitary leader was a monster of its kind. As tall as Jim, clashing in its horny armor, it rushed toward the fugitives.

"It's going to reach the tunnel before we do," Jim panted. "We've got to kill the thing — and do it before the rest get to us. . . ."

The monster was on them. Blindly, ferociously it hurled its bulk at the things that smelled like termites however little they resembled them. The termite-paste was, in this instance, the most deadly of challenges.

Jim stepped to the fore, with his spear point slanted to receive the onslaught, spear butt grounded at his feet.

Whether the six-legged horror would have had wit enough to comprehend the nature of the defense offered, and would have striven to circumvent it, had time been given it, is a question that will never be answered. For the thing wasn't given the time.

In mid-air it seemed to writhe and try to change the direction of its leap. But it was on the point and had transfixed itself before its intelligence, however keen, could have functioned.

The fight, though, was by no means over. With five feet of steel piercing it through, it whirled with hardly abated vitality toward Dennis. Its gargoyle head came close and closer.

Dennis sprang sideways along its length, lifted the pointed bar he held, and dashed it down on what looked to him a vital spot — the unbelievably slender trunk that held its spatulate abdomen to its armored chest.

There was a crack as the bar smashed down on the weak point. The monster sank quivering to the ground. An instant later it was up, but now its movements were dazed and sluggish as it dragged its half-paralyzed abdomen after it, and fumbled and caught on the heavy bar that transfixed it.

Jim caught the bar and tugged it. "My spear!" he cried. "Denny — help!"

Together the two wrenched to jerk the spear loose from the horny armor of the dying ant. The rest of the pack were very near now.

"We'll have to let it go. . . ." panted Denny.

But at that instant their desperate efforts tore it loose from the convulsively jerking hulk. They darted into the tunnel mouth with the racing horde scarcely twenty yards behind them.

Without hesitation the ants poured in after them. Jim and Dennis leaped forward, in pitch darkness, now and then bumping heavily against a wall as the tunnel turned, but having at least no trouble with their footing: the floor was as smooth as though man-made.

Behind them they could hear the armored horde crashing along in the blackness. The smashing noise of their progress was growing louder. The two had run perhaps fifty yards in the darkness. Another fifty, and they would be caught!

But now, just as their eyes — sharpened also by the danger they were in — began to grow accustomed to the gloom, they saw ahead of them a thing that might have stepped straight out of a horrible dream.

Six feet of vulnerable, unarmored body, amply protected by horny head and shoulders and ten feet of awful, scissor-mandibles, faced them. The creature was doing a strange sort of war dance, swaying its terrible bulk back and forth rhythmically, while its feet remained immovable. An instant it did this, then it charged at the two men. Simultaneously the crashing of the fierce horde behind sounded with appalling nearness — the noise and odor of the ants preventing the huge termite guard in front of the men from recognizing and approving the smell of the termite-paste that covered their bodies.

"Follow me!" snapped Denny, remembering that the hideous attacking thing before them was blind, and gaining from that knowledge swift inspiration.

Jim gathered his muscles to follow at command. But he almost shouted aloud as he saw Denny leap — straight toward the enormous, snapping mandibles.

In an instant, however, Denny's idea was made clear. With a slide that would have done credit to any baseball player, the entomologist catapulted on his chest past the snapping peril. Jim followed, with not a foot to spare. They were not past the soft rear-parts of the thing, but they were at least past its horrible jaws. And before the monster could turn its unwieldy bulk in the tunnel, the ants were upon it.

For a few seconds, blinded to their own danger by the fascination of the struggle going on before them, the two men witnessed the grim watcher of the tunnel as it drove back wave after wave of attacking ants.

Two at a time, the invaders charged that wall of living horn. And two at a time they were swept against the walls, or slashed in two by the enormous mandibles. One against an army; but it was a full minute or so before the one began to weaken.

"Come," whispered Dennis, at last. "If what I think is going to happen occurs, this will be no place for us."

They went ahead, with the din of battle dying behind them, till they saw a small tunnel branching off beside the main stem. Into this they squeezed. But as Jim started to go farther down its constricted length, Dennis stopped him.

"We're fairly safe here, I think. We'll stay and watch. . . ."

Silently, motionless, they lurked in the entrance of the side-avenue, and peered out at the main avenue they had just left. And now that avenue began to buzz with traffic.

First, more of the horrors with the enormous scissor-mandibles began to stream past them. In twos and threes, then in whole squads, they lumbered by, bound for the ant army that had invaded their sanctum.

Not quite too far ahead to be out of sight, the defenders halted. Several of their number went forward to help the dying Horatius. The rest lined up in a triple row across a wide patch in the tunnel, presenting a phalanx it would appear that nothing could beat.

"How do they know enough to gather here from distant parts of this hollow mountain?" whispered Jim to Denny. "How do they know their city is besieged just at this spot, and that their help is needed?"

Dennis shrugged. His eyes were shining. This was the kind of thing he had come here for. This unhampered observation of a strange and terrible race at war and at work — it was well worth all the personal risks he might run.

"No man can answer your question, Jim. They're blind — they can't see their danger so as to know how to combat it. They couldn't hear, and be alarmed by, the vibrations of battle for a distance of more than a few yards. My only guess is that they are constantly and silently commanded by the unknown intelligence, the ruling brain, that hides deep in the earth beneath us and directs these 'soldier' termites in some marvelous way — though itself never seeing or hearing the actual dangers it guards against."

"The queen?" suggested Jim.

Again Denny shrugged. "Who knows? She might be the brains, as well as the egg layer, of the tribe. But don't talk too much. The vibration of our voices might lead them to us in spite of their blindness."

* * * *

NOW the main avenue before them was humming with a new kind of traffic. From side to side it was being filled with a new sort of termite. These were smaller than the soldiers, and entirely unprotected by either horn armor plate or slashing mandibles.

Each of these carried an unwieldy block of gleaming substance. And each in turn dropped its block in a growing wall behind the savage defenders against the ants, and fastened it in place with a thick and viscous brown liquid that dried almost immediately into a kind of cement.

"The workers," whispered Dennis, enthralled. "The building blocks are half-digested wood. The cement is a sort of stuff that exudes from their own bodies. In ten minutes there will be a wall across the tunnel that no ants on earth could penetrate!"

"But the home guards, the brave lads and all that sort of thing, will be shut off on the outside of the wall with the enemy. And there are hundreds of the enemy," protested Jim.

"A necessary sacrifice," said Denny. "And so perfect is their organization that no one, including the soldiers to be sacrificed, ever makes any objection."

Jim shivered a little. "It's terrible, somehow. It's — it's inhuman!"

"Naturally. It's insectian, if there is such a word. And a wise man once predicted that the termite organization, being so much more perfect a one than man's, indicated the kind of society man would at some time build up for himself. In ten or twelve more centuries we, too, might go off in millions and deliberately starve to death because the ruling power decided there were too many people on earth. We, too, might devour our dead because it was essential not to let anything go to waste. We, too, might control our births so that we produced astronomers with telescopes in their heads instead of regular eyes, carpenters with hammer and saw instead of hands, soldiers with poison gas sacs in their chests so they could breathe death and destruction at will. It would be the perfect state of society."

"Maybe — but I'm glad I'll be dead before that times comes," said Jim with another shiver.

By now the wall ahead of them was complete. On the other side of it the soldier termites stolidly fought on to their certain death. On the near side, the workers retreated to unknown depths in the great hollow mountain behind them. The main avenue was once more clear, and, save for a few workers hastening on unknown errands, deserted.

"That act's over," sighed Dennis. "But it may well be no more than a curtain raiser to the acts to come. Shall we be on our way? We're hardly on the fringe of the termitary yet — and I want to get at the heart of it, and into the depths far beneath it. Depths of hell, we'll probably find them, Jim. But a marvelous hell, and one no man has ever before seen."

They left their little haven and moved along the main tunnel toward the heart of the termitary, walking easily upright in this tunnel which was only one of many hundreds in the vast, hollowed mountain — which loomed into the outer sunshine to almost a height of a yard.

CHAPTER V
Trapped

ON along the tunnel they went. And as they progressed, Dennis got the answer to something that had troubled him a great deal before their entrance here — a problem which had been solved, rather amazingly, of itself.

Termitaries, as far as the entomologist knew, were pitch-black places which no ray of light ever entered. He had been afraid he would be forced to stumble blindly in unlit depths, able to see nothing at all, on a par with the blind creatures among whom he moved. Yet he and Jim could see in this subterranean labyrinth.

He observed now the reason for that. The walls on all sides, made of half-digested cellulose, had rotted just enough through long years to be faintly phosphorescent. And that simple natural fact was probably going to mean all the difference between life and death: it gave the two men at least the advantage of sight over the eyeless savage creatures among whom, helped by the termite-smell given by the paste, they hoped to glide unnoticed.

However, even the termite-paste, and the fact that the termitary citizens were blind, didn't seem enough to account for the immunity granted the two men as they began to come presently to more crowded passages and tunnels near the center of the mound.

On every side of them now, requiring the utmost in agility to keep from actually brushing against them, were hordes of the worker ter-mites, and dozens of the frightful soldiers. Yet on the two men moved, ever more slowly, without one of the monsters attempting to touch them. It was odd — almost uncanny.

"Surely the noise of our walking, tiptoe as we may, must be heard by them — and noted as different from theirs," whispered Dennis. "Yet they pay no attention to us. If it is due to the paste, I must say it's wonderful stuff!"

Jim nodded in a puzzled way. "It's almost as if they wanted to make our inward path easy. I wonder — if it's going to be different when we try to get out again!"

Dennis was wondering that, too. It seemed absurd to suspect the things of being intelligent enough to lay traps. But it did look almost as though they were encouraging their two unheard-of visitors from another world to go on deeper and deeper into the heart of the eerie city (all the tunnels sloped down now), there perhaps to meet with some ghastly imprisonment.

He gave it up. Sufficient for the moment that they were unmolested, and that he had a chance at first hand to make observations more complete than the world of entomology had ever dreamed of.

They stumbled onto what seemed a death struggle between one of the giant soldiers and an inoffensive-looking worker. The drab, comparatively feeble body of the worker was wriggling right in the center of the great claws which, with a twitch, could have sliced it in two endwise. Yet the jaws did not twitch; and in a few moments the worker drew unconcernedly out and moved away.

"The soldier was getting his meal," whispered Denny, enthralled. "Their mandibles are enlarged so enormously that they can't feed themselves. The workers, who digest food for the whole tribe, feed them regularly. Then if a soldier gets in the least rebellious, he can simply be starved to death at any time."

"Ugh!" Jim whispered back. "Fancy being official stomach to three or four other people! More of your wonderful 'organization,' I suppose."

They went on, down and down, till Denny calculated they had at last reached nearly to the center of the vast city. And now they stumbled into something weird and wonderful indeed. Rather, they half fell into it, for it lay down a few feet and came as a complete surprise in the dimness; and not till they had recovered from their near fall and looked around for a few seconds did they realize where their last few steps — the last few steps of freedom they were to have in the grim underground kingdom — had taken them.

They were in a chamber so huge that it made the largest of man-made domes shrink to insignificance by comparison.

A hundred yards or more in every direction, it extended. And far overhead, lost in distance, reared the arched roof. A twenty-story building could have been placed under that roof without trouble.

Lost in awe, Dennis gazed about him; and he saw on the floor, laid in orderly rows in countless thousands, that which gave further cause for wonderment: new-hatched larvae about the size of pumpkins but a sickly white in color — feeble, helpless blobs of life that one day develop into soldiers and workers, winged rulers or police. The termite nursery.

"Whew!" gasped Jim, wiping his face. "From the heat in here you'd think we were getting close to the real, old-fashioned hell instead of an artificial, insect-made one. What are all these nauseating-looking blobs of lard lying about here, anyway?"

Denny told him. "Which is the reason for the heat," he concluded. "Jim, it's twenty degrees warmer in here than it is outdoors. How — *how* — can these insects regulate the temperature like that? The work of the ruling brain again? But where, and what, can that brain be?"

"Maybe we'll find out before we leave this place," said Jim, more prophetically than he knew. "Hello — we can't get out through the door we entered. We'll have to find another exit. Look."

Dennis looked. In the doorway they had just come through was a soldier — a giant even among giants. Its ten-foot jaws, like a questing, gigantic vise, were opening and closing regularly and rapidly across the opening of the portal. It made no attempt to enter the great nursery, just stood where it was and sliced the air rhythmically with its jaws.

"We haven't a chance of walking through *that* exit!" Dennis agreed. "Let's try the other side."

But before they could half cross the great room — walking between rows of life that weakly stirred like protoplasmic mud on either side of them — a soldier appeared at that door, too. Like the first, it stationed itself there, and began the same regular, swift slicing movements of jaws that compassed the doorway from side to side and halfway from top to bottom.

"We might possibly be able to run through that giant's nut-cracker before it smashed shut on us," said Jim dubiously. "But I'd hate to try it. There's a door at the end, too."

They made for this, running now. But a third soldier appeared to block the way out with those deadly, clashing mandibles.

"You're *sure* they can't see?" demanded Jim, clutching his spear while he hesitated whether to try an attack on the fearful guard or to turn tail again. "Because they certainly act as if they did!"

"Direct commands from the ruling brain," Denny surmised soberly. "Somewhere, perhaps half a mile down in the earth, Something is able to see us through solid walls, read in our minds our intentions of what we're to do next, and send out wordless commands to these soldiers to execute countermoves."

"Rot!" said Jim testily. "These things are bugs, not supermen. And the fact that they're now bigger than we are, and much better armed, doesn't keep them from being just bugs. There's no real brain-power in evidence here."

But an instant later he changed his mind. They approached the fourth and last exit from the giant chamber. And here there was no guard. They were able to race out of it without interference. The oddity of that was glaring.

"Denny," gasped Jim, "we're being *herded*! Driven in a certain direction, and for a certain reason, by these damned things! Do you realize that?"

Dennis did realize it. And a moment later, when he glanced behind, he realized it more.

Behind them, marching in orderly twos that filled the tunnel from side to side, moved a body of the soldiers. As the men moved, they moved; never coming nearer and never dropping behind.

Experimentally, Dennis stopped. The grim soldiers stopped, too. Dennis walked back toward them a step or two, spear held ready.

The monsters did not try to attack. On the other hand they did not give ground, either; and as Denny got to within a few yards of them, one in the front line suddenly opened and shut his ponderous jaws.

They clashed together a matter of inches from Denny's torso — a clear warning to get on back in the direction he had come.

Jim came and stood beside him, heavy shoulder muscles bunched into knots, standing on the balls of his feet as a boxer stands before flashing in at an opponent.

"Shall we have it out with them here and now?" said Jim, his jaws set. "We wouldn't have a chance — but I'm beginning to get awfully doubtful about the fate these things have in store for us. I can't even guess at what it may be — but I've an idea it may be a lot worse than a quick, easy death!"

Denny shook his head. "Let's see it through," he muttered, looking at the nightmare jaws of their guard. Two sweeps of those jaws and he and Jim would lie in halves.

They started back down the corridor, the monstrous shepherds moving as they did. The way descended so steeply now that it was difficult for them to keep their footing. Then, yards below the level of the horrible nursery, the tunnel narrowed — and widened again into a chamber which had no other opening save the one they were being herded into. A blind end to the passageway.

"The bug Bastille," said Jim with a mirthless grin. "Here, I guess, we're going to wait for the powers-that-be to judge us and give us our sentence."

The giant soldiers halted. Two of them stood in the narrowed part of the tunnel, one behind the other, blocking it with a double, living barrier. Their jaws commenced moving regularly, savagely back and forth, open and closed. Blind these guards might be; but no living thing, even though it bristled with eyes, could creep out unscathed through the animated threshing machine those jaws made of that doorway. The two men were more securely held in their prison cell than they would have been by two-inch doors of nickel-steel. They could only wait there, helpless prisoners, to learn the intentions of the unknown Something that ruled the great city, and that held them so easily in its grasp.

CHAPTER VI
In the Food Room

RESTLESSLY, Jim paced back and forth in the narrow dank cell. At the doorway the two guards opened and closed their jaws, regularly, rhythmically, about sixty to the minute. Hours, the two men calculated, they had been there. And still the clashing of those jaws rang steadily, maddeningly in their ears.

Clash-clash-clash. The things seemed as tireless as machinery. Clash-clash-clash. And into that savage, tireless movement, Denny read a sort of longing refrain.

"Try — to — es — cape! Try — to — es — cape!"

He shivered. At any time, did he and Jim grow too fearful of the dark future or too nerve-wracked by the terrific suspense, they could step into these gigantic, steel-hard jaws. But to be sliced in two . . .

Jim stopped his pacing, and stared speculatively at the wall of their cell. For the dozenth time he raised his ponderous spear and thrust the pointed end at the wall with all his strength. And for the dozenth time he was rewarded only by seeing a flake no larger than his clenched fist fall out.

"Might as well be cement!" he rasped. "God, we're caught like flies in a spiderweb!"

"Well, you wanted excitement," remarked Dennis, a bit acidly. The strain was telling on him more than on the less finely strung Holden; but he was struggling to keep himself in hand.

"So I did want excitement," said Jim. "But I want at least a sporting chance for my white-alley, too. But —"

He stopped; and both stared swiftly toward the door.

The ponderous, gruesome clashing of jaws had stopped. The two nightmare guards stood motionless, as though at command. Then they moved into the cell, straight toward the two men.

"It's come!" said Jim through set teeth. He swung his spear up, ready to shoot it at the horny breastplate of the nearest monster with all his puny strength. "We're going to catch it now!"

But Dennis gazed more intently; and he saw that the blind but ferocious creatures showed no real signs of molesting them. Instead, they were edging to one side. In a moment, as the two men moved warily to keep their distance, they found suddenly that the soldiers were behind them, and that the doorway was free to them.

The glimpse of freedom, however, was not inspiring. The meaning of the move was too apparent: they were again being herded.

Whatever reigning power it was that had let them penetrate so deeply into the trap, and then had surrounded and imprisoned them — was now going to honor them with an audience.

"His Majesty commands," commented Jim, reading the sinister gesture as clearly as Denny had. "I'll wager we're about to meet your 'unknown intelligence,' Denny. But be it 'super-termite' or be it Queen — whatever it may be — I want just one chance to use this spear of mine!"

Reluctantly he stepped forth before the fearful guard; reluctantly, but in full command of his nerves now that the wearing inactivity was ended and something definite was about to happen. Which proves but once again the wisdom of the gods in not allowing man to read the future. For could Jim Holden have foreseen the precise experience awaiting them, his nerve control — and Denny's, too — might not have been so firm.

Again their way led sharply down, through tunnels loftier and broader and glowing more brilliantly with phosphorescence which was a testimonial to their greater age.

The efficiency of their herding was perfect. At each side entrance along the way stood one of the ghastly soldiers, jaws clashing with monotonous deadliness. Now and again several of the monsters appeared straight ahead, barring the avenue, and leaving no choice but to turn to right or left into off-branching tunnels. Small chance here of missing the path! And always behind them marched their two particular guards, closing off their retreat.

"How do you suppose they sense our approach?" wondered Jim, who had noticed that the menacing jaw-clashing began while they were still fairly far from whatever side entrance was being barred to them. And again: "You're *sure* they can't see?"

"There isn't an eye in the lot of them," said Denny. "They must sense our coming by the vibration of our footsteps."

But when they tried tiptoeing, on noiseless bare feet, the result was the same. Surely the things could not hear them for more than a few feet; yet with no sound to guide them, the blind guards commenced automatically opening and closing those invulnerable jaws with the distant approach of the two men just the same. They could only ascribe it to the same force that seemed able to follow them, step by step and thought by thought, though it was far away and out of sight — the ruling brain of the termite tribe.

Ever hotter it grew as they descended, till at length a blast of heat like a draft from a furnace met them as they rounded a corner and stepped into a corridor that no longer led downward. They knew that they were very near the ruler's lair now, on the lowest level, deep in the foundations of the vast pile.

Dennis wiped perspiration, caused as much by emotion as by heat, from his face. He alone of all students on earth was going to penetrate the very heart of the termite mystery. He alone was going to have at least a glimpse of the baffling intelligence that science had guessed about for so many decades He . . . alone. For it was hardly likely that he would ever get back up to the surface of earth to share his knowledge.

How different was this adventure from what he had hoped it might be! He had thought that the two of them might simply enter the termitary, mingle — perilously, but with at least a margin of safety — with the blind race it housed, and walk out again whenever they pleased. But from the moment of entering they'd had no chance. They had been hopelessly in the clutch of the insects; played with, indulged, and finally trapped, to be led at last like dogs on a leash to the lair of the ruling power.

They rounded another corner and now, ahead of them, they saw what must be the end of this last and deepest of all the tunnels. This end showed as a glare of light. Real light, not the soft gleam of the rotting wood walls which was already paling feebly in comparison. The glare ahead of them, indeed, had something of the texture of electric light. Neither Jim nor Dennis could repress a sudden start; it was like coming abruptly onto a man-made fact, a bit of man-made world in the midst of this insect hell.

The damp heat was almost paralyzing now. Their limbs felt weak as they stumbled toward the light. But they were inexorably herded forward, and soon were at the threshold of the oddly illuminated chamber.

Now the two stopped for an instant and sniffed, as a peculiar odor came to their nostrils. It was a vague but fearsome odor, indescribable, making their skin crawl. A smell of decay — of death — and yet somehow of rank and fetid life. A combination of charnel-house and menagerie smell.

Denny blanched as an inkling of what was before them came to his mind. He remembered the swooping wasp, that had so narrowly missed them at the start of their adventure. The wasp, he knew, was not the only insect that had certain dread ways of stocking its larder and keeping the contents of that larder fresh! The termites did not customarily follow these practices. Yet — yet the odor coming from the place before them certainly suggested . . . But he tried to thrust such apprehensions from his thoughts.

They entered the chamber. The two gigantic soldiers stopped on the threshold behind them and took up their standard guard attitudes. The men stared about them. . . .

It was huge, this chamber, almost as huge as the nursery chamber they had blundered into. The source of the light was not apparent. It seemed to glow from walls and floor and ceiling, as though it were a box of glass with sunshine pouring in at all six sides.

And now horror began to mingle with awed interest, as they took in more comprehensively the sights in that place, and saw precisely what it contained.

Denny's apprehensions had been only too well founded. For larder, food storeroom, the chamber certainly was. But what a storeroom! And in what state the "food" that stocked it was!

All along the vast floor were laid rows of inert, fantastic bodies. Insects. The whole small-insect world seemed to be represented here. One or more of everything that crawled, flew, walked or bored, seemed gathered in this great room. Grubs, flies, worms, ants, things soft and slimy and things grim and armored, were piled side by side like cordwood.

These hulks, nearly all larger than the two quarter-inch men, lay stark and motionless where they had been dropped. From them came the odor that had stopped Jim and Denny on the threshold — the strange odor of blended life and death. And the reason for the queer odor became apparent as the two gazed more closely at the motionless hulks.

These things, like figures out of a delirium in their great size and exaggerated frightfulness, were rigid as in death — but they were nevertheless not dead! Helpless as so many lumps of stone, they were still horribly, pitifully alive. Paralyzed, in some inscrutable termite fashion, probably fully conscious of their surroundings, they could only lie there and wait for their turn to come to be devoured by the ferocious creatures that had dragged them down to this, the bowels of the mound city.

Besides these things bound in the rigidity of death, there was more normal life. There were termites in that vast storeroom, too; but they were specialized creatures, such as termitary life abounds in, that were so distorted as to be hardly recognizable as termites.

Along one wall of the place, hanging head down and fastened there for life, was a row of worker termites whose function was obviously that of reservoirs: their abdomens, so enormously distended as to be nearly transparent, glistened in varying colors to indicate that they contained various liquids whose purpose could only be guessed at.

Living cisterns, never to move, never to know life even in the monotonous, joyless way of the normal worker, they hung there to be dipped into whenever the master that reigned over this inferno, or his immediate underlings, desired some of their contents!

In addition, there were several each of two forms of termite soldier such as they had not seen before, standing rigidly at attention about the place.

At the door, of course, were the two creatures with the enormous mandibles that had escorted the pigmy men to the larder. But these others were as different as though they belonged to a different race.

Three had heads that were hideously bulbous in form, and which were flabby and elastic instead of armored with thick horn as were the heads of the usual soldiers. Like living syringes, these heads were; perambulating bulbs filled with some defensive or offensive liquid to be squirted out at the owner's will.

The third kind of soldier was represented in the spectacle of termites with heads that were huge and conical, resembling bungs, or the tapered cylindrical corks with which one plugs a bottle. These, Denny knew from his studies, had been evolved by termite biology for the purpose of temporarily stopping up any breach in termitary mound-wall or tunnel while the workers could assemble and repair the chink with more solid and permanent building material.

But how fantastically, gruesomely different these colossal figures looked, here in the deepest stronghold of termitedom, than as scurrying little insects viewed under an entomologist's glass! And how appallingly different was the viewpoint from which they were now being observed — here where the human observers were equal in size, and doomed at any moment perhaps to be paralyzed and piled with the helpless live things that made up the rest of the "larder"!

And the presiding genius of this mysterious, underground storeroom — where was it? Denny and Jim looked about over the rows of live food, and among the termite soldiers with their odd heads, in vain for a creature that might conceivably be the super-insect that so omnipotently ruled the mound.

Off in a corner they saw two more termites — standard worker types, standing motionless side by side, with a queer sort of mushroom growth linking them together — a large, gray-white ball borne mutually on their backs. But that was all. The listing of those two workers concluded the roll-call of termites in the chamber as far as the two men could see. And the two were — just ordinary workers.

"I guess His Majesty is out," said Jim. But his voice, in spite of the attempted levity of the words, was low-pitched and somber. "Most impolite to keep us waiting —"

He stopped as Denny sharply threw up his hand. And he too gazed at the maneuver that had caught Denny's wary attention.

This was nothing save that the various soldiers in the chamber — seven of them, besides the two that never left their stations at the door — had moved. But they had moved in concert, almost as harmoniously in unison as if performing some sort of drill.

In a single line they filed across the rows of inert, palpitating, paralyzed bodies; and in a line they surrounded Jim and Denny in a hollow square about twenty feet across. There they took up their stations, the three soldiers with the syringe-heads, and the four with the unwieldy craniums that resembled bungs.

So perfectly had the move been executed, so perfectly and in unison had it been timed, that there could be little doubt it had resulted from a direct order. But where was the thing to give the command? Where was the head-general? In some far place, on his way to inspect the new and odd kind of prisoners, and giving orders to hold them yet more closely in anticipation of that inspection?

Jim turned to Denny and started to voice some of his thoughts. But the words were killed by the light that had appeared suddenly in Denny's eyes. In them had appeared a gleam of almost superstitious terror.

"Jim!" gasped Denny, raising his hand and pointing with trembling forefinger. "Jim — *look*!"

Jim turned to gaze, and his spear, clutched with almost convulsive desperation till this moment, sagged to the floor from his limp hinds.

The thing Denny had pointed at was the curious, large mushroom growth supported jointly on the backs of the two worker termites. It had been across the chamber from them when they first saw it. Now it was moving toward them, steadily, borne by the team of workers. And now, clearly, for the first time, they saw what it really was.

It was a head, that mushroom growth. Rather, the whitish-gray, soft-looking thing was a brain. For it had long ago burst free of the original insect skull casing in which it had been born. Evidence that it had once been a normal, termite head was given by the fact that here and there, on sides and top of the huge, spongy-looking mass, were brownish scales — fragments of the casing that had once contained its bulk.

Set low down under the sphere, with the whitish-gray mass beetling up over them like a curving cliff, were eyes; great, staring, dull things of the type termites have during the short-winged periods of their existences. Like huge round stones, those eyes regarded the two men as the team of termites marched closer.

Hanging down from the great mass was an abortive miniature of a body — soft, shriveled abdomen, almost nonexistent chest, and tiny, sticklike legs that trailed helplessly along the floor as the termites — in the manner of two men who support a helpless third man between them — bore it forward.

Here, then was the Intellect that ruled the tribe, the super-termite, the master mind of the mound! This travesty of a termite! This thing with wasted limbs and torso, and with enormous, voracious brain that drained all sustenance constantly from the body! It was, in the insect world, a parallel to the dream that present-day Man sometimes has of Man a million years in the future: a thing all head and staring eyes, with a brain so enlarged that it must be artificially supported on its flabby torso.

"I guess His Majesty is out," Jim had said, with a shaky attempt at lightness.

But he now realized his mistake. His Majesty hadn't been out. His Majesty had been with them all along — a four-foot, irregular sphere of grayish-white nerve matter and intricately wrinkled cortex dependent for movement on borrowed backs and legs — and was now peering at them out of the only pair of eyes in the termitary as though in doubt as to what to do first with his helpless-seeming captives.

CHAPTER VII
"Clinging Brown Stuff"

BEMUSED, appalled, the two gazed at this almost disembodied brain that held them captive. It continued to come steadily toward them, carried by its two faithful slaves; and the grotesque termite soldiers, that had closed about them in a hollow square, parted to let it through.

Such was the bewitchment of the two men as they stared at the monstrosity, that they did not hear the slight clashing of horn that accompanied a swift movement of one of the soldiers behind them.

The first thing they knew of such a movement was when they felt their arms pinioned to their sides with crushing force, and looked down to find a pair of hard, jointed forelegs coiled about their bodies. In answer to some voiceless command, one of the termites with the conical heads had approached behind them and wound a leg around each.

Sweat stood out on Denny's forehead at the repellent touch of that living bond. He turned and twisted wildly.

Jim was struggling madly in the grip of the other foreleg. Great shoulders bulging with the effort, muscles standing in knots on his heavy arms, he nearly succeeded in breaking free. Denny felt the tie that bound him relax ever so little as the monster centered its attention on the stronger man.

With a last effort, he tore his right arm free, and wriggled partly around in the thing's grip. He raised the spear and plunged it slantingly down into the hideous body.

This type of termite was armored more poorly than the others. Only its head was plated with horn; chest and abdomen were soft and vulnerable as those of any humble worker in the mound. The spear tore into it for two-thirds its length. There was a squeak — the first sound they had heard — from the wounded monster. The clutching forelegs tightened terribly, then began to loosen, quivering spasmodically as they slowly relinquished their grasp.

Denny bounded free and again sent the length of his spear into the loathsome body. Jim, meanwhile, had leaped toward his fallen spear. He stooped to pick it up — and was lost!

Obeying another wordless order, one of the ghastly, syringe-headed monsters had stepped out of line with the start of the short struggle. This one bounded on Jim just as he leaned over for his weapon.

Denny shouted a warning, started to run to his friend's aid. The dying termite, with a last burst of incredible vitality, caught his leg and held him.

In an instant it was done. The termite with the distorted head had drenched Jim with a brown, thick liquid that covered him from shoulder to feet — and Jim was writhing helplessly on the floor.

Denny burst loose at last from the feebly clutching foreleg. He straightened, poised his spear, and with a strength born of near madness shot it at the syringe-headed thing's chest.

But this one was different, armored to the full save for its soft cranium. The steel bar glanced harmlessly from the heavy horn breastplate. In answer, the monster wheeled and drenched Dennis, too, with the loathsome liquid.

On the instant Dennis was helpless. As Jim had done, he sank to the floor, his body constricted in a sheath that tightened as it dried and which bound him as securely as any straitjacket might have done.

The two rolled on the floor, trying to shed the terrible coating of hardening fluid that contracted about them. But they were as impotent as two flies that had rolled in the sticky slime of some super-flypaper. At last they gave it up.

Panting, helpless as mummies, they glared up at the stony eyes of the ruler-termite. The team of workers moved, bearing their burden of almost bodiless, mushroom brain like well-oiled machines.

Their forelegs went out. The two men were shoved along the floor ahead of the monarch — and were laid in one of the lines of paralyzed insects so patently held as the ruler's private food supply!

The great, stony eyes were next bent, as though in curiosity, on the spears that had done such damage to the termite with the conical head. In the true insect world there was no such phenomenon as those glittering steel bars; and it appeared that the over-developed brain of the monarch held questions concerning their nature.

The team of termites wheeled, and walked over to the nearest spear, trailing the feeble, atrophied legs of their rider as they went. They squatted close to the floor, and the staring eyes examined the spears at close range. Then the owner of the eyes apparently sent out another command; for one of the guards at the door left its post and drew near, scissor-mandibles opened in obedience.

The hard mandible's clashed over one of the steel bars. The jaws crunched shut, with a nerve-rasping grind. They made, naturally, no impression on the bar. The guard retired to its post at the doorway.

The termite-ruler seemed to think this over, for a moment. Then at some telepathic order, its two bearers picked up the spear and carried it, and their physically helpless ruler, over to one of the living cisterns — one filled with a dark red liquid.

One of the beasts of burden reached up and thrust an end of the spear into the hugely distended abdomen filled with the unknown red liquid. The spear was withdrawn, with about a foot of its blunt end reddened by the fluid. The termite laid it down; the staring, dull eyes watched it. . . .

Slowly the end of the bar dulled with swift oxidation; slowly it turned brownish and flaked away, almost entirely consumed. The acid — if that was what the red stuff was — was awesomely powerful, at least with inorganic substances.

The termite team turned away from the bar, as if it were now a matter of indifference to the bloated brain borne on their backs. It approached the men again.

"I suppose," groaned Jim, "that our turn is next. The thing will probably have us dipped into the red stuff, to see if we're consumed, too."

But here His Majesty's curiosity was interrupted while he partook of nourishment.

The clashing jaws of the two termite soldiers at the door stopped for a moment. Jim and Dennis struggled to turn their heads — all of them they could move — to see what the cessation of jaw-clashing might mean.

Three worker termites squeezed past. They approached one of the line of paralyzed insect hulks, and sank their mandibles into a garden slug. They tugged at this until they had it under the live cistern of red liquid into which the spear had been thrust.

One of the three flicked drops of the reddish stuff onto the inert slug, till it was well sprinkled. Then they dragged the carcass back to the termite-ruler.

They got it there barely in time. In a matter of seconds after they had dropped it before the monarch, the slug had collapsed into a half-liquid puddle of decomposed protoplasm on the floor. One of the main functions — if not *the* main function — of the red acid, it seemed, was to act as a powerful digestive juice for His Majesty's food, predigesting it before it was taken into the feeble body for nourishment.

The termite team settled down over the semi-liquid mess that had been the slug, and tilted back. Now, under the huge globe of the brain, Jim and Denny saw exposed a small, soft mouth fringed by the tiny rudiments of atrophied mandibles. The repulsive little mouth touched the acid-softened mass. . . .

The withered abdomen filled out. The whitish-gray lump of brain-matter grew slightly darker. It looked as though the mass of the dead slug were as large as the total bulk of the termite ruler; but not until the meal was nearly gone did the voracious feeding stop.

The three workers that had spread the banquet before their monarch, left the chamber. The guards resumed their interrupted jaw-clashing, which seemed senseless now: the captives, though not paralyzed as were the other captives there, were held so helpless by the dried and hardened fluid that escape was out of the question.

The misshapen burden of the termite team seemed to relax a little, lethargically, as though so gorged with food as to render almost inactive the grotesquely exaggerated brain. The stony eyes became duller. Plainly the captives were to have a brief respite while the huge meal was assimilated.

"If I could get loose for just one minute," Jim took the opportunity to whisper to Denny, "and get at my spear — I think there would be one termite-ruler less in the world!"

Denny nodded. He had been thinking along the same lines as Jim: that bloated, swollen brain seemed a very vulnerable thing. Soft and boneless and formless, contained only by the dirty-white, membranous skin, it did appear a tempting target for a spear thrust. And now, sluggish with its meal, it seemed less alert and on guard.

Jim went on with his thought.

"I think you scientists are wrong about *all* the termites having intelligence," he whispered. "I believe that thing has the only reasoning mind in the mound. Look at those two guards at the door, for instance. There's no earthly need for them to keep guard as eternally as they do. We can't even move, let alone try to escape. They're utterly brainless, commanded to guard the entrance with their mandibles, and continuing to guard it accordingly although the need for it is past."

Jim worked almost unthinkingly at his bonds. "If we could kill the wizened, little, big-headed thing, we might have a chance. There'd be nothing left to guide the tribe, no ruling power to direct them against us. We might even . . . escape!"

"Through the entire city — with untold thousands of these horrible things on our trail?" objected Denny gloomily.

"But if the untold thousands were dummies, used to being directed in every move by this master brain," urged Jim, "they might just blunder around while we slipped through the lines. . . ."

His words trailed into silence. Escape seemed so improbable as to be hardly worth talking about. Quiet reigned for a long time.

It was broken finally by Dennis.

"Jim," he breathed suddenly, "can you see my legs?"

With difficulty Jim turned his head. "Yes," he said. "Why?"

"It seems to me I can move my left knee — just a little!"

Jim looked more closely. "By heaven!" he exclaimed. "Denny, *I think the brown stuff is cracking*! Maybe it was never intended to be more than a temporary bond, to hold an enemy helpless just long enough for it to be killed! Maybe it hardens as it dries so that it loses all resiliency! Maybe —"

He stopped. A faint quivering of the ruler's withered little legs heralded its reawakening consciousness.

"Act helpless!" whispered Denny excitedly, as he too saw that faint stir of awakening. "Don't let the thing get an idea of what we're thinking. Because . . . we *might* get our moment of freedom. . . ."

Both lay relaxed on the floor, eyes half closed. And in the hardening substance that covered them all over like a shell of cloudy brown bakelite, appeared more minute seams as it dried unevenly on the flexible human flesh beneath it. Whether Jim's guess that it was only a temporary bond was correct, or whether it had been developed to harden relentlessly only over unyielding surfaces of horn such as the termites' deadliest enemy, the ants, wear for armor, will never be known. But in a matter of moments it became apparent that it was going to prove too brittle to continue clamping flesh as elastic as that of the two humans!

By now the termite-ruler seemed to have recovered fully from its gargantuan meal. And while, of course, there was no expression of any kind to be read in the stony, dull eyes, its actions seemed once more to indicate curiosity about these queer, two-legged bugs that wandered in here where they had no business to be.

The team of workers bore it close again, lowered the great head close to Denny. One of the team began chipping at the brown shell where it encased and held immovably to his body Denny's left hand.

A bit of the shell dropped away, exposing the fingers. Delicately, accurately, the worker's normal-sized but powerful mandibles edged the little finger away from the rest — and closed down over it. . . .

"Denny!" burst out Jim, who could just see, out of the corners of his eyes, what was being done. "My God . . . Denny. . . ."

Dennis himself said nothing. His face went white as chalk, and great drops of perspiration stood out on his forehead. But no sound came from his tortured lips.

The finger was lifted to the terrible little mouth under the gigantic head. The mouth received it; the worker nuzzled with its mandibles for another finger. The monarch, having tried the taste of this latest addition to his larder, had found it good.

Jim writhed and twisted in his weakening bonds. There was a soft snapping as several now thoroughly dried sections of the brown substance cracked loose. The termite team whirled around; the ruler stared, as though in sudden realization of danger.

More furiously Jim fought his bonds. Dennis was still, recovering slowly from the nauseating weakness that had followed the pain of his mutilated hand. There was less blood flow than might have been expected, due, perhaps, to the fact that the nipping mandibles had pinched some of the encasing shell tight over the wound.

With a dull crack, a square foot of the brown stuff burst from Jim's straining chest. But now the monarch moved to correct the situation.

The two giant soldiers at the doorway started across the great room toward them. Simultaneously, a second of the syringe-headed termites moved to renew the bonds that were being broken.

But the move had come a shade too late. Jim kicked his legs free with a last wild jerk, and staggered to his feet. His arms were still held, in a measure, in spite of his utmost efforts to free them of the clinging brown stuff. But he could, and did, run away from the body of soldiers surrounding the monarch just before the deadly syringe of the first attacking termite could function against him.

The great, flabby head hurtled his way. But he knew what to expect, now. As the slimy brown stream, directed by the agitated termite-ruler, squirted toward him, he leaped alertly aside — leaped again as the head swung around — and saw with savage hope that the monster had exhausted its discharge!

The two soldiers from the doorway closed in on him now. With their apparent command of the situation, the monstrosities with the bung- and syringe-heads closed in more tightly around their monarch. Theirs, evidently to protect that vulnerable big brain, and leave the attacking to others.

Jim fled down between the rows of paralyzed insects. The two great guards from the doorway, mandibles reaching fiercely toward the fugitive, followed. And there commenced, there in that deep-buried insect hell, a chase for life.

CHAPTER VIII

The Coming of the Soldiers

FOR a moment Jim was handicapped in fleetness and agility by the fact that his arms were hampered. But the two hideous guards, though each was a dozen times more powerful than any man its size, were handicapped in a chase, too — by the very weight of their enormous mandibles. In their thundering chase after Jim, they resembled nothing so much as two powerful but clumsy battleships chasing a relatively puny but much more agile destroyer.

Behind the great bulk of a paralyzed June bug, Jim halted for a fraction while he tore his arms at last free of the clinging brown stuff. The guards rushed around the June bug at him.

He leaped for the row of hanging cisterns; and there, while he dodged from one to another of the loathsome vats, he thought over a plan that had come to his racing mind. It wasn't much of a plan, and it seemed utterly futile in the face of the odds against him. But he had boasted, before starting this mad adventure, that Man's wits were superior to any bug's. It was time now to see if his boast had been an empty one.

He feinted toward the far end of the laboratory. The guards, acting always as if they had a dozen eyes instead of none, rushed to prevent this, cutting across his path and closing the exit with clashing jaws.

Jim raced toward the spot where Denny lay. This was within twenty yards of the spot where, behind his ring of guards, the big-brained ruler now cowered. But, while one of the syringe-monsters sent a brown stream blindly toward the leaping, shifting man, no other attacking move was made. The soldiers remained chained to their posts. Jim retrieved his spear — and the first part of his almost hopeless plan had succeeded!

It was good, the feel of that smooth steel. He balanced the ponderous weapon lightly. An ineffective thing against the plates of living armor covering the scissor-mandibles. But it was not against them — at least not directly — that he was planning to use it now!

Once more he darted toward the living cisterns. The soldiers followed close behind.

Under the bulging abdomen of the termite containing the reddish acid, Jim halted as though to make a defiant last stand against the guards. They stopped, too, then began to advance on him from either side, more slowly, like two great cats stalking a mouse.

Muscles bunched for a lightning-quick move, eyes narrowed to mere slits as he calculated distances and fractions of a second. Jim stood there beneath the great acid vat. The mandibles were almost within slicing distance now.

The guards opened wide their tremendous jaws, forming two halves of a deadly horn circle that moved swiftly to encompass him. They leaped. . . .

With barely a foot left him, Jim darted back, then poised his spear and shot it straight toward the bulging, live sack that held the acid above the guards.

The acid spurted from the spear hole. Jim clenched his fists and unconsciously held his breath till his chest ached, as the scarlet liquid spread over the great hulks that twisted and fought in ponderous frenzy to untangle legs and antennae and mandibles from the snarl their collision had made of them.

The acid bit through steel and human flesh. On the other hand, it had not harmed the horny flipper of the termite worker that had flicked it onto the garden slug. Did that mean that the flipper was immunized to the stuff, like the lining of the stomach, which is unharmed by acids powerful enough to decompose other organic master? Or did it mean that *all* horn was untouched by it?

He groaned aloud. The two great insects had drawn apart by now, and had sprung from under the shattered acid vat. Again they were on the trail. The maneuver had been fruitless! The chase was on again, which meant — since he could not hope to elude the blind but ably directed creatures forever — that all hope was lost. . . .

Then he shouted with triumph. A massive foreleg dropped from one of the guards, to crash to the floor. Whether or not the acid was able to set on the horny exterior of the termites, it was as deadly to their soft interiors as to any other sort of flesh! The acid had found the joint of that foreleg and had eaten through it as hot iron sinks through butter!

Still the injured creature came on, with Jim ever retreating, twisting and dodging from one side of the huge room to the other, leaping over the smaller paralyzed insects and darting behind the larger carcasses. But now the thing's movements were very slow — as were the movements of its companion.

Another leg fell hollowly to the floor, like an abandoned piece of armor; and then two at once from the second termite.

Both stopped, shuddering convulsively. The agony of those two enormous, dumb and blind things must have been inconceivable. The acid was by now spending its awful force in their vitals, having seeped down through every joint and crevice in their living armor. They were hardly more than huge shells of horn, kept alive only by their unbelievable vitality.

One more feeble lunge both made in concert, toward the puny adversary that had outwitted them. Then both, as though at a spoken command, stopped dead still. Next instant they crashed to the floor, shaking it in their fall.

For a second Jim could only stand there and gaze at their monstrous bodies. His plan had succeeded beyond all belief; and realization of this success left him dazed for an instant. But it was only for an instant.

Recovering himself, he raced to the acid vat to recover the spear he'd punctured it with — only three feet of it was left: the rest had been eaten away by the powerful stuff — and then wheeled to help Denny.

By now the crackling brown stuff had fallen from Denny, too — enough, at least for him to struggle to his feet and hasten its cracking by tearing at it with partially loosened hands. As Jim reached him, he freed himself entirely save for the last few bits that stuck to him as bits of shell cling to a newborn chick.

They turned together toward the corner where the termite-ruler was cowering behind the guards that surrounded it. Intellect to a degree phenomenal for an insect, this thing might have; but of the blind fierce courage possessed by its subjects, it assuredly had none! In proof of this was the fact that when the half dozen specialized soldiers ringing it round might have leaped to the aid of the two clumsy door guards and probably have ended the uneven fight in a few minutes, the craven monarch had ordered them to stay at their guard-posts rather than take the risk of remaining unguarded and defenseless for a single moment! Increasing intelligence apparently had resulted (as only too often it does in the world of men) in decreasing bravery!

An attack on the thing, closely guarded as it was, seemed hopeless. Those enormous, flat-topped heads held ready to present their steely surfaces as shields! Those armored terrors with the syringe-heads — one of which still held a full cargo of the terrible brown fluid that at a touch could bind the limbs of the men once more in the straitjacket embrace! What could the two do against that barrier?

Nevertheless, without a word being spoken, and without a second's hesitation, Jim and Denny advanced on the bristling ring — and the heart of termite power it enclosed. Not only was the slimmest of hopes of escape rendered impossible while the super-termite lived to direct its subjects against them — but also they had a reckoning to collect from the thing if they could. . . .

Denny glanced down at his hand, from which slow red drops still oozed.

At their approach, the guarding ring shifted so that the soldier whose head was still bulging with the brown liquid, faced them. The two men stopped, warily. They must draw the sting from that monster before they dared try to come closer.

Jim feinted, leaping in and to one side. The guard turned with him,

moved forward a bit as though to discharge a brown stream at him —
but held its fire. Jim moved still closer, then leaped crabwise to one
side as the brain behind the guards telepathed in a panic for its blind
minion to release some of its ammunition. The flood missed Jim only
by inches.

Denny took his turn at gambling with death. He shouted ringingly,
and ran a dozen steps straight at the monster that was the principal menace. At the last moment he flung himself aside as Jim had done — but
this time the stream was not to be drawn.

Still most of the deadly liquid was left; the thing's head bulged with
it. And no real move could be made till that head was somehow emptied.

"Your spear!" panted Denny, who was armed only with the three-
foot club which was all that was left of the spear that had entered the
acid bag.

Jim nodded. As he had done under the acid vat, he drew it back for
a throw — and shot it forward with all the power of his magnificent
shoulders.

The glittering length of steel slashed into the flabby, living syringe.
A fountain of molasseslike liquid gushed out.

The move had not been elaborately reasoned out; it had been a natural; almost instinctive one, simply a blow struck for the purpose of
draining the dread reservoir of its sticky contents. But the results — as
logical and inevitable as they were astounding and unforeseen — were
such that the move could not have been wiser had all the gods of war
conspired to help the two men with shrewd advice.

The searching spear-point had evidently found the brain behind the
syringe of the thing; for it reared in an agony that could only have been
that of approaching death, and ran amuck.

No longer did the ruling brain that crouched behind it have the power
to guide its movements, it seemed. The telepathic communications had
been snapped with that crashing spear-point. It charged blindly, undi-
rected, in havoc-wreaking circles. And in an instant the whole aspect of
the battle had been changed.

The ring of living armor presented by the other soldiers was broken
as the enormous, dying termite charged among them. Furthermore, the
fountain of thick brown liquid exuding from its head, smeared the limbs
of the soldiers the blind, crazed thing touched, as well as its own.

In thirty seconds or less the wounded giant was down, still alive, but
wriggling feebly in a binding sheath of its own poison. And with it, so
smeared as to be utterly out of the struggle, were three of the others.

Quick to seize the advantage, Jim leaped to wrench his spear from the conquered giant's head. And side by side he and Denny started again the charge against the ruler's guards, which, while still mighty in defense, were by their very nature unable to attack.

Three of these guards were left. Two of them were the freaks with the great, armored, bung-heads — and the soft and vulnerable bodies. The third was of the syringe type, with invulnerable horn breastplate and body armor — but with a head that, now its fatal liquid was exhausted, was useless in battle.

"Take 'em one by one," grunted Jim, setting the example by swinging his spear at the body of the nearest guard. "We'll get at that damn thing with the overgrown brains yet!"

His spear clanged on iron-hard horn as the termite swung its unwieldy head to protect its unarmored body. The force of the contact tore the spear from his hand; but almost before it could drop, he had recovered it. And in that flashing instant Denny had darted in at the side of the thing and half disembowelled it with a thrust of the acid-blunted point of his three-foot bar, and a lightninglike wrench up and to the side.

"Only two left!" cried Jim, stabbing at the flabby head of the syringe-monster that loomed a foot above his own head. "We'll do it yet, Denny!"

But at that moment a clashing and rattling at the doorway suddenly burst in on the din of the eery fight. Both men stared at each other with surrender in their eyes.

"Now we *are* all through!" yelled Jim, almost calm in his complete resignation. "But we'll try to reach that devilish thing before we're doomed!"

IN the heat of the swift, deadly fray, the two men had forgotten for the moment, that these few soldiers ranged against them were not all the fighters in the mound city. But the quaking intellect they were striving to reach had not forgotten! At some time early in the one-sided struggle it had sent out a soundless call to arms. And now, in the doorway, struggling to force through in numbers too great for the entrance's narrow limits, were the first of the soldier hordes the ruler had commanded to report here for fight duty. And behind them, as far as the eye could see, the tunnel was blocked by yet others marching to kill the creatures that menaced their leader. The abortive effort at escape, it seemed, was doomed.

The strength of desperation augmented Jim's naturally massive muscular power. He whirled his spear high over his head, clubwise. Disdaining now to try for a thrust behind and to one side of the great conical head that faced him, he brought the bar down with sledge-hammer force on the horn-plated thing.

As though it had been a willow wand, the big bar whistled through the air in its descent. With a crack that could be heard even above the crashing mandibles of the soldiers pouring across the hundred-yard floor toward the scene of battle, the bar landed on the living buckler of a head.

The head could not have been actually harmed. But the brain behind it was patently jarred and numbed for an instant. The great creature stood still, its head weaving slowly back and forth. Jim swung his improvised club in another terrific arc. . . .

Denny darted around behind the ponderously wheeling bulk of the last remaining guard to the team of worker termites. He, too, swung his arms high — over the bloated brain-bag that cowered down between the backs that bore it — leaping here and there to avoid the blunt mandibles of the burden bearers. He, too, brought down his three-foot length of bar with all the force he could muster, the sight of that swollen, hideous head atop the withered remnants of termite body lending power to his muscles.

And now, just as the nearest of the soldiers reached out for them, the termite-ruler lay helpless on the backs of its living crutches, with its attenuated body quivering convulsively, and its balloonlike, fragile head cleft almost in two halves. It was possible that even that terrific injury might not be fatal to a thing so great and flexible of brain, and so divorced from the ills as well as the powers of the flesh. But for the moment at least it was helpless, an inert mass on the patient backs of the termite team.

"To the acid vat," snapped Jim. "We'll make our last stand there."

Dodging the nearest snapping mandibles, Denny ran beside his companion to where the termite, dead now, with its distended abdomen deflated and the last of the acid trickling from the hole caused by Jim's spear, still hung head down from the ceiling.

The powerful ruler of this vast underground city was crushed — for the moment at least. But the fate of the two humans seemed no less certain than it had before. For now the huge chamber was swarming with the giant soldiers. In numbers so great that they crashed and rattled against each other as they advanced, they marched toward the place where the broken monarch still quivered in weak convulsions — and behind which, near the acid vat, the two men crouched.

CHAPTER IX
The Cannibalistic Orgy

AT first Jim and Dennis could only comprehend the *numbers* of the foe — could only grip their bars and resolve to die as expensively as possible. But then, as a few seconds elapsed during which they were amazingly not charged by the insects, they began to notice the *actions* of the things.

They were swarming so thickly about the spot where their leader had fallen that all the men could see was their struggling bodies. And the movements of these soldiers were puzzling in the extreme.

The things seemed, of a sudden, to be fighting among themselves! At any rate, they were not hurrying to attack the unique, two-legged bugs by the deflated acid bag.

Instead, they seemed to be having a monstrous attack of colic as they rolled about their vanquished monarch. With their antennae weaving wildly, and their deadly jaws crashing open and shut along the floor, they were fairly wallowing about that section. And the crowding ring of soldiers surrounding the wallowers were fighting like mad things to shove them out of place.

Over each other they struggled and rolled, those on the top and sides of the solid mass pressing to get in and down. In stark astonishment, the two men watched the inexplicable conflict — and wondered why they had not already been rushed and sliced to pieces by the steely, ten-foot mandibles.

In Dennis' mind, as he watched, wide-eyed, the crazy battle of the monsters around the spot, a memory struggled to be recognized. He had seen something vaguely like this before, on the upper earth, what was it?

Abruptly he remembered what it was. And with the recollection — and all the possibilities of deliverance it suggested — he shouted aloud and clutched Jim's arm with trembling fingers.

That scene of carnage suggested to his mind the day he had seen a cloud of vultures fighting over the carcass of a horse in the desert. The mad pushing, the slashing and rending of each other as all fought for the choice morsels of dead flesh! It was identical.

The termites, he knew, were deliberately cannibalistic. A race so efficiently run, so ingenious in letting nothing of possible value go to waste, would almost inevitably be trained to consume the bodies of dead fellow beings. And now — now . . .

The gruesome monarch, that thing of monstrous brain and almost nonexistent body, was no longer the monarch. It was either dead, or utterly helpless. In that moment of death or helplessness — was it being fallen upon and eaten by the horde of savage things it normally ruled? Did the termite hordes make a practice of devouring their helpless and worn-out directing brains as it was known they devoured all their worn-out, no longer potent queens?

It certainly looked as if that was what the leaderless horde of soldiers was doing here! Or, at any rate, trying to do; accustomed to being fed by the workers, with mandibles too huge to permit of normal self-feeding, they would probably be able to hardly more than strain clumsily after the choice mass beneath them and absorb it in morsels so small as to be more a source of baffled madness than of satisfaction.

Which latter conjecture seemed certainly to support the theory that the soldier termites were not trying to help their fallen monarch, but were trampling and slashing it to death in an effort to devour it!

"Quick!" snapped Denny, realizing that it was a chance that must not be overlooked; that even if he were wrong, they might as well die trying to get to the doorway as be crushed to death where they stood. "Run to the exit!"

"Through that nightmare army?" said Jim, astounded. "Why, we haven't a chance of making it!"

"Come, I say!" Denny dragged him a few feet by main force. "I hope — I believe — we won't be bothered. If a pair of jaws crushes us, it will probably be by accident and not design — the brutes are too busy to bother about us now."

Still gazing at Denny as though he thought him insane, Jim tarried no longer. He began to edge his way, by Denny's side, toward the distant door.

IN a very few feet Denny's theory was proved right. None of the gigantic insects tried to attack them. But even so that journey to the exit, a distance of more than the length of a football field, was a ghastly business.

On all sides the giant, armored bodies rushed and shoved. The clash of horn breastplates against armored legs, of mandibles and granitic heads against others of their kind, was ear-splitting. The monsters, in their effort to indulge the cannibalistic instinct — at once so horrible to the two humans, and so fortunate for them — were completely heedless of their own welfare and everything else.

Like giant ice cakes careening in the break-up of a flood, they crunched against each other; and like loose ice cakes in a flood, every now and then one was forced clear up off its feet by the surrounding rush, to fall back to the floor a moment later with a resounding crash.

It would seem an impossibility for any two living things as relatively weak and soft as men to find a way through such a maelstrom. Yet — Jim and Denny did.

Several times one or the other was knocked down by a charging, blind monster. Once Denny was almost caught and crushed between two of the rock-hard things. Once Jim only saved himself from a pair of terrific, snapping jaws that rushed his way, by using his short spear as a pole and vaulting up and over them onto the monster's back, where he was allowed to slide off unheeded as the maddened thing continued in its rush. But they reached the door!

There they gazed fearfully down the corridor, sure there would be hundreds more of the soldiers crowding to answer the last call of their ruling, master mind. But only a few stragglers were to be seen, and these, called to the grim feast by some sort of instinct or perhaps some sense of smell, rushed past with as little attempt to attack them as the rest.

The two men ran down the tunnel, turned a corner into an ascending tunnel they remembered from their trip in, raced up this, hearts pounding wildly with the growing hope of actually escaping from the mound with their lives — and then halted. Jim cursed bitterly, impotently.

Branching off from this second tunnel, all looking exactly alike and all identical in the degree of their upward slant, were five more tunnels! Like spokes of a wheel, they radiated out and up; and no man could have told which to take. They stopped, in despair, as this phase of their situation, unthought of till now, was brought home to them.

"God! The place is a labyrinth! How can we ever find, our way out?" groaned Jim.

"All we can do is keep going on — and up," said Denny, with a shake of his head.

At random, they picked the center of the five underground passages, and walked swiftly along it. And now they began to come in contact again with the normal life of the vast mound city.

Here soldiers were patrolling up and down with seeming aimlessness, while near-by workers labored at shoring up collapsing sections of tunnel wall, or at carrying staggering large loads of food from one unknown place to another. But now there seemed to be a certain lack of system, of coordination, in the movements of the termites.

"Damned funny these soldiers aren't joining in the rush with the rest to get to the laboratory in answer to the command of the ruler," said Jim, warily watching lest one of the gigantic guards end the queer truce and rush them. "And look at the way the workers move — just running aimlessly back and forth with their loads. I don't get it."

"I think I do," said Denny. He pitched his voice low, and signed for Jim to walk more slowly, on tiptoe. "These soldiers aren't with the rest because only a certain number was called. It's simple mathematics: if all the soldiers in the mound tried to get in that room back there where the ruler was, they'd get jammed immovably in the tunnels near-by. The king-termite, with all the astounding reasoning power it must have had, called only as many as could crowd in, in order to avoid a jam in which half the soldiers in the city might be killed.

"As for the aimless way the workers are moving — you forget they haven't a leader any more. They are working by habit and instinct only, carrying burdens, building new wall sections, according to blind custom alone, and regardless of whether the carrying and building are necessary."

"In that case," sighed Jim, "we'd have a good chance to getting out of here — if we could only find the path!"

"I'm sure we can find the path, and I'm sure we can get out," said Denny confidently. "For in a mound of this size there must be many paths leading to the upper world, and there is no reason — with the omnipotent ruling brain dead and eaten — why any of these creatures should try to stop or fight us."

Which was good logic — but which left entirely out of consideration that one factor which man so often forgets but is still inevitably governed by: the unpredictable whims of fate. For on their way out they were to blunder into the one place in all the mound which was — death or no death of the ruling power — absolutely deadly to them; and were to arouse the terrible race about them to frenzies that were based, not on any reasoned thought processes, or which in any case they were of themselves incapable, but on the more grim and fanatic foundations of unreasoned, primal, outraged instinct.

CHAPTER X
The Termite Queen

THE slope of the upward-leading tunnels had become less noticeable, from which fact the two men reasoned hopefully that they were near ground level. And now they began to see termite workers bearing a new sort of burden: termite eggs, sickly looking lumps that had only too obviously been newly laid.

A file of workers approached. In a long line, each with an egg, looking for all the world like a file of human porters bearing the equipment of a jungle expedition. Slowly, the things moved — carefully — bound for some such vast incubator as the one Jim and Dennis had stumbled into some hours before.

"We want to go in the opposite direction from them," Denny whispered. "They're coming from the Queen termite's den — and we don't want to blunder in there!"

They about-faced, and moved with the workers till they came to the nearest passage branching away from the avenue on which the file marched. Denny dabbed at his forehead.

"Lucky those things came in time to warn us," he said. "From what little science knows of the termites, I can guess that the Queen's chamber would be a chamber of horrors for us!"

They walked on, searching for another main avenue, such as the one they had left; which might be an artery leading to the outside world. But they had not gone far when they were again forced to change their course.

Ahead of them, marching in regular formation, came a band of soldiers larger than the usual squad. They filled the tunnel so compactly that the two men did not dare try to squeeze past them.

"Here," whispered Jim, pointing to a side tunnel.

They stole down it; but in a moment it developed that their choice had been an unlucky one: the crash of the heavy, armored bodies continued to follow them. The soldiers had turned down that tunnel, too.

"Are they after us again?" whispered Jim.

Denny shrugged. There was still a remnant of the disguising termite-paste on their bodies to fool the insects. It seemed impossible that the ruling brain behind them had survived the cannibalistic rush and taken command of the mound again? But — was anything impossible in this world of terror?

Steadily the two were forced to retreat before the measured advance of the guards. And now the tunnel they were in broadened — and abruptly ended in another of the vast chambers that seemed to dot the mound city at fairly regular intervals. But this one appeared to be humming with activity, if the noise coming from within it was any indication.

The two passed at the threshold, dismayed at the evidence of super-activity in the chamber ahead of them. But while they paused there, the soldiers behind them rounded a corner. They could not go back. There were no more of the opportune side entrances to dodge into. All they could do was retreat still farther — into the vast room before them.

They did so, reluctantly, moving step by step as the marching band behind them crashed rhythmically along. But once inside the great chamber, they shrank back against the wall with whispered imprecations at the final, desperate trick fate had played on them.

Their path of retreat, leading around labyrinthine corners and by-passages, had doubled back on them without their having been aware of it. They were in the very place Dennis had wished so much to avoid — the chamber of the Queen termite!

High overhead, almost lost in the dimness, was the arching roof. Around the circular walls were innumerable tunnel entrances. At each of these stood a termite guard — picked soldiers half again as large as the ordinary soldiers, with mandibles so great and heavy that it was a marvel the insects could support them.

Hurrying here and there were worker termites. And these were centering their activities on an object as fearful as anything that ever haunted the mind of a madman.

Up and back, this object loomed, half filling the enormous room like a zeppelin in a hangar. And like a zeppelin — a blunt, bloated zeppelin — the object was circular and tapered at both ends. But the zeppelin was a living thing — a horrible travesty of life.

At the end facing the two men was a tiny dot of a head, almost lost in the whitish mass of the enormous body. Around this a cluster of worker termites pressed, giving nourishment to the insatiable mouth. At the far end of the vast shape another cluster of termites thronged. And these bore away a constant stream of termite eggs — that dripped from the zeppelinlike, crammed belly at the rate of almost one a second.

Her Highness, the Queen — two hundred tons of flabby, greasy flesh, immobile, able only to eat and lay eggs.

"My God," whispered Jim. Utterly unstrung, he gazed at that mighty, loathsome mass, listening to its snapping jaws as it took on the tons of nourishment needed for its machinelike functioning. "My God!"

Instinctively he whirled to run back through the entrance they had come through. But now, with the admittance of the soldier band that had pressed them in here, the entrance was guarded again by one of the giants permanently stationed there.

"What had we better do?" he breathed to Denny.

Dennis stared helplessly around. He had noticed that the termites in here were acting differently from the others they had encountered since leaving the lair of the termite-ruler. These were moving uneasily, restlessly, stopping now and again with waving, inquisitive antennae. It looked ominously as though they had sensed the presence of intruders here in the sanctum where their race was born, and were dimly wondering what to do.

"We might try each tunnel mouth, one by one, on the chance that we can find a careless guard somewhere," Dennis muttered at last. "But for heaven's sake don't touch any of the brutes! I think that at the slightest signal the whole mob of the things would spring on us and tear us to pieces. Most of the paste is rubbed off by now."

Jim nodded. He had no desire to brush against one of the colossal, special guard of soldiers if he could help it, or against any of the relatively weak workers that might give the signal of alarm.

Stealing silently along among the blind, instinctively agitated monsters, they worked a circuitous way from one exit to another. But nowhere did any chance of getting out of the place present itself. Across each tunnel mouth was placed one of the enormous guards, twelve-foot mandibles opened like a waiting steel trap.

Halfway around the tremendous room they went, without mishap, but also without finding an exit they could slip through. And then, in the rear of the vast bulk of the Queen, it happened.

One of the worker termites, bearing an egg in its mandibles, faltered, and dropped its precious burden. The thing fell squashily to the floor within a foot of Jim, who had brushed against the wall to let the burden bearer pass without touching him. Jim, attempting to sidestep away from the spot, as the worker put out blind feelers, to search for the dropped egg, lost his balance for a fraction of a second — and stepped squarely on the nauseous ovoid!

Frantically he stepped out of the mess he had created, and the two stood staring at each other, holding their breaths, fearful of what might result from that accidental destruction of budding termite life.

The worker, feeling about for its burden, came in contact with the shattered egg. It drew back abruptly, as though in perplexity: soft and tough, the egg should not have broken merely from being dropped. Then it felt again. . . .

For a few seconds nothing whatever occurred. The two breathed again, and began to hope that their fears had been meaningless. But that was not to be.

The worker termite finally began to rush back and forth, antennae whipping from side to side, patently trying to discover the cause of the tragedy. And Jim and Dennis rushed back and forth, too, engaged in a deadly game of blind man's buff as they tried to avoid the questing antennae — which, registering sensation by touch instead of smell, was not to be fooled by the last disappearing traces of the termite-paste.

The game did not last long. One of the feelers whipped against Dennis' legs — and hell broke loose!

The worker emitted a sound like the shriek of a circular saw gone wild. And on the instant all its fellows, and the gigantic guards at the exits, stiffened to rigid attention.

Again came the roaring sound, desolate, terrible, at once a call to arms and a funeral dirge. And now every termite in the dim, cavernous chamber began the battle dance Jim and Dennis had seen performed by the termite guard when it was confronted by the horde of ants. Not moving their feet, they commenced to sway back and forth, while long, rhythmic shudders convulsed their grotesque bodies. It was a formal declaration of war against whatever mad things had dared invade the fountain-spring of their race.

Jim and Dennis leaped toward the nearest exit, determined to take any risk on the chance of escaping from the horde of things now aware of their presence and ravening for their blood. But in this exit — the only one accessible to them now — the guard had commenced the jaw-clashing that closed openings more efficiently than steel plates could have done. An attempt to pass those enormous mandibles presented no risk; what it presented was suicide.

By now the dread war dance had stopped. All the termites in the chamber were converging slowly toward the spot where the termite had given the rasping alarm. Even the workers, ordinarily quick to run from danger, were advancing instead of retreating. Of all living things in the room only the Queen, unable to move her mountainous bulk, did not join in the slow, sure move to slash to pieces the hated trespassers.

Again the questing antennae of the worker that had given the alarm touched one of the men. With a deafening rasp it sprang toward them, blind but terrible.

Dennis swung his steel club. It clashed against the scarcely less hard mandibles of the worker, not harming them, but seeming to daze the insect a little.

Jim followed the act by plunging his longer spear into the soft body. No words were wasted by the two men. It was a fight for life again, with the odds even more heavily against them than they had been in the ruler's lair.

Behind them, blocking the only exit they had any chance whatever of reaching, the guard continued its clashing mandible duty. If only it, too, would join in the blind search for the trespassers, thus giving them an opportunity of slipping out! But the monster gave no indication of doing such a thing.

Another worker termite flung its bulk at them. Its mandibles, tiny in comparison with those of the great guards but still capable of slicing either of the men in two, snapped perilously close to Jim's body. There was a second's concerted action: Dennis' club lashed against the thing's head, Jim's spear tore into the vulnerable body.

Ringing them round, the main band of the termites moved closer. They moved slowly, in no hurry, apparently only too sure the enemy could not possibly get away from them. And the two worker termites killed were mere incidents compared to the avalanche of mandible and horn that would be on them in about thirty seconds.

However, the two dead termites gave Jim a sudden inspiration. He glanced from the carcasses to the mechanically moving, deadly jaws of the guard that barred the nearest exit.

"Denny," he panted, "feed it this."

He pointed first toward the nearest carcass and then toward the rock-crushing, steadily snapping jaws.

"I'll try to hold the bridge here —"

But Dennis was on his way, catching Jim's idea with the first gesture.

He stooped down, and caught the dead termite by two of its legs. Close to two hundred pounds the mass weighed; but strength is an inconstant thing, and increases or decreases according to the vital needs of life-preservation.

Clear of the floor, Denny lifted the bulk, and with its repulsive weight clasped in his arms, he advanced toward the mighty guard.

Behind him, Jim glared desperately at the third termite that was about to attack. No feeble worker this, but one of the most colossal of all the Queen's guard.

Towering over Jim, mandibles wide open and ready to smash over its prey, the giant reared toward him. And behind him came the main body of the horde. It was painfully evident that the clash with the lone soldier would be the last single encounter. After that the hundreds of the herd would be on the men, tearing and trampling them to bits.

During the thing's steady, inexorable approach, which had taken far less time than that required to tell of it, Jim had clenched his fingers around his spear and calculated as to the best way to hold the monster off for just the few seconds needed by Denny to try the plan suggested.

The monster ended its slow advance in a lunge, that, for all its great bulk, was lightning quick. But a shade more quickly, Jim sidestepped the terrible mandibles, leaped back along the armored body till he had reached the unarmored rear, and thrust his spear home with all his force.

The hideous guard reared with pain and rage. But this was no worker termite, to be killed with a thrust. As though nothing had happened, the huge hulk wheeled around. The mandibles crashed shut with deafening force over the space Jim had occupied but an instant before.

And now the inner circle of the multiple ring of death was within a few yards. Jim leaped to put himself behind the living barrier of the attacking soldier. But it was only a matter of a few seconds now, before he and Denny would be caught in the blind bull charges of the wounded soldier or by the surrounding ring of maddened termites.

"Denny?" he shouted imploringly over his shoulder, not daring to take his eyes off the danger in front of him.

"Soon!" he heard Dennis pant.

The entomologist had got almost up to the twelve-foot jaws that closed the exit. He paused a moment, gathering strength. Then he heaved the soft mass of the dead termite into the clashing mandibles.

"Jim!" he cried, as the burden left his arms.

Jim turned, raced the few yards intervening between the ring of death and the doorway. Together they waited to see if their forlorn hope would work. . . .

It could not have lasted more than a second, that wait, yet it seemed at least ten minutes. And then both cried aloud — and crouched to repeat the maneuver that had saved them from death when they had first entered this insect hell.

For the enormous, smashing jaws had caught the body of the worker termite with ferocious eagerness, and were worrying the inanimate carcass with terrible force.

The great jaws were occupied just an instant before the monster sensed that it was one of his own kind that he was mangling so thoroughly. But in that instant Jim had slid on his chest along the floor past the armored head and shoulders, and Dennis had leaped to follow.

But Dennis was not to get off so lightly.

The charging ring of termites had closed completely in by now. The snapping mandibles of the nearest one were up to him. They opened; shut.

They caught Denny on the back swing, knocking him six feet away instead of slicing him wide open. Denny got to his feet almost before he had landed; but between him and the exit was the bulk of the termite that had felled him, and in the doorway the guard had dropped the body it was slashing to bits, and had recommenced its slashing jaw movements.

"Jim! For God's sake. . . ." shrieked the doomed man.

Beside himself, he managed to hurdle clear over the massive insect between him and the doorway. But there he stopped, with the guard's great mandibles fanning the air less than a foot from him. "Jim!" came the agonized cry again.

And behind the gigantic termite, in the tunnel, with at least a possibility of safety lying open before him, Jim heard and answered the call.

Savagely he plunged his spear into the unarmored rear of the guard, tore it out, thrust again. . . .

The thing heaved and struggled to turn, shaking the tunnel with its rasping anger — and taking its attention at last away from the duty of closing that tunnel mouth.

With no room to run and slide, Denny fell to the floor and commenced to creep through the narrow space between the trampling guard's bulk and the wall. He felt his left arm and shoulder go numb as he was crushed for a fleeting instant against the wood partition. Broken, he thought dimly. The collar-bone. But still he kept moving on.

HE moved in a haze of pain and weakness. He did not see that he had passed clear of the menacing hulk — that his slow crawling had been multiplied in results by the fact that the termite guard had finally, stopped trying to turn in the narrow passage and had rushed ahead into the Queen's chamber, to turn there and come dashing back. He did not see that Jim was finally disarmed and completely helpless, with his spear buried beyond recovery in the bulk of the maddened guard. He hardly felt Jim's supporting arm as it was thrust under him, to half drag and half lead him along the tunnel away from the horde behind.

He only knew that they were moving forward, with the din behind them — as the grim cohorts of the Queen fought to all crowd ahead in the narrow passage at once — keeping pace with them in spite of all they could do to make haste. And he only knew that finally Jim gave a great shout, and that suddenly they were standing under a rent in a tunnel roof through which sunlight was pouring.

Several worker termites were laboring to close up the chink and cut off the sunlight; but these, not being of the band outraged by the destruction of the egg in the Queen's chamber, moved swiftly away as the two men advanced.

Jim reached up and tore with frantic hands at the crumbling edges of the rotten wood overhead. Ignoring his gashed and bleeding fingers, he widened the breach till he, could pull himself up through it. Then he reached down, caught Denny's sound arm, and raised him by main strength.

They were in the clear air of the outer world once more, on a terrace in the mound low down near its base.

Jim and Dennis half slid, half fell down the near terrace slope to the jungle of grass stalks beneath. And there Denny bit his lip sharply, struggled against the weakness overcoming him — and fainted.

Jim caught him up over his shoulder, and staggered forward through the jungle. Behind, the termites poured out through the broken wall in an enraged flood, braving even the sunlight and outer air in their chase of the invaders that had, profaned the Queen's chamber.

"Matt!" shouted Jim with all the strength of his lungs, forgetting that his voice could not be heard by normal human ears. "Matt!"

But if Matthew Breen could not hear, he could see. The slightest inattention at his guard duty at that second would have resulted in two deaths. But he was on the alert.

Jim saw the sun blotted out swiftly, saw a huge, pinkish-gray wall swoop down between him and Denny, and the deadly horde of termites pursuing them. Then he saw another pinkish-gray wall, in which was set something — a shallow, regular, hollowed plateau — that looked familiar. The patty-dish in which he and Denny had been carried to this place of death and horror.

Jim knew he could not clamber into that great plateau; he was too exhausted. But the necessity was spared him.

The patty-dish scooped down under him, uprooting huge trees, digging up square yards of earth all around him. He was flung from his feet to roll helplessly beside the unconscious Dennis, as men and earth and all were shifted from the dish's rim to its center.

Like gigantic express elevator the dish soared dizzily up in the tremendous hand that held it, over the vast pile of the mound city, over all the surrounding landscape, and was borne back toward Matt's automobile — and toward the laboratory where the bulk of their bodies waited, in protoplasmic form, in the dome of the glass bell.

CHAPTER XI
Back to Normal

"I THINK," said Jim, loading his pipe, "that now I really will settle down. No other adventures could seem like much after the one" — he repressed a shiver — "we've just passed through."

"And I think," said Dennis, following his own line of thought, "that as far the world of science goes, my exploring has been for nothing. Try to tell sober scientists of the specially evolved, huge-brained thing that rules the termite tribe and forms and holds the marvelous organization it has? Try to tell them — now that Matt has to stubbornly decided to keep secret his work with element eighty-five — that we were reduced to a quarter of an inch in height, and that we went through a mound and saw at first hand the things we describe? They'd shut me in an asylum!"

The two were sitting in Denny's apartment, once more conventionally clothed, and again their normal five feet eleven, and six feet two.

The reassembling of Denny's body had done odd things. Jim had set the broken bone with rough skill before stepping under the glass bell; and the fracture had been healed automatically by the growing deposit of protoplasmic substance resulting when Matt threw his switch.

But Denny's missing finger had baffled the reversing process. With no tiny pattern to form around, the former substance of his finger had simply gathered in a shapeless knob of flesh and bone like a tumorous growth sprouting from his hand. It would have to be amputated.

But the marvels performed under Matthew Breen's glass bell were far secondary to the two men. The things they had recently seen and undergone, and the possibility of telling folks about them, occupied their attention exclusively.

"Then you're not going to write a monograph on the real nature of termites, as you'd planned?" Jim asked Denny.

Denny shrugged dispiritedly. "People would take it for a joke instead of a scientific treatise if I did," he said.

Jim puffed reflectively at his pipe. A thought had come, to him that seemed to hold certain elements of possibility.

"Why not do this," he suggested: "Write it up first as a straight story, and see if people will believe it. Then, if they do, you can rewrite it as scientific fact."

And eventually they decided to do just that. And — here is their story.

THE PLANETOID OF PERIL

HARLEY 2Q14N20 stopped for a moment outside the great dome of the Celestial Developments Company. Moodily he stared at their asteroid development chart. It showed, as was to be expected, the pick of the latest asteroid subdivision projects: the Celestial Developments Company, established far back in 2045, would handle none but the very best. Small chance of his finding anything here!

However, as he gazed at the chart, hope came suddenly to his face, and his heart beat high under his sapphire blue tunic. There was an asteroid left for sale there—one blank space among the myriad, pink-lettered Sold symbols. Could it be that here was the chance he had been hunting so desperately?

He bent closer, to read the description of the sphere, and the hope faded gradually from his countenance. According to its orbit and location, and the spectroscopic table of its mineral resources, it was a choice planetoid indeed. Of course such a rich little sphere, listed for sale by the luxurious Celestial Developments Company, would cost far more than he could ever rake together to pay for an asteroid.

Shaking his head, he adjusted his gravity regulator to give him about a pound and a half of weight, and started to float on. Then, his lips twisting at his own absurd hopefulness, he stopped again; and after another moment of indecision turned into the archway that led to the concern's great main office. After all, it wouldn't hurt to inquire the price, even though he knew in advance it would be beyond his humble means.

A youngster in the pale green of the one-bar neophyte in business promptly glided toward him.

"Something for you to-day, sir?" he asked politely.

"Yes," said Harley. "I'm looking around for a planetoid; want to get a place of my own out a way from Earth. Something, you understand, that may turn out to be a profitable investment as well as furnishing an exclusive home-site. I see on your chart that you have a sphere left for sale, in the Red Belt, so I came in to ask about it."

"Ah, you mean asteroid Z-40," said the youngster, gazing with envious respect at the ten-bar insignia, with the crossed Sco drills, that proclaimed Harley to be a mining engineer of the highest rank. "Yes, that is still for sale. A splendid sphere, sir; and listed at a remarkably low figure. Half a million dollars."

"Half a million dollars!" exclaimed Harley. It was an incredibly small sum: scarcely the yearly salary of an unskilled laborer. "Are you sure that's right?"

"Yes, that's the correct figure. Down payment of a third, and the remaining two thirds to be paid out of the exploitation profits—"

Here the conversation was interrupted by an elderly, grey-haired man with the six-bar dollar-mark insignia of a business executive on his purple tunic. He had been standing nearby, and at the mention of asteroid Z-40 had looked up alertly. He glided to the two with a frown on his forehead, and spoke a few curt words to the neophyte, who slunk away.

"Sorry, sir," he said to Harley. "Z-40 isn't for sale."

"But your young man just told me that it was," replied Hartley, loath to give up what had begun to look like an almost unbelievable bargain.

"He was mistaken. It's not on the market. It isn't habitable, you see."

"What's wrong—hasn't it an atmosphere?"

"Oh, yes. One that is exceptionally rich in oxygen, as is true of all the spheres we handle. With a late model oxygen concentrator, one would have no trouble at all existing there."

"Is its speed of revolution too great?"

"Not at all. The days are nearly three hours long: annoying till you get used to it, but nothing like the inferior asteroids of the Mars Company where days and nights are less than ten minutes in duration."

"Well, is it barren, then? No minerals of value? No vegetation?"

"The spectroscope shows plenty of metals, including heavy radium deposits. The vegetation is as luxuriant as that of semi-tropic Earth."

"Then why in the name of Betelguese," said Harley, exasperated, "won't you sell the place to me? It's exactly what I've been looking for, and what I'd despaired of finding at my price."

"I'm forbidden to tell why it isn't for sale," said the executive, starting to float off. "It might hurt our business, reputation if the truth about that bit of our celestial properties became widely known—Oh, disintegrate it all! Why wasn't the thing erased from the chart weeks ago!"

"Wait a minute." Harley caught his arm and detained him. "You've gone too far to back out now. I'm too eager to find some such place as your Z-40 to be thrown off the subject like a child. *Why* isn't it for sale?"

The man tightened his lips as though to refuse to answer, then shrugged.

"I'll tell you," he said at last. "But I beg of you to keep it confidential. If some of our investors on neighboring asteroids ever found out about the peril adjoining them on Z-40, they'd probably insist on having their money back."

He led the way to a more secluded spot under the big dome, and spoke in a low tone, with many a glance over his shoulder to see if anyone were within earshot.

"Z-40 is an exceptionally fine bit of property. It is commodious; about twenty miles in diameter. Its internal heat is such that it has a delightful climate in spite of the extreme rarity of atmosphere common to even the best of asteroids. It has a small lake; in fact it has about everything a man could want. Yet, as I said, it is uninhabitable."

His voice sank still lower.

"You see, sir, there's already a tenant on that sphere, a tenant that was in possession long before the Celestial Developments Company was organized. And it's a tenant that can't be bought off or reasoned with. It's some sort of beast, powerful, ferocious, that makes it certain death for a man to try to land there."

"A beast?" echoed Harley. "What kind of a beast?"

"We don't know. In fact we hardly even know what it looks like. But from what little has been seen of it, it's clear that it is like no other specimen known to universal science. It's something enormous, some freak of animal creation that seems invulnerable to man's smaller weapons. And that is why we can't offer the place for sale. It would be suicide for anyone to try to make a home there."

"*Has* anyone ever tried it?" asked Harley. "Any competent adventurer, I mean?"

"Yes. Twice we sold Z-40 before we realized that there was something terribly wrong with it. Both buyers were hardy, intrepid men. The first was never heard of after thirty-six hours on the asteroid. The second man managed to escape in his Blinco Dart, and came back to Earth to tell of a vast creature that had attacked him during one of the three-hour nights. His hair was white from the sight of it, and he's still in a sanitarium, slowly recovering from the nervous shock."

Harley frowned thoughtfully. "If this thing is more than a match for one man, why don't you send an armed band with heavy atomic guns and clear the asteroid by main force?"

"My dear sir, don't you suppose we've tried that? Twice we sent expensive expeditions to Z-40 to blow the animal off the face of the sphere, but neither expedition was able to find the thing, whatever it is. Possibly it has intelligence enough to hide if faced by overwhelming force. When the second expedition failed, we gave it up. Poor business to go further. Already, Z-40 has cost us more than we could clear from the sale of half a dozen planetoids."

For a long time Harley was silent. The Company was a hard headed, cold blooded concern. Anything that kept them from selling an asteroid must be terrible indeed.

His jaw set in a hard line. "You've been honest with me," he said at length. "I appreciate it. Just the same—I still want to buy Z-40. Maybe I can oust the present tenant. I'm pretty good with a ray-pistol."

"It would be poor policy for us to sell the asteroid. We don't want to become known as a firm that trades in globes on which it is fatal to land."

"Surely my fate is none of your worry?" urged Harley.

"The asteroid," began the executive with an air of finality, "is not for—"

"Man, it's *got* to be!" cried Harley. Then, with a perceptible effort he composed himself. "There's a reason. The reason is a girl. I'm a poor man, and she's heiress to fabulous—Well, frankly, she's the daughter of 3W28W12 himself!" The executive started at mention of that universally known number. "I don't want to be known as a fortune hunter; and my best bet is to find a potentially rich asteroid, cheap, and develop it—incidentally getting an exclusive estate for my bride and myself far out in space, away from the smoke and bustle of urban Earth. Z-40, save for the menace you say now has possession of it, seems to be just what I want. If I can clear it, it means the fulfillment of all my dreams. With that in view, do you think I'd hesitate to risk my neck?"

"No," said the executive slowly, looking at the younger man's powerful shoulders and square-set chin and resolute eyes. "I don't think you would. Well, so be it. I'd greatly prefer not to sell you Z-40. But if you want to sign an agreement that we're released of all blame or responsibility in case of your death, you can buy it."

"I'll sign any agreement you please," snapped Harley. "Here is a down payment of a hundred and seventy thousand dollars. My name is Harley; sign 2Q14N20; unmarried—though I hope to change that soon, if I live—occupation, mining engineer, ten-bar degree; age, thirty-four. Now draw me up a deed for Z-40, and see that I'm given a stellar call number on the switchboard of the Radivision Corporation. I'll drop around there later and get a receiving unit. Good day." And, adjusting his gravity regulator to lighten his weight to less than a pound, he catapulted out the archway.

Behind him a prosaic business executive snatched a moment from a busy day to indulge in a sentimental flight of fancy. He had read once of curious old-time beings called knights, who had undertaken to fight and slay fire-eating things called dragons for the sake of an almost outmoded emotion referred to as love. It occurred to him that this brusque man of action might be compared to just such a being. He was undertaking to slay a dragon and win a castle for the daughter of 3W28W12—

The romantic thought was abruptly broken up by the numeral. It jarred so, somehow, that modern use of numbers instead of names, when thinking of sentimental passages of long ago. "The rose is fair; but in all the world there is no rose as fair as thou, my princess 3W28W12. . . ." No, it wouldn't do.

Cursing himself for a soft-headed fool, he went to deliver a stinging rebuke to somebody for not having blocked Z-40 off the asteroid chart weeks before.

"Harley 2Q14N20," recited the control assistant at Landon Field. "Destination, asteroid Z-40. Red Belt, arc 31.3470. Sights corrected, flight period twelve minutes, forty-eight seconds past nine o'clock. All set, sir?"

Harley nodded. He stepped inside the double shell of his new Blinco Dart—that small but excellent quantity-production craft that had entirely replaced the cumbersome space ships of a decade ago—and screwed down the man-hole lid. Then, with his hand on the gravity bar, he gazed out the rear panel, ready to throw the lever at the control assistant's signal.

The move was unthinkingly, mechanically made. Too many times had he gone through this process of being aimed by astronomical calculation, and launched into the heavens, to be much stirred by the wonder of it. The journey to Z-40 in the Dart was no more disquieting than, a century and a half ago, before the United States had fused together into one vast city, a journey from Chicago to Florida would have been in one of the inefficient gasoline-driven vehicles of that day.

All his thoughts were on his destination, and on a wonder as to what could be the nature of the thing that dwelt there.

He had just come from the sanitarium where the man who'd bought Z-40 before him was recovering from nervous exhaustion. He'd gone there to try to get first hand information about the creature the executive at the Celestial Developments Company had talked so vaguely of. And the tale the convalescent had told him of the thing on the asteroid was as fantastic as it was sketchy.

A tremendous, weirdly manlike creature looming in the dim night—a thing that seemed a part of the planetoid itself, fashioned from the very dirt and rock from which it had risen—a thing immune to the ray-pistol, that latest and deadliest of man-made small-arms—a thing that moved like a walking mountain and stared with terrible, stony eyes at its prey! That was what the fellow said he had faintly made out in the darkness before his nerves had finally given way.

He had impressed Harley as being a capable kind of a person, too; not at all the sort to distort facts, nor to see imaginary figures in the night.

There was that matter of the stone splinter, however, which certainly argued that the wan, prematurely white-haired fellow was a little unbalanced, and hence not to be believed too implicitly. He'd handed it to Harley, and gravely declared it to be a bit of the monster's flesh.

"Why, it's only a piece of rock!" Harley had exclaimed before he could check himself.

"Did you ever see rock like it before?"

Turning it over in his hands, Harley had been forced to admit that he never had. It was of the texture and roughness of granite, but more heavily shot with quartz, or tridymite than any other granite he'd ever seen. It had a dull opalescent sheen, too. But it was rock, all right.

"It's a piece of the thing's hide," the man had told him. "It flaked off when it tried to pry open the man-hole cover of ray Dart. A moment after that I got Radivision arc directions from London Field, aimed my sights, and shot for Earth. It was a miracle I escaped."

"But surely your ray-pistol—" Harley had begun, preserving a discreet silence about the man's delusion concerning the stone splinter.

"I tell you it was useless as a toy! Never before have I seen any form of life that could stand up against a ray-gun. But *this* thing *did*!"

This was another statement Harley had accepted with a good deal of reservation. He had felt sure the weapon the man had used had a leak in the power chamber, or was in need of recharging, or something of the kind. For it had been conclusively proved that all organic matter withered and burned away under the impact of the Randchron ray.

Nevertheless, discounting heavily the convalescent's wild story, only a fool would have clung to a conviction that the menace on Z-40 was a trivial one. There was *something* on that asteroid, something larger and more deadly than Harley had ever heard of before in all his planetary wanderings.

He squared his shoulders. Whatever it was, he was about to face it, man against animal. He was reasonably certain his ray-gun would down anything on two legs or ten. If it didn't—well, there was nothing else that could; and he'd certainly provide a meal for the creature, assuming it ate human flesh. . . .

A mechanic tapped against the rear view panel to recall his wandering attention. The control assistant held up his hands, fingers outspread, to indicate that there were ten seconds left.

Harley's hand went to his throat, where was hung a locket—a lovely but useless trinket of the kind once much worn by Earth women—and his fingers tightened tenderly on it. It had belonged to Beatrice 3W28W12's great-great-grandmother, and Beatrice had given it to him as a token.

"With luck, my dear," he whispered aloud. "With luck. . . ."

There was a slight vibration. He threw the gravity bar over to the first notch. Earth dropped, plummet-like, away from him. He pushed the bar to the limit leg; and, at a rate of hundreds of miles a second, was repelled from Earth toward Z-40, and the thing that skulked there.

WITH a scarcely perceptible jar, he landed on the small sphere that, he hoped, was to be his future home. Before opening his man-hole lid, he went from panel to panel of the Dart and cautiously reconnoitered. He had elected to land beside the little lake that was set like a three hundred-acre gem on the surface of Z-40, and it was more than possible that the enemy had its den nearby.

However, a careful survey of the curved landscape in all directions failed to reveal a glimpse of anything remotely threatening. He donned his oxygen concentrator—in appearance a simple tube of a thing, projecting about six inches above his forehead, and set in a light metal band that encircled his head. Adjusting his gravity regulator so he wouldn't inadvertently walk clear off into empty space—he calculated his weight would be less than a twentieth of an ounce here—he stepped out of the Dart and gazed around at the little world.

Before him was the tiny lake, of an emerald green hue in the flashing sunlight. Around its shores, and covering the adjacent, softly rolling countryside as far as eye could reach, was a thick growth of carmine-tinted vegetation: squat, enormous-leaved bushes; low, sturdy trees, webbed together by innumerable vines. To left and right, miniature mountains reared ragged crests over the abbreviated horizon, making the spot he was in a peaceful, lovely valley.

He sighed. There was everything here a man could wish for—provided he could win it! Loosening his ray-pistol in its holster, he started to walk slowly around the lake to choose a site for the house he intended to build. On the opposite shore he found a place that looked suitable.

A few yards back from the water's edge, curling in a thick crescent like a giant sleeping on its side, was a precipitous outcropping of rock; curious stuff, rather like granite, that gleamed with dull opalescence in the brilliant sunlight. With that as a sort of natural buttress behind the house, and with the beautiful lake as his front dooryard, he'd have a location that any man might envy.

He returned to his Dart, hopped back across the lake in it, and unloaded his Sco drill[1]. With this he planned to sink a shaft that would serve in the future as the cellar for his villa, and in the present as an entrenchment against danger.

But now the swift night of Z-40 was almost upon him. The low slant of the descending sun warned him that he had less than ten minutes of light left, until the next three-hour day should break over the eastern rim. He placed the drums and the flexible hose of the Sco drill so that he could begin operations with it as soon as the dawn broke, and started to walk toward the precipitous outcropping of quartziferous stone immediately behind the home-site he had picked. He would climb to the top of this for a short look around, and then return to the Dart—in which double-hulled, metal fortress he thought he would be safe from anything.

He had almost reached the rock outcropping when the peculiarities of its outline struck him anew. He'd already observed that the craggy mound rather resembled a sleeping, formless giant. The closer he got to it the more the resemblance was heightened and the greater grew his perplexity.

It sprang straight up from the carmine underbrush, like a separate heap of stone cast there by some mighty hand. One end of it tapered down in a thick ridge; and this ridge had a deep, horizontal cleft running along it which made it appear as though it were divided into two leglike members. In the center the mound swelled to resemble a paunchy trunk with sagging shoulders. This was topped by a huge, nearly round ball that looked for all the world like a head. There were even rudimentary features. It was grotesque—one of those freak sculptures of nature, Harley reflected, that made it seem as though the Old Girl had a mind and artistic talent of her own.

---

1   This implement, invented by Blansco 9X247A in 2052, is not so much a "drill" as a compressor. It is somewhat superficially defined in the Universal Dictionary, 2061 edition, as "a portable mechanism which, by alternating gaseous blasts of extreme heat and cold, breaks down the atoms of inorganic matter, causing them to collapse together in dense compression." Thus a cubic yard of earth can be reduced in size, in a few moments, to a pebble no larger than a pea; which pebble would weigh, on Earth, close to a ton.

He scrambled through the brush till he reached that part of the long mound that looked like a head. There, as the sun began to stream the red lines of its descent over the sky, he prepared to ascend for his view of the surrounding landscape.

He'd got within twenty feet of the irregular ball, and had adjusted his gravity regulator to enable him to leap to its top, when he stopped as abruptly as though he had been suddenly paralyzed. Over the two deep pits that resembled nostrils in the grotesque mask of a face he thought he had observed a quiver. The illusion had occurred in just the proper place for an eyelid. It was startling, to say the least.

"I'm getting imaginative," said Harley. He spoke aloud as a man tends to do when he is alone and uneasy. "I'd better get a tighter grip on my nerves, or—good God!"

Coincident with the sound of his voice in the thin, quiet air, the huge stumps that looked like legs stirred slightly. A tremor ran through the entire mass of rock. And directly in front of Harley, less than twenty feet from where he stood, a sort of half-moon-shaped curtain of rock slid slowly up to reveal an enormous, staring eye.

Frozen with a terror such as he had never felt before in a life filled with adventure, scarce breathing, Harley glared at the monstrous spectacle transpiring before him. A hill was coming to life, A granite cliff was growing animate. It was impossible, but it was happening.

The half-moon curtains of rock that so eerily resembled eyelids, blinked heavily. He could hear a faint rasping like the rustle of sandpaper, as they did so. One of the great leg stumps moved distinctly, independent of the other one. Three columnar masses of rock—arms, or tentacles, with a dozen hinging joints in each—slowly moved away from the parent mass near the base of the head, and extended toward the Earth man.

Still in his trance, with his heart pounding in his throat till he thought it would burst, Harley watched the further awful developments. The eyelids remained opened, disclosing two great, dull eyes like poorly polished agates, which stared expressionlessly at him. There was a convulsion like a minor earthquake, and the mass shortened and heightened its bulk, raising itself to a sitting posture. The three hinged, irregular arms suddenly extended themselves to the full in a thrust that barely missed him. They were tipped, those arms, with immense claws, like interlocking, rough-hewn stone fingers. They crashed emptily together within a few feet of Harley. Then, and not till then, did the paralysis of horror loose its grip on the human.

He tore his ray-pistol from its holster and pointed it at the incredible body. An angry, blue-green cone of light leaped from the muzzle, and played over the mighty torso. Nothing happened. He squeezed the trigger back to the guard. The blue-green beam increased in intensity, and a crackling noise was audible. Under that awful power the monster should have disappeared, dissolved to a greasy mist. But it didn't.

The light beam from the ray-gun died away. The power was exhausted. It was only good for about ten seconds of such an emergency, full-force discharge, after which it must be re-charged again. The ten seconds were up. And the gigantic creature against which it had been directed had apparently felt no injury from a beam that would have annihilated ten thousand men.

The now useless ray-pistol slipped from his limp fingers. Stupefied with horror at the futility of the deadly Randchron ray against this terrible adversary, he stood rooted to the spot. Then the thing reached for him again; and his muscles were galvanized to action—to instinctive, stupid, reasonless action.

Screaming incoherently, mad with horror of the stone claws that had clutched at him, he turned and ran. In great leaps he bounded away from the accursed lake and made for the taller trees and thicker vegetation at a distance from the shore. It was the worst thing he could have done. There was a chance that he could have reached his Dart, had he thought of it, and soared aloft out of reach. But he thought of nothing. All he wanted to do, in that abysmal fear that can still make a mindless animal out of a civilized man, was to run and hide—to get away from the fearful monster that had risen up to glare at him with those stony, pitiless eyes, and to reach for him with two-fingered bands like grinding rock vises.

JUST as the sun fell below the rim of the asteroid, plunging it into a darkness only faintly relieved by the light of the stars, he crashed into the deeper underbrush. A trailing creeper tripped him in his mad flight. He fell headlong, to lie panting, sobbing for breath, in the thick carpet of blood-colored moss.

Behind him, from the direction of the lake, he heard a sudden clangor as of rock beating against metal. This endured only a short time. Then the solid ground beneath him shook slightly, and an appalling crash of trees and underbrush to the rear told him that the stone colossus was on his trail.

He leaped to his feet and continued his great bounds over the sharply curved surface of the asteroid, banging against tree trunks, bruising himself against stones, falling in the darkness to rise again and flee as before in a mad attempt to distance the crashing sound of pursuit behind him.

Then he felt himself writhing in thin air as his flying course took him over the edge of a cliff. Down, down he fell, to land in a dense bed of foliage far below. Something hit his head with terrific force. Pinwheels of light flashed before his eyes, to fade into velvety nothingness. . . .

SLOWLY, uncertainly he wavered back to consciousness. For a moment he was aware of nothing save that he was lying on some surface that was jagged and uncomfortable, and that it was broad daylight. He opened his eyes, and saw that he was reclining, across a springy bed formed of the top of a tree. Ahead of him loomed a cliff about a hundred feet high.

Remembrance suddenly came to him. The unreasoning rush through the underbrush. The nightmare creature lumbering swiftly after him. The fall over the cliff into the top of this tree.

With a cry, he sat up, expecting to see the stone giant nearby and poised to leap. But it was nowhere in sight; nor, listen as intently as he would, could he hear the sounds of its crashing path through the brush. Somehow, for the moment at least, he had been saved. Perhaps his disappearance over the cliff edge had thrown it off his track.

He became aware of the fact that it was difficult for him to breathe. His lungs were heaving in a vain effort to suck in more oxygen, and his tongue felt thick as though he were being strangled. Then he saw that his oxygen concentrator had been knocked from his head when he fell, and was dangling from a limb several feet away. It was almost out of breathing range. Had it fallen on through the branches to the ground he would have died, in his unconsciousness, in the rarified atmosphere. He reached for it; settled the band around his head again.

After once more listening and peering around to make sure the rock colossus was not about, he descended the tree that had saved his life, and began to walk in the direction he judged the lake to be. He would get into his Dart, cruise aloft out of harm's way, and perhaps think up some effective course of action.

He was thinking clearly, now. And, in the glare of daylight, no longer an unreasoning animal fleeing blindly over a dim-lit foreign sphere, he was unable to understand his panic of the night. Afraid? Of course he had been afraid! What man wouldn't have been at sight of that monstrous thing? But that he, Harley 2Q14N20, should have lost his head completely and gone plunging off into the brush like that, seemed unbelievable. To the depths of his soul he felt ashamed. And to his own soul he made the promise that he would wipe out, in action, that hour of cowardice.

As he wound his way through the squat, carmine forest, he tried to figure out the nature of the thing that had crashed balefully after him in the black hours.

It had seemed made of rock—a giant, primitive stone statue imbued with life. But it was impossible that it should really be fashioned of rock. At least it ought to be impossible. Rock is inorganic, inanimate. It simply couldn't have the spark of life in it. Harley had seen many strange creations, on many strange planets, but never had he seen inorganic mineral matter endowed with animation. Nor had anyone else.

Yet the thing *looked* as though made of stone. Of some peculiar, quartz-suffused granite—proving that the wan, white-haired man he had talked to in the sanitarium had not been mad at all, but only too terribly sane. The creature's very eyes had had a stony look. Its eyelids had rasped like stone curtains rubbing together. Its awful, two-fingered hands, or claws, had ground together like stones rubbing.

Was it akin to the lizards, the cold-blooded life of Earth? Was this rocky exterior merely a horny shell like that of a turtle? No. Horn is horn and rock is rock. The two can't be confused.

The only theory Harley could form was that the great beast was in some strange way a link between the animal and the mineral kingdoms. Its skeletal structure, perhaps, was silicate in substance, extending to provide an outside covering that had hardened into actual stone, while forming an interior support to flesh that was half organic, half inorganic matter. Some such silicate construction was to be found in the sponge, of Earth. Could this be a gigantic relative of that lowly creature? He did not know, and couldn't guess. He wasn't a zoologist. All he knew was that the thing appeared to be formed of living, impregnable stone. He knew, also, that this fabulous creature was bent on destroying him.

At this point in his reflections, the glint of water came to his eyes between the tree trunks ahead of him. He had come back to the lake.

For moments he stood behind one of the larger trees on the fringe and searched around the shore for sight of the rock giant. It was nowhere in evidence. Rapidly he advanced from the forest and ran for the Dart. From a distance it appeared to be all right: but as he drew near a cry rose involuntarily to his lips.

In a dozen places the double hull of the little space craft was battered in. The man-hole lid was torn from its braces and bent double. The glass panels, unbreakable in themselves, had been shoved clear into the cabin; their empty sash frames gaped at Harley like blinded eyes. Never again would that Blinco Dart speed through the heavens!

He went to the spot where he had left his Sco drill, and a further evidence of the thing's cold blooded ferocity was revealed. The intricate mechanism had been wrenched into twisted pieces. The drums were battered in and the flexible hose lengths torn apart in shreds. The inventor himself couldn't have put it in working order again.

He was hopelessly trapped. He had no means of fighting the colossus. He had no way of escaping into space, nor of returning to Earth and trying to raise a loan that would allow him to come back here with men and atomic guns. He hadn't even a way of intrenching himself in the ground against the next attack.

For an instant his hair prickled in a flash of the blind panic that had seized him a few hours before. With a tremendous effort of will he fought it down. This—the destruction of his precious Dart and drill—was the result of one siege of insensate fear. If he succumbed to another one he might well dash straight into the arms of death. He sank to the ground and rested his chin on his fist, concentrating all his intellect on the hopeless problem that faced him.

The surface of Z-40 was many square miles in extent. But, if he tried to hide himself, he knew it was only a question of time before he would be hunted down. The asteroid was too tiny to give him indefinite concealment. Flight, then, was futile.

But if he didn't try to conceal himself in the sparse forest lands, it meant that he must stay to face the monster at once—which was insanity. What could he do, bare-handed, against that thirty-foot, three-tentacled, silicate mass of incredible life!

It was useless to run, and it was madness to stay and confront the thing. What, then, could he do? The sun had slid down the sky and the red of another swift dusk was heralding the short night before he shook his head somberly and gave the fatal riddle up.

He rose to his feet, intending to make his way back to the concealment—such as it was—of the forest. It might be that he could find safety in some lofty treetop till day dawned again. Then he stopped, and listened. What was that?

From far away to the left he could hear faint sounds of some gargantuan stirring. And, coincident with the flickering out of the last scrap of sunlight, a distant crashing came to his ears as an enormous body smashed like an armored ship through trees and thorn bushes and trailing vines. The rock thing had found his trail and was after him again.

A second time Harley fled through the dim-lighted night, stumbling over boulders and tripping on creepers. But this time his flight was not that of panic. Frightened enough, he was; but his mind was working clearly as he leaped through the forest away from the source of the crashing.

The first thing he noted was that though—as far as his ears could inform him—he was managing to keep his lead, he wasn't outdistancing his horrible pursuer by a yard. Dark though the night was, and far away as he contrived to keep himself, the colossus seemed to cling to his trail as easily as though following a well-blazed path.

He climbed a tree, faced at right angles to the course he had pursued, and swung for the next tree. It was a long jump. But desperation lent abnormal power to his muscles, and the gravity regulator adjusted to extremely low pitch, was a great help. He made it safely. Another swinging leap into the dark, to land sprawling in a second tree; a third; a fourth. Finally be crouched in a tangle of boughs, and listened. He was a quarter of a mile from the point where he had turned from his first direction. Perhaps this deviation would throw the rock terror off.

It didn't. He heard the steady smashing noise stop. For an instant there was a silence in the darkness of the asteroid that was painful. Then the crashing was resumed, this time drawing straight toward where he was hidden. Somehow the thing had learned of his change of direction.

He continued his flight into the night, his eyes staring glassily into the darkness, his expression the ghastly one of a condemned man. And as he fled the crashing behind him told how he was followed—easily infallibly, in spite of all his twisting and turning and efforts at concealment. What hellish intelligence the monster must possess!

He ran for eternities. He ran till his chest was on fire, and the sobbing agony of his breathing could be heard for yards. He ran till spots of fire floated before his eyes and the blood, throbbing in his brain, cut out the noise of the devilish pursuit behind him. At long last his legs buckled under him, and he fell, to rise no more.

He was done. He knew it. His was the position of the hunted animal that lies panting, every muscle paralyzed with absolute exhaustion, and glares in an agony of helplessness at the hunter whose approach spells death.

The crashing grew louder. The tremor of the ground grew more pronounced as the vast pursuer pounded along with its tons and tons of weight. Harley gazed into the blackness back along the way he had come, his eyes sunk deep in the hollows fatigue had carved in his face, and waited for the end. The dark night darkened still more with the approach of another swift, inexorable dawn.

There was a terrific rending of tree trunks and webbed creepers. Dimly in the darkness he could see something that towered on a level with the tallest trees, something that moved as rapidly and steadily as though driven by machinery. Fear so great that it nauseated him, swept over him in waves; but he could not move.

The first grey smear of dawn appeared in the sky. In the ghostly greyness he got a clearer and clearer sight of the monster. He groaned and cowered there while it approached him—more slowly now, eyeing him with staring, stony orbs in which there was no expression of any kind, of rage or bate, of curiosity or triumph.

Great stumps of legs, with no joints in them, on which the colossus stalked like a moving stone tower—a body resembling an enormous boulder carved by an amateurish hand to portray the trunk of a human being—a craggy sphere of rock for a head, set directly atop the deeply riven shoulders—a face like the horrible mask of an embryonic gargoyle—a mouth that was simply a lipless chasm that opened and closed with the sound of rocks grinding together in a slow-moving glacier—the whole veiled thinly by trailing lengths of snapped vines, great shattered tree boughs, bushes, all uprooted in its stumping march through the forest! Harley closed his eyes to shut out the sight. But in spite of himself they flashed open again and stared on, as though hypnotized by the spectacle they witnessed.

THE grey of dawn lightened to the first rose tint of the rising sun. As though stung to action by the breaking of day, the thing hastened its ground-shaking pace. With one last stride, it came to Harley's side and loomed far above, the unwinking eyes glaring down at him.

The three arms, hinged at equidistant points at the base of the horrible head, slowly lowered toward his prostrate form. There was a grating noise as the creature hinged in the middle and bent low, bringing its enormous, staring eyes within two yards of his face.

One of its hands closed over his leg, tentatively, experimentally, as though to ascertain of what substance he was made. He cried aloud as the rock vise, like a gigantic lobster claw, squeezed tight. The thing drew back abruptly. Then the chasm of its mouth opened a little, for all the world as though giving vent to soundless, demoniac laughter. All three of the vise-like hands clamped over him—lightly enough, considering their vast size, and intimating that the colossus did not mean to kill him for a moment or two—but so cruelly that his senses swam with the pain of it.

He felt the grip relax. The vast stone pincers were lifted from him; slithered to the ground beside him.

The first blinding rays of the sun were beating straight on the colossal figure, which glittered fantastically, like a huge splintered opal, in their brilliance.

It glared down at Harley. The abyss of a mouth opened as though again giving vent to silent, infernal laughter. Then, with the noise of a landslide, the giant form settled slowly to the ground. The rock half-moons of curtains dropped over the expressionless, dull eyes. The whole great figure quivered, and grew still. It lay without movement, stretched along the ground like a craggy, opalescent hill.

DAZED, stunned by such fantastic behavior, Harley struggled wearily to his feet. He had been a dead man as surely as though shot with a ray-gun. One twitch of those terrible rock pincers would have broken him in two pieces. It had seemed as though that deadly twitch were surely forthcoming. And then the thing had released him—and had lain down to go to sleep! Or was it asleep?

He took a few slow steps away from it, expecting to see the three great tentacles flash out to capture him as a cat claws at a mouse that thinks it is escaping. The arms didn't move. Astounding as it was, Harley was free to run away if he chose. Why was that?

A hint of a clue to the creature's action began to unfold in his mind. When he had first laid eyes on it, in daylight, it was asleep. It had not pursued him during the preceding day, which argued that again it was asleep. And now, with the first touch of dawn, it was once more quiet, immobile.

The answer seemed to be that it was entirely nocturnal; that for some obscure, unguessable reason sunlight induced in it a state of suspended animation. It seemed an insane theory, but no other surmise was remotely reasonable.

But if it were invariably sunk in a coma during daylight, why had it delayed killing him just a moment ago? Its every act indicated that it possessed intelligence of a high order. It was more than probable that it realized its limitation—why hadn't it acted in accordance with that realization?

On thinking it over, he believed he had the answer to that, too. He remembered the way the gaping mouth had seemed to express devilish mirth. The thing was playing with him. That was all. It had saved him for another night of hopeless flight and infallible trailing through the forests of Z-40.

He gazed at the monster in a frenzy of impotent rage and fear. If only he could kill it somehow in its sleep! But he couldn't. In no way could he harm it. Secure in its silicate covering, it was impervious to his wildest attempts at destruction. And it knew it, too; hadn't it laughed just before sinking down to slumber through the asteroidal day?

With his Sco drill he might have pierced that silicon dioxide armor till he reached the creature's gritty flesh. Then he could have used his ray-pistol, possibly disintegrating all its vitals and leaving only an empty rock shell sprawling hugely there in the trampled underbrush.

But he had neither drill nor pistol. The one had been wrecked by the monster; the other he had dropped in his madness of fright, after completely exhausting its power chamber.

Half crazed by the hopelessness of his plight, he paced up and down beside the great length of animated stone. Trapped on an asteroid—utterly unarmed—alone with the most pitiless, invulnerable creation Nature had placed in a varied universe! Could Hell itself have devised a more terrible fate?

Shuddering, he turned away. He had some two and a half hours of grace, before the sun should set again and darkness release the colossus from its torpor. There was only one thing he could do: place the diameter of the sphere between the thing and himself, and try to exist through another night of terror.

His hands went to his belt to adjust the gravity regulator strapped about his waist. By reducing his weight to an ounce or two, he could make the long journey possible for his fatigue-numbed muscles—

His hands clenched into fists, and his breath whistled between his set teeth as a wild hope came to him. The touch of the regulator had brought inspiration. A way to defeat the gigantic creature stretched on the ground beside him! A way to banish it forever from the surface of this lovely little world where all was perfect but the monstrous thing with which it was cursed!

Trembling with the reaction wrought in him by the faint glow of hope, he began to race toward the lake and his wrecked Blinco Dart. It wasn't hard to find the way; the rock giant had left a trail as broad as a road; trees broken off like celery stalks, bushes smashed flat, tracks that looked like shallow wells sunk into the firm ground. Fifty yards to a step, he leaped along this path, praying that one object, just one bit of machinery in the Dart had escaped the general wreckage.

Arrived at the little shell at last, he was forced to pause a moment and compose himself before he could step into the battered interior. Everything hinged on this one final chance!

Drawing a long breath, he entered the cabin and made his way to the stern repellor. A groan escaped his lips. It was ruined. Evidently the thing had reached in the man-hole opening with one of its three mighty tentacles, and, with sure instinct, had fastened its stone claws on the repellor housing. At any rate, it was ground to bits. But—there was the bow repellor.

He went to that, and the flame of hope came back to his eyes. It was untouched! He threw back the housing to make sure. Yes, the inter-sliding series of plates, that reversed or neutralized gravitational attraction at a touch, were in alignment.

He bent to the task of disconnecting it from the heavy bed-plate to which it was bolted, his fingers flying frenziedly. Then back to the torpid colossus he hurried, clutching the precious repellor tight in his arms lest he should drop it, walking carefully lest he should fall with it.

There he was faced by a new difficulty that at first seemed insurmountable. How could he fasten the repellor to that great, impenetrable, opalescent bulk?

A second time he bounded back toward the Dart, to return with the heavy bow and stern bed-plates from its hull.

ONCE more the orange ball of the sun was sinking low. The terrible brevity of those three-hour days! He had less than ten minutes, Earth time, in which to work.

One of the thing's arms, or tentacles, was pointing out away from the parent mass. It was twice the diameter of his body, and was ponderously heavy; but by rigging a fulcrum and lever device, with a stone as the fulcrum and a tough log as the lever, he managed to raise it high enough to thrust one of the bed-plates under it. The other massive metal sheet he laid across the top.

The lower rim of the sun touched the horizon. A tremor ran through the colossus. In frantic haste, racing against the flying seconds, Harley clamped the two plates tight against the columnar tentacle with four long hull-bolts from the Dart. He set the repellor in position on the top bed-plate, and began to fasten it down.

He felt another tremor run through the stone column on which he was squatting. With a rasping sound, one of the half-moon rock-curtains the thing had for eyelids blinked open and shut. He shot the last bolt into place and tightened it.

The stone claws, just behind which he had fastened the repellor, ground savagely shut. The great tentacle began to lift, and carried him with it—toward the chasm of a mouth. That chasm opened wide. . . .

Harley straightened up and jumped for the ground. As he jumped, he kicked the repellor control bar hard over.

There was a shrieking of wind as though all the hurricanes in the universe were battling each other. He felt himself turned over and over, buffeted, torn at, in a mad aerial whirlpool. The whirlpool calmed as the abruptly created vacuum, caused by the monster's rapid drive upward, passed after it into space. Far overhead there was one fleeting glimpse of a pinpoint of dull opalescence reflecting the rays of the dying sun. Then the pinpoint disappeared in fathomless space. With his gravity regulator adjusted to the point where it almost neutralized his weight, he fell slowly back toward the ground. . . .

ALMOST immediately after he had landed in the darkness that blanketed the surface of the planetoid, a big space yacht settled down near him. A searchlight bored a hole in the blackness, to bathe him in cold light. Down the beam came a band of men from Earth, pushing atomic cannon and gazing apprehensively about them. In the lead was an elderly man with the six-bar dollar-mark insignia of a business executive on his purple tunic.

He hastened to Harley's side. Harley only dimly heard what he said. Something to the effect that the man had been worried after selling the fatal asteroid. Had got in touch with the Radivision Corporation and learned that this call number was dead. Had come with men and big guns to rescue him, if it wasn't too late, and take him back to Earth. Had cruised for half an hour before locating him. "I've been calling myself a murderer ever since I let you have Z-40, Mr. 2Q14N20," he concluded. "I was sure we'd get here only to find you'd been killed. But I see you've managed to escape from the creature so far—though by the look of you, it must have been a narrow shave."

At this Harley shook off some of the gathering dizziness that hazed his mind. He threw back his shoulders. "Managed to *escape*? I did better than that. I got rid of the thing forever! Yes, I'll return to Earth with you, but only because I need a new Blinco Dart. I'm coming back to Z-40 at once. Perfect little paradise, now that I've got rid of that—animated—rock pile—"

The belated rescuers caught him as he collapsed.

THE RADIANT SHELL

"AND THAT, gentlemen," said the Secretary of War, "is the situation. Arvania has stolen the Ziegler plans and formulae. With their acquisition it becomes the most powerful nation on earth. The Ziegler plans are at present in the Arvanian Embassy, but they will be smuggled out of the country soon. Within a month of their landing in Arvania, war will be declared against us. That means"—he glanced at the tense faces around the conference table—"that we have about three months to live as a nation—unless we can get those plans!"

There was a hushed, appalled silence, broken at last by General Forsyte.

"Nonsense! How can a postage-stamp country like Arvania really threaten us?"

"The day has passed, General," said the Secretary, "when a nation's power is reckoned by its size. The Ziegler heat ray is the deadliest weapon yet invented. A thousand men with a dozen of the ray-projectors can reduce us to smoking ruins while remaining far outside the range of our guns. No! I tell you that declaration of war by Arvania will be followed by the downfall of the United States inside of three months!"

Again the hushed, strained silence descended over the conference table, while one white-faced man gazed at another and all speculated on the incredible possibility of a world in which there was no United States of America.

"We must get the plans," nodded Forsyte, convinced at last. "But how? March openly on the Arvanian Embassy?"

"No, that would be declaration of war on *our* part. The World Court, which knows nothing of the Ziegler plans, would set the League at our throats."

"Send volunteers unofficially to raid the place?"

"Impossible. There is a heavy guard in the Arvanian Embassy; and I more than suspect the place bristles with machine guns."

"What *are* we to do?" demanded Forsyte.

The Secretary seemed to have been waiting for that final question.

"I have had an odd and desperate plan submitted me from an outside source. I could not pass it without your approval. I will let you hear it from the lips of the planner."

He pressed a buzzer. "Bring Mr. Winter in," he told his secretary.

The man who presently appeared in the doorway was an arresting figure. A man of thirty-odd with the body of an athlete, belied somewhat by the pallor of an indoor worker, with acid stained, delicate hands offset by forearms that might have belonged to a blacksmith, with coal black hair and gray eyes so light as to look like ice-gray holes in the deep caverns of his eye-sockets. This was Thorn Winter.

"Gentlemen, the scientist, Mr. Winter," announced the Secretary. "He thinks he can get the Ziegler plans."

Thorn Winter cleared his throat. "My scheme is simple enough," he said tersely. "I believe I can walk right into the Embassy, get the plans—and then walk right out again. It sounds kind of impossible, but I think I can work it by making myself invisible."

"Invisible?" echoed Forsyte. "Invisible!"

"Precisely," said Thorn in a matter-of-fact tone. "I have just turned out a camouflage which is the most perfect yet discovered. It was designed for application to guns and equipment only. I'd never thought of trying to cover a human body with it, but I am sure it can be done."

"But . . . invisible . . ." muttered Forsyte, glancing askance at Winter.

"There's no time for argument," said the Secretary crisply. "The question is, shall we give this man permission to try the apparently impossible?"

All heads nodded, though in all eyes was doubt. The Secretary turned to the scientist.

"You are aware of the risk you run? You realize that if you are caught, we cannot recognize you—that we must disclaim official knowledge of your work, and leave you to your fate?"

Thorn nodded.

"Then," said the Secretary, his voice vibrant, "yours is the mission. And on your effort hangs the fate of your country. Now—what help will you require?"

"Only the assistance of one man," said Thorn. "And, since secrecy is vital, I'm going to ask you, sir, to be that man."

The Secretary smiled; and with that smile he seemed to be transformed from a great leader of affairs into a kindly, human individual. "I am honored, Mr. Winter," he said. "Shall we go at once to your laboratory?"

IN THE great laboratory room, the Secretary glanced about almost uneasily at the crowding apparatus that was such an enigma to one untrained in science. Then his gaze returned to Winter's activities.

Thorn was carefully stirring fluids, poured drop by drop from various retorts, in a mixing bowl. All the fluids were colorless; and they combined in a mixture that had approximately the consistency of thin syrup. To this, Thorn added a carefully weighted pinch of glittering powder. Then he lit a burner under the bowl, and thrust into the mixture a tiny, specially constructed thermometer.

"You can really make yourself invisible?" breathed the Secretary.

"I can," said Thorn, "if the blisters don't upset my calculations by making my body surfaces too moist for this stuff to stick to. I'm going to have you paint me with it, you see, and it was never intended to cover flesh."

He regulated the burner anxiously, and then began to take off his clothes.

"Ready," he said at last, glancing at the thermometer and turning off the burner. He stood before the wondering Secretary, a fine, muscular figure. "Take this brush and cover me with the stuff. And be sure not to miss any of me!"

And then the Secretary saw why Thorn had said the colorless paint was never intended to be applied to human flesh. For it was still seething and smoking in the cauldron.

"Good heavens!" he said. "Don't you want to wait till it cools a little?"

"Can't," said Thorn. "It has to be applied hot or it loses its flexibility."

The Secretary dipped the brush and began to paint the naked flesh of the scientist. Not a quiver touched that flesh as an almost microscopically thin, colorless layer formed into a film after the brush strokes. But the Secretary's fingers shook a little.

"My God, man!" he said finally. "Doesn't it hurt?"

"It's a little like being boiled in oil," replied Thorn grimly. "Outside of that it's all right. Hurry, before the stuff gets too cool."

The clinging thin shell covered him to his chest, then to his throat. At that point he reached into a drawer in a workbench beside him and drew out two small, hollow hemispheres of glass. These he cupped over his eyes.

"What are those for?" asked the Secretary.

"So my eyes can be covered with the film. If they weren't, I'd present the somewhat remarkable spectacle of a pair of disembodied eyes walking down the street."

Painfully, agonizingly, the hot film was applied to throat and face; over the glass spheres that cupped around the eyes; over a tight leather cap covering the scientist's hair; and over a sort of football nose-guard which extended down an inch below the end of Thorn's nose in a sort of overhanging offset that would allow him to breathe and still keep his nostrils hidden. The Secretary stepped back.

Before him stood a figure that looked not unlike a glazed statue of a man. The effect was that of a body encased in clear ice—and like clear ice, the encasing shell sparkled and glittered radiantly in the sunlight that poured in at the windows.

Thorn moved. His glazed arms and legs and torso glistened with all the colors in the spectrum; while under the filmed bulges of glass his eyes looked as large as apples. The Secretary felt a chill of superstitious fear as he gazed at that weird and glittering figure with its enormous glazed eyes.

"But you aren't invisible," he said at length.

"That comes now," said Thorn, walking ahead of the Secretary while on the ceiling above him danced red and yellow and blue rainbows of refracted light.

He stepped onto a big metal plate. Suspended above was a huge metal ring, with its hole directly over the spot on which he stood.

"Soft magnets," explained Thorn. "As simply as I can put it, my process for rendering an object invisible is this: I place the object, coated with the film, on this plate. Then I start in motion the overhead ring, creating an immensely powerful, rapidly rotating magnetic field. The rotating field rearranges the atoms of this peculiarly susceptible film of mine so that they will transmit light rays with the least possible resistance. It combs the atoms into straight lines, you might say. With that straight-line, least-resistance arrangement comes invisibility."

"I don't quite see—" began the Secretary.

"Refraction of light," said Thorn hurriedly. "The light rays strike this film, hurtle around the object, it coats—at increased speed, probably, but there are no instruments accurate enough to check that—and emerge on the other side. Thus, you can look at a body so filmed, and not see it: your gaze travels *around* it and rests on objects in a straight line behind it. But you'll see for yourself in a moment. Pull that switch, there, will you? And leave it on for two full minutes after you have ceased to see me."

Straight and tall, a figure encased in shimmering crystal, the scientist stood on the metal plate. Hesitant, with the superstitious dread growing in his heart, the Secretary stood with his hand on the switch. That hand pulled the switch down. . . .

Soundlessly the overhead metal ring began to whirl, gathering speed with every second. And then, though he had known in advance some-thing of what was coming, the Secretary could not suppress a shout of surprise.

The man before him on the metal plate was vanishing.

Slowly he disappeared from view—slowly, as an object sinking deeper and deeper into clear water disappears. Now the face was but a white blob. Now the entire body was but a misty blur. And now a shade, a wavering shadow, alone marked Winter's presence.

The Secretary could not have told the exact instant when that last faint blur oozed from sight. He only knew that at one second he was gazing at it—and at the next second his eyes rested on a rack of test-tubes on the wall beyond the plate.

He looked at his watch. Sweat glistened in tiny points on the hand that held the switch. It was all so like death, this disappearance—as if he had thrown the switch that electrocuted a man.

The specified two minutes passed. He cut off the power. The great ring lost speed, stopped whirling. And on the plate was—nothing.

At least it seemed there was nothing. But a moment later a deep voice sounded out: "I guess I'm invisible, all right, according to the expression on your face."

"You are," said the Secretary, mopping his forehead, "except when you speak. Then I have the bizarre experience of seeing glimpses of teeth, tongue and throat hanging in mid-air. I'd never have believed it if I hadn't witnessed it myself! That paint of yours is miraculous!"

"A little complicated, but hardly miraculous. It has a cellulose base, and there is in it a small per cent of powdered crystal—but the rest I'll keep locked in my brain alone till my country has need of it."

The glimpses of teeth and tongue and throat ceased. In spite of him-self, the Secretary started as an unseen hand touched his shoulder.

"Now,"—there was ringing resolution in the deep voice—"for the Arvanian Embassy. Please drive me there—and be as quick as you can about it. I can't last very long with this film sealing most of the pores of my body."

The Secretary started for the laboratory door. Beside him sounded the patter of bare feet. He opened the door and walked into the hallway. Behind him, apparently of itself, the door clicked shut; and the footsteps again sounded beside him.

The Secretary walked to the curb where his limousine waited. His chauffeur jumped out and opened the door. The Secretary paused a mo-ment, one foot on the running board, to draw a cigar from his pocket and light it. During that moment the car pressed down on that side, and as suddenly rocked back up again.

The chauffeur stared wide-eyed at his employer.

"Did you do that, sir?" he asked.

"Do what?" said the Secretary.

"Push down on the running board with your foot."

"Of course not," said the Secretary, his eyebrows raising. "You could have seen my leg move if I had. But why do you ask?"

"It felt like somebody got into this car," mumbled the man.

"Did you see anybody get in?" said the Secretary with a shrug. And, shaking his head, with a fuddled look in his eyes, the chauffeur turned away and got into the driver's seat.

The Secretary glanced at the rear seat. On the far side, the cushion was heavily depressed. He sat on the near side, feeling his knee strike another, unseen knee.

"Drive to the Bulgarian Embassy," he told his man.

Up Sixteenth Street the car swung, past the various embassies which looked more like palatial private villas than offices of foreign nations. Toward the end of the line, a smaller building than most of the others, was the Arvanian Embassy. Next to it was the Bulgarian.

The car stopped in front of the Bulgarian Embassy, and the Secretary got out. Again he paused, while the chauffeur held the door open, to hold a match to his cigar. Again the car sagged down on that side, and slowly swayed up again.

"Hey—" said the chauffeur. But meeting the Secretary's calmly inquiring gaze, he stopped. Scratching his head, he went back to the wheel, while the Secretary walked toward the building entrance.

Behind him, moving on soundless bare feet along the sidewalk, Thorn Winter hastened, cloaked in invisibility, toward the Arvanian Embassy—and the plans that spelled America's destruction if they remained in Arvanian hands.

The embassy building was a three-storied oblong house of white stone topping a terrace that started its climb from the sidewalk of Sixteenth Street. The doors at the head of the wide stone staircase were of bronze; and they were closed, and, Thorn surmised, efficiently barred. The windows at front and sides were also closed, in spite of the warmth of the sunny spring afternoon.

Beside the building, leading up in a short steep hill, was the driveway. Up this Thorn started. The front of the house was hopelessly barred; but at the rear entrance there might be a chance.

Up the driveway, then, he walked, a little startled at the fact that he cast no shadow—feeling as a ghost might feel. The pavement was hot to his thinly filmed feet. A little dubious as to the effect of heat on the vital shell that hid him, he stepped off into the cool grass beside the drive; and came soon to the rear of the embassy.

There was no porch or veranda, simply two stone steps leading up to a stout oak door which opened onto the embassy kitchens. From behind this door came the sound of crockery and the hum of voices. The Arvanian chef evidently was preparing afternoon tea.

Walking boldly to the very steps, Thorn began the vigil that should end when someone came in or out of that door, allowing him to slip inside the building before the portal was barred shut again.

For nearly half an hour Thorn stood there before something happened that at once helped him, and, at the same time, nearly proved his undoing.

A light delivery van sped up the driveway. The wheels stirred up a cloud of dust. It was a very small cloud of very fine dust. Thorn at first thought nothing of it, because he was so engrossed in the conviction that here ought to be provided an entrance into the house.

The truck driver got out, took a crate from the body of the van, and went with it to the back door. After a moment of waiting, the door opened. Thorn noticed that it was opened very cautiously, only an inch or so. He caught a glimpse of a heavy chain stretched across the inch opening, and saw a strip of bearded, resolute face.

The door was unchained. The driver walked in, while the door stood open. Thorn started to glide in after him. . . .

Mere chance made him glance at a window near the door. This window framed another bearded, resolute face. And the eyes in that face were like saucers as they stared full at Thorn!

For an instant Thorn knew icy fear. His invisibility! Had something happened to strip him of that concealing mantle? But what *could* have happened?

He glanced down at himself and saw the reason for the guard's saucer-eyed expression.

A little of the light cloud of dust stirred up by the truck wheels had settled over him and clung to the encasing shell. As he moved, these dust specks moved. The effect to the staring guard, Thorn realized, must be that of seeing a queer, fine dust column moving eccentrically over a grassy lawn where no dust column had any business to be.

Quickly Thorn moved toward the garage, with the eyes of the amazed guard following him. The scientist was savage at the delay; but it was vital that he rid himself of that clinging dust.

Behind the garage he broke off a feathery spray from a vine, and stroked it lightly over himself. That, too, presented a curious spectacle: a leafy branch suddenly detaching itself from the parent vine and dancing here and there in mid-air.

When the all-important task was done, Thorn raced back to the rear doorway. By great good luck it was still open. He stole in, just making it as the truck driver, staggering under a load of empty crates, came up the cellar stairs and went out to his truck.

Thorn drew a deep breath. He was inside the Arvanian Embassy. The place was a three-storied stone trap in which, if the slightest slip revealed him to its tenants, he would surely meet his death. But, anyway, he was inside! And the threatening Ziegler plans waited somewhere near at hand for him to find and take!

Even had Thorn not known in advance that trouble was brewing, he could have surmised that something sinister was being hatched in the Arvanian Embassy. For, in this big sunny kitchen five men lounged about in addition to the white-coated chef and his beardless stripling of an assistant. And each of the five had a holster strapped openly over his coat with the butt of an automatic protruding in plain sight.

Thorn looked about. Across from the great range, beside which he was standing and holding his breath for fear some one of the seven men should become aware of his presence, was the door leading to the front part of the house. He started toward that door, walking on tiptoe. A shudder crept up his spine as he tiptoed across the floor directly in front of the armed guards who would have shot him down without compunction could they have seen him. He was not yet used to his invisibility; knowing himself to be substantial, feeling his feet descend solidly on the floor, he still could hardly credit the fact that human eyes could not observe him.

He got to the door. He put out his hand to open it, then realized just in time that he could not do that. A door stealthily opening and closing again, with no apparent hand to manipulate it? Such a spectacle would start a riot!

In a frenzy of impatience, he stood beside the door, waiting till someone else should swing it open. And in a moment it chanced that the stripling assistant chef came toward him with a tray. The boy pushed the swinging door with his foot, and walked into the butler's pantry. After him, treading almost on the lad's heels, came Thorn.

The boy sat the tray down, and turned to reach into an upper shelf. The space in the pantry was constricted, and he turned abruptly. The result was that he suddenly drew back as though a hot iron had seared him, and went white as chalk. Then he dashed back into the kitchen.

"A hand!" Thorn heard him gibbering in Arvanian. "A hand! I touched it with mine! Something horrible is in there!"

With his heart pounding in his throat, Thorn leaned close to the swing-door to hear what happened next. Would there be a rush for the butler's pantry? An investigation? He eyed the farther door—the dining room door. But he dared not flee through that save as a last resort. In the dining room sounded voices; and again the sight of a door opening and closing of itself would lead to uproar.

"A hand?" he heard one of the guards say in the kitchen. "An unseen hand? Thou art empty in the head, young Gova."

There followed some jeering sentences in colloquial Arvanian that were too idiomatic for Thorn's knowledge of the language to let him understand. A general guffaw came from the rest; and, as no move was made toward the pantry, Thorn decided he was saved for another few moments.

Gasping, he raised his hand to wipe the perspiration off his forehead, then realized there was no perspiration there. His film-clogged pores could exude nothing; he had only the sensation of perspiring.

Now the problem was to get through the next door. Thoughtfully, Thorn gazed at it. He saw that this, too, was a swing-door. Further, he saw that now and then it creaked open a few inches, and swung sluggishly back. Beyond it somewhere a window was open, and spasmodic gusts moved the swinging slab of wood.

The next time the door moved with the wind, Thorn caught it and augmented the movement a bit. Twice he did that, each time swinging it back a trifle further. Next time, he figured, he could open it enough to slide into the room.

Two glimpses he had had, with the openings of the door, into the room beyond. These glimpses had showed him a great oval table on which was set the debris of afternoon tea, and around which were grouped tense, eager men. Dark of hair and complexion were these men, with the arrogant hawk noses and ruthless small eyes of the typical Arvanian. Several of them were garbed in military uniforms and armed with swords. They were talking in tones too low for Thorn to distinguish words through the film over his ears. He would have to get in there to hear them.

For the third time the wind pushed at the door. For the third time Thorn caught its edge and swung it—six inches, eight, almost enough to slip through. . . .

"Shut thou the window!" crackled a voice suddenly. "Fool! What if some of these documents blew away?"

There was a slam, and the breeze was cut off. Thorn quickly let go of the door, and watched it fall back in place again.

He was cursing his luck when he heard the same commanding voice say: "Kori, see if there be one who listens in the butler's pantry. It seemed the door opened wider than the wind would warrant."

There was the scrape of a chair. Then the door was abruptly thrust open and coldly alert eyes in a hostile, wary face, swept over the pantry.

"No one here, Excellency," said Kori; and he returned to his place at the table.

BUT with him came another, unseen, to stand against the wall beside a great mahogany buffet, and to listen and watch. Kori had, not unnaturally, held the door open while he glanced around the pantry. And under Kori's outstretched arm, so close as almost to brush against his uniformed legs, had stolen Thorn.

"Then, gentlemen, it is all arranged?" said the man at the head of the oval table—a spare, elderly individual with bristling gray mustachios and smoldering dark eyes. "The plans leave for Arvania to-morrow night, to arrive in our capital city in ten days. Then day and night manufacture of the Ziegler projectors—and declaration of war. Following that, this great city of Washington, and the even greater cities of New York and Chicago, and all, this fine land from Atlantic to Pacific, shall become an Arvanian possession to exploit as we like!"

There was an audible "Ah!" from the score of men around the table—broken by a voice in the main double doorway of the dining room: "Gentlemen, your pardon, I am late."

Thorn looked at the speaker. He was a young fellow with an especially elaborate uniform and a face that appeared weak and dissipated in spite of the arrogant Arvanian nose. Then a bark came to Thorn's ears—and a cold feeling to the pit of Thorn's stomach. The newcomer had brought a dog with him!

Even as he gazed apprehensively at the dog—a rangy wolfhound— the brute growled deep in its throat and stared at the corner by the buffet where Thorn was instinctively trying to make himself smaller.

The dog growled again, and stalked warily toward the buffet.

"Grego, down," said his master absently. Then, to the spare man at the head of the table: "I have been next door, talking to the American Secretary of War. A dull fellow. Convinced, is he, that Arvania harbors only kind thoughts for this great stupid nation. They shall be utterly unprepared for our attack—Grego! What ails the brute?"

The wolfhound had evaded several outstretched hands and got to the buffet. There it crouched and cowered, fangs showing in a snarl, eyes reddening wickedly, while the growl rattled louder in its shaggy throat.

"Perhaps the heat has affected him," said one.

All were looking at the dog now, marveling at its odd behavior. But of all the eyes that observed it a pair of unseen eyes watched with the utmost agitation.

Thorn stared, almost hypnotized, at the creature. A dog! What rotten luck! Men might be fooled by the masking invisibility, but there was no deceiving a dog's keen nose!

The wolfhound started forward as though to leap, then settled back. Plainly it longed to spring. Equally plainly it was afraid of the being that so impossibly was revealed to its nostrils but not to its eyes. Meanwhile, one tearing sweep of blunt claws or sharp fangs—and a fatal rent would appear in Thorn's encasing shell!

The dog snapped tentatively. Thorn flattened still harder against the wall, with discovery and death hovering very closely about him. Then the beast's master intervened.

"Grego! Here, sir! A council room is no place, for thee, anyway. Here, I say! So, then—"

He hastened to the dog and caught its collar. Twisting the leather cruelly, he dragged the protesting, snarling brute to the doors and slid them shut with the wolfhound barking and growling on the outside. "Someone put him in his kennel," he said through the panels. A scuffling in the hall told of the execution of the order. The council room became quiet again, and Thorn leaned against the wall and closed his eyes for an instant.

"We were saying, Soyo," the leader addressed the dog's owner, "that the Ziegler plans start for Arvania to-morrow night. All is arranged. These innocent looking bits of paper"—he thumped a small packet of documents lying before him—"shall deliver mighty America to us!"

A subdued cheer answered the man's words—while Thorn stared at the packet of papers with unbelieving eyes. It had never occurred to him that the Ziegler plans might be in that very room, on the table with the rest of the welter of letters, thumbed documents, and cups and saucers. And there they were—the vital projector plans—not in a safe or hidden in some fantastic place, but right before his eyes!

Involuntarily his hand extended eagerly toward the packet, then was withdrawn. Not now. *He* was invisible—but the papers, if he grasped them, would not be. Clenched in his unseen hand, they would be perfectly visible, moving in jerks and starts as he raced for the door.

Like lightning his mind turned over one plan after another for making away with that precious packet. Each scheme seemed impossible of fulfilment.

"The biggest difficulty is in getting them out of the country," the spare, elderly man was saying. "But we have solved that. Solved it simply. I myself shall bear them, sewn in my clothes, to our native land. The American authorities could search, on some pretext, any other of our number who tried to smuggle them out. But *me* they dare not lay a finger on. That would be an overt act."

Thorn's thoughts whirled desperately on. Wait till later and follow whoever left the room with the plans? But he hated to let them get out of his sight.

And at this point he became suddenly aware that the man named Kori was gazing fixedly at him.

Thorn was between the section of the table where Kori sat, and the angular buffet-end. Kori could not possibly see anything but the shining mahogany, thought Thorn. And yet the man's eyes were narrowing to ominous slits as he started in his direction.

Thorn held his breath. Was the shielding film changing in structure? Were the repolarized atoms slowly losing their straight-line arrangement, allowing light rays to penetrate through to his body instead of diverting them to form a pocket of invisibility around him? The film had never acted like that before—but never before had Thorn applied it to living flesh with its disintegrating heat and moisture.

"Excellency," said Kori at last, a hard edge to his voice, "look thou at that buffet. No, no—the end nearest my chair."

"Well?" said the elderly man. "I see nothing."

Thorn breathed a sigh of relief. But the relief was to be of short duration.

"Come to my place, if thou wilt, and see from here," said Kori.

The leader got up and came to Kori's place. Kori pointed straight at Thorn.

"There—seest thou anything out of the ordinary?"

"I see nothing," said the leader, after a moment. "Thine eyes, Kori, are not good."

"They are the eyes of a hawk," said Kori stubbornly. "And they see this—the vertical line of the end of that buffet does not continue straightly up and down. At its middle, the line is broken, then continues up—a fraction of an inch to the side! Like an object seen under water, distorted by the sun-rays that strike the surface!"

Thorn fairly jumped away from the buffet and stood against bare wall. Fool! Of course the light refraction would not be perfect! Why hadn't he thought of that—thought to stand clear of revealing vertical lines!

"There, it is gone," said Kori, blinking. "But something, Excellency, made that distortion of line. And something made Soyo's wolfhound act as it did! Something—"

"Art thou attempting to say a spy listens unseen in this room?" demanded the gray-mustachioed Arvanian.

"Something is odd—that is all I say."

All eyes were ranging along the wall against which Thorn leaned his back. All eyes finally turned to Kori. "It is nonsense." "I see nothing whatever." "Kori has drunk of champagne in place of tea!" were some of the exclamations.

And then occurred the thing that, in Thorn's perilous position, was like the self-signing of his own death warrant.

He sneezed.

That agony of helplessness, as a man's nose wrinkles and twitches and—in spite of the most desperate attempts at repression—the betraying sound forces its way out! How many men have lost their lives because of that insistent soft nasal explosion which can be smothered, but not entirely hushed!

Thorn had felt the sneeze coming on for seconds. He had fought it frantically, with life itself at stake. But he could not hold it back. In his naked body, beginning to burn with fever from the long-clogged pores and insulated not at all by the film from the coolness of the room, the seeds of that soft explosion had been planted—and they *would* bear fruit!

So he had sneezed!

Instantly there was chaos. Men looked at each other, and back at the blank wall from which had come the painfully muffled sound. Then all sprang to their feet.

"Champagne, is it!" Kori exulted savagely. "Did I not say my eyes were those of a hawk?"

"Double guard all doors!" roared the Arvanian leader, to the guards outside. "Someone is in the house! And you in here," he went on in a lower tone, "see that this unseen one dies!"

Soyo and several other men whipped out automatics and pointed them at the wall. Thorn dropped to the floor. But with his quick action came Kori's voice.

"No, no! The sword, gentlemen. It is not so noisy, and covers a wider sweep."

Thorn shivered. Far rather would he have had bullets as his lot than cold steel. The prospect of being hacked to pieces, of gradually emerging from invisibility as a lump of gashed and bleeding flesh, turned him faint.

THE Arvanians split up into orderly formation. Two went to guard the door to the butler's pantry, and two to cover the closed sliding doors to the outer hall. Six, with drawn swords sweeping back and forth before them, walked slowly toward the wall from which the sneeze had come.

Thorn set his jaws—only just catching himself in time to prevent his lips from opening in the half-snarl instinctive to the most civilized of men when danger is threatening. That lip motion would have revealed his teeth for an instant!

The sensation of perspiring heavily flamed over him again. There were so many trifling things to keep in mind! And each, if neglected, meaning certain death!

The nearest of the marching six stopped with his foot almost touching Thorn's hand. The dancing sword the man carried almost grazed the scientist's shoulder on its down sweep.

Thorn could not stay there. Lying flat along the baseboard, he would be stabbed at any instant by an inquiring sword point.

The six spread a little. A very little. But there was room enough for Thorn to slide between the two men nearest him and roll soundlessly under the table.

There was no sanctuary for him there. The cursed Kori, with his hawk eyes, glanced under the table after stabbing vainly along the wall.

"The carpet!" he bellowed. "See how the nap is pressed down! He is under there, comrades!"

The thrusting swords raked under the table a half second or so after Thorn had rolled out the other side, upsetting a chair in his hurry.

"After him!" panted Soyo. "By the living God, this is wizardry! But he must not get away—"

"He won't!" snapped the elderly leader. "Men, form a line at the far end of the room and march slowly, shoulder to shoulder, to this end. The spy must be caught!"

The move was executed. All the men in the room, save the four guarding the doors, lined up and advanced slowly, swerving and slashing their swords. Like a line of workers hand-harvesting a wheat field they came—foot by foot toward the corner where Thorn turned this way and that in a vain effort to escape.

The line reached the table. Over and under and around it the swords slashed viciously, leaving no space unprobed.

Thorn clenched his fists. He gazed at the packet containing the Ziegler plans. He gazed at the guarded door leading back to the kitchen. Then he tensed himself and leaped.

"The plans!" shouted Kori hoarsely. "Look—"

The vital packet, as far as the eye could see, had suddenly grown wings, soared from the table top, and was floating rapidly, convulsively, toward the door.

"Stop him!" yelled Soyo. "Stop—"

At that instant the heads of the two who guarded the door were dashed together. The door itself slammed open. The Ziegler plans sped into the butler's pantry.

The door to the kitchen began to open just as Kori reached the pantry. An oath burst from the Arvanian's lips. He flung his sword. In the air, shoulder high, appeared suddenly a small fountain of blood. Kori yelled triumphantly.

Thorn, feeling the warm drip following the glancing slash in his shoulder, knew the veil of invisibility had at last been rent. Abandoning efforts at noiselessness, knowing that his whereabouts was constantly marked by the packet in his hand, anyway, he fled through the kitchen to the rear door.

The bolt jerked back, under the astonished eyes of the five guards who had not yet realized precisely what the commotion was all about— and who only saw a packet of papers waving in mid-air, a trickle of blood appearing out of nothing, and a bolt banging open in its slot for no reason whatever.

Thorn's fingers worked feverishly at the chain. But before he could begin to get it undone, the guards had recovered from their surprise and had joined the Arvanians who poured in from the dining room under Kori's lead.

With a score of men crowding the kitchen, Thorn looped back in his tracks like a hunted creature, and sought the cellar door. Four men he upset, one after another, aided by the fact that his twisting body could be only approximately placed by the papers and the wound.

Then Kori's hand swept through the air above the waving packet, to clamp over Thorn's wrist.

With an effort—that bulged the muscles of that blacksmith's forearm of his till it seemed they must burst through the film, Thorn whirled

Kori clear off his feet and sent him stumbling into the charge of three guards. But in the meantime the cellar was barred to him by a double line of men.

Fighting for his life—and, far more important, the existence of his country—Thorn lashed out with his invisible right fist while his left clutched the plans.

A score of men arrayed in a death struggle against one! But the odds were not twenty to one. Not quite. The score could mark Thorn's general whereabouts—but they could not see his flying right fist! That was an invisible weapon that did incredible damage.

But if they could not see the fist to guard against it, they could see the results of the fist's impacts. Here a nose suddenly crumpled and an instant later gushed red. There a head was snapped back and up, while its owner slowly sagged to the floor. And all the while the still dripping wound and the packet of documents kept with devilish ingenuity between the body of some swordless guard and the impatient blades of the Arvanian nobles.

Almost, it seemed to Thorn, he would win free. Almost, it appeared to the Arvanians, the unseen one would reach the big window near the door—which the path of his wreckage indicated was his goal. But one of the wildly swinging fists of a guard caught Thorn at last.

It landed on the glass cup over his right eye, cutting a perfect circle in the skin around the eyesocket, and tearing the film over the glass!

Now there were three things about the lithe, invisible body that the Arvanians could see: the crumpled papers, a slowly drying patch of blood that moved shoulder high in the air, and a blood-rimmed, ice-gray eye that glared defiance at them from apparently untenanted atmosphere.

Then came what seemed must be the end. Soyo appeared in the pantry doorway with a machine gun.

"Everybody to the end of the kitchen by the window!" he cried. "To the devil with silence—we'll spray this room with lead, and let the sound of shots bring what consequences it may!"

The men scattered. The machine gun muzzle swept toward the place where the eye, the papers, and the blood spot were to be seen.

That spot was now at one end of the great kitchen range on which a few copper pots simmered over white-hot electric burners. At the other end of the range, in the end wall of the kitchen, was a second window. It was small, less than a yard square, and had evidently been punched through the wall as an afterthought to carry off some of the heat of the huge stove.

Soyo's face twisted exultantly. The machine gun belched flame.

Chasing relentlessly after the dodging, shifting blood spot, a line of holes appeared in the wall following instantly on the tap—tap—tap of the gun.

Eye and papers and blood spot appeared to float through the air. One of the copper pots on the range flew off onto the floor. The glass of the small ventilating window smashed to bits. In the jagged frame its broken edges presented, the Arvanians saw for a flashing instant the seared, blistered soles of a pair of human feet.

"Outside!" bawled Kori. "He jumped onto the range and dove through the window! After him!"

After precious seconds had been wasted, the rear door was unchained and wrenched open. The Arvanians, swords and guns drawn, raced out to the rear yard.

His Excellency's town car, that had been standing in front of the open garage doors, leaped into life. With motor roaring wide open, it tore toward the Arvanians, some of whom leaped aside and some of whom were hurled to right and left by the heavy fenders. . . .

Startled people on Sixteenth Street saw a great town car swaying down the asphalt seemingly guided by no hand other than that of fate; some said afterward they saw a single eye gleaming through the windshield, but no one believed that. Equally startled people saw the car screech to a stop in front of the home of the Secretary of War. After it, scarcely a full minute later, three motors with the Arvanian coat of arms on them came to a halt.

"My dear fellow," said the Secretary blandly to the livid Arvanian Ambassador, "no one has come in here with papers or anything else. I saw a man jump out of your town car and run south on Connecticut Avenue. That's all I know."

"But I tell you—" shrieked the Arvanian.

He stopped, impaled on the Secretary's icy cold glance.

"Your story is rather incredible," murmured the Secretary. "Valuable plans stolen from your Embassy by an invisible man? Come, come!"

Dark Arvanian eyes glared into light American ones.

"By the way," said the Secretary affably, "I am thinking of giving a semi-official banquet to celebrate future, friendly relations between our two countries. Do you approve?"

The Arvanian Ambassador tugged at his collar to straighten it. World dominion had been in his fingers—and had slipped through—but he would not have been a diplomat had he let his face continue to express the bitterness in his heart.

"I think such a banquet would be a splendid idea," he said suavely.

MAROONED UNDER THE SEA

Editor's note: This document, written on a curious kind of parchment and tied to a piece of driftwood, was reported to have been picked out of the sea near the Fiji Islands. The first and last pages were so water soaked as to be indecipherable.

. . . Yacht *Rosa* was due to leave the San Francisco harbor in two hours.

We were going on some mysterious cruise to the South Seas, the details of which I did not know.

"Professor George Berry, the famous zoologist, and myself are going to do some exploring that is hazardous in the extreme," Stanley had said. "For purely mechanical reasons we need a third. You are young and have no family ties, so I thought I'd ask you to go with us. I'd rather not tell you what it's all about until we are on our way."

That was all the explanation he had given. It was sufficient. I was fed-up with life just then: I had enough money to avoid work and was tired of playing.

"I must warn you that you'll risk your life in this," he had continued, in answer to my acceptance of his invitation.

And I had replied that the hazard, whatever it might be, only made the trip appear more desirable.

So here I was, on board the yacht, about to sail for far places on some scientific mission which had so far been kept veiled in secrecy and which was represented as "hazardous in the extreme." It sounded attractive!

Stanley came aboard accompanied by a lean, wiry man with iron gray hair and cool, alert black eyes.

"Hello, Martin," Stanley greeted me. "I want you to meet Professor Berry, the real leader of this expedition. Professor, this young red-head is Martin Grey, a sort of nephew by adoption who knows more about night life than most cabaret proprietors—and not much of anything else. He has shaken the dangers of the gold-diggers to face with us the dangers of the tropic seas."

The professor gripped my hand, and his cool black eyes gazed into mine with a kind of friendly frostiness.

"Don't pay any attention to him," he advised me. "Twenty years ago, when I first met him, he was on his way to Africa to shoot elephants because some revue beauty had just thrown him over and he felt he ought to do something big and heroic about it. It was shortly afterward that he decided to stay a bachelor all his life, and became such a confirmed woman hater."

He smiled thinly at Stanley's prod in the ribs, and the two went below, talking and laughing with the intimacy of old friendship.

I stayed on deck and soon found myself watching, with no little wonder, an enormous truck and trailer arrangement that drew up on the dock heavily loaded with a single immense crate. It was for us. I speculated as to what it could possibly contain.

It was a twenty or twenty-five-foot cube solidly braced with strap-iron and steel brackets. It evidently contained something fragile. The yacht's donkey engine lowered a hook for it, and swung it over the side and into the hold as daintily as though it had been packed with explosives.

The last of the ship's stores followed it over the side: the group of newspaper reporters who had been trying to pump the captain and first mate for a story were warned to leave, and we were ready to go. Precisely where and for what purpose?

I was to find out almost immediately.

Even as the yacht nosed superciliously away from the dock, the steward approached me with the information that lunch was ready. I went to the small, compactly furnished dining salon, where I was joined by Stanley and the professor.

THERE were only the three of us at the table. Stanley Browne, noted big game hunter and semi-retired owner of the great Browne Glassworks at Altoona, a man fifteen years my senior but tanned and fit looking; Professor Berry, well known in scientific circles; and myself, known in no branch of activity save the one Stanley had jested about—the night life of my home city, Chicago.

"It's time you knew just what you're up against," said Stanley to me after the consomme had been served. "Now that we've actually sailed, there's no longer any need for secrecy. Indeed there never has been urgent need of it: the Professor and myself merely thought we might provoke incredulity and comment if we stated the purpose of our trip publicly."

He buttered a roll.

"We—the Professor and you and I—are going in for some deep sea diving. And when I say deep, I mean deep. We are going to investigate conditions as they exist one mile down from the surface of the ocean."

"A mile!" I exclaimed. "Why—"

There I stopped. I had only a layman's knowledge of such matters. But I knew that the limit of man's submersion, till then at any rate, was a matter of a few hundred feet.

"Sounds incredible, doesn't it," said Stanley with a smile. "But that's what we're going to do—if the Professor's gadget works as he seems to think it will."

"I don't think it, I know it," retorted the Professor. "And man, man, the things we may see down there! New and unknown species—a world no human has ever seen before—perhaps the secret of all of life—"

"Dragons, sea-serpents, and what not!" Stanley finished with a grin.

"Or, possibly—nothing at all." The Professor shrugged. "I mustn't let my scientific curiosity run away with me. Perhaps we'll find no new thing down down. Our deep sea dredging and classification may already embrace most of the forms of life in the greater depths."

"If it does I want my money back," said Stanley. "When you asked me to finance this expedition for you, I agreed on condition that you would show me a thrill—some *real* big game, even if I would not be able to shoot it. If we draw blank—"

"The mere descent should satisfy you, my adventuring friend," replied the Professor brusquely. "I think you'll find that thrilling enough."

"But—a mile under the surface!" I marveled, feeling not entirely comfortable. "The pressure! Enormous! It can't be done! That is, I mean, can it be done?"

"It had better be," said Stanley with a humor that I did not entirely appreciate. "If it isn't, the three of us are going to be pressed out like three sheets of tissue paper! For we are assuredly going down that far in the Professor's gadget."

"Was that the thing I saw hoisted aboard just before we left?"

"That was it. We'll stroll around after lunch and look it over."

If I had taken this cruise in search of distraction—I was surely going to be successful! That was plain!

"Just where are we going?" I asked. "You said something about the South Seas, but you've named no special part of them."

"We're bound for Penguin Deep. That's a delightful little dimple in the Kermadec Trough, which," Stanley explained, "is north-northeast of New Zealand almost halfway up to the Fiji Islands. Penguin Deep is ticketed at five thousand one hundred and fifty feet, but it probably runs deeper in spots."

The rest of the meal was consumed in silence. I hardly tasted what I ate; I remember that. Over five thousand feet down—where no man had ever ventured before! Could we make it?

I tried to recall my neglected physics lessons and compute the pressure that far down. I couldn't. But I knew it must be an appalling total of tons to the square inch. What possible arrangement could they have brought in which to make that awful descent?

And, if the descent were accomplished, what in the world would we see when we got down there? Gigantic, hitherto unknown fishes? Marine growths, hair animal and half vegetable?

Decidedly, hot rolls and salad, cutlets and baked potatoes, good as they were, could not distract attention from the crowding questions that assailed me. And I could see that Stanley and the Professor were also far away in their thoughts—probably already exploring Penguin Deep.

AFTER lunch we went forward to look at the Professor's gadget, as Stanley insisted on calling it.

It had been carefully unpacked by the crew while we ate, and it shimmered in the electric lighted hold like a great bubble.

It was a giant glass sphere, polished and flawless. Inside it could be made out various objects—a circular bench arrangement on a wooden flooring, batteries that filled the cup between the floor and the bottom arc of the sphere, tall metal cylinders, a small searchlight set next to a mechanism that was indeterminate. At three equidistant points on the sides there were glass handles, as thick as a man's thigh, cast integral with the walls. On the top there was a smaller handle.

At first glance the sphere seemed all in one piece, with the central objects cast inside like a toy ship in a sealed bottle. Then a mathematically precise ring of prismatic reflections showed me that the top third of the ball was a separate piece, fitting conically down like the tapered glass stopper of a monstrous perfume bottle. The handle on the top was for the purpose of lifting this giant's teapot lid, and allowing entrance into the sphere.

"Isn't it a beauty?" murmured Stanley. "It ought to be," he added. "It cost me eighty-six thousand to make it in my own glass factory. Eleven castings before this one came along that was reasonably free of flaws. Twenty-two feet six inches over all, walls five feet thick, new formula unbreakable glass, four men working a month to grind the lid into place, tolerance limits plus or minus zero."

He slapped the Professor's shoulders. "Let's go in and look over the apparatus."

* * * *

To accommodate the huge ball a well had been constructed in the Rosa's hold. This brought the deck we were standing on up to within six feet of the top ring, above which was rigged a chain hoist for lifting the ponderous lid.

The hoist was revolved, the conical top was swung free, and we clambered into our unique diving shell.

The tall cylinders were revealed as great flasks of compressed air. The indeterminate thing beside the searchlight turned out to be a hand pump, geared to work against heavy pressure. From the suction chamber of this three tubes extended.

"We inhale the air of the chamber," the Professor explained to me, "and exhale through the tubes into the pump cylinder. Breathe in through the nose and out through the mouth. The pump piston is forced down by this geared handle, sending the used air out of the shell through this sixteenth-inch hole. A ball check valve keeps the water from squirting in when the exhaust pressure is released."

He pointed to a telegraphic key which completed a circuit from the batteries in the bottom of the ball to a thread of copper cast through the lid.

"That's your plaything, Martin. You are to raise or lower us by pressing that key. It controls the donkey engine electrically, so that we guide our own destinies though we are a mile beneath our power plant. Stanley works the pump. I direct the searchlight, write down notes, and, I sincerely hope, take snapshots of deep sea life."

For a moment my part of the labor seemed so easy as to be unfair. Merely to sit there and punch a little key at raising and lowering time! But as I thought it over it began to appear more difficult.

The *Rosa* could not anchor, of course, in a mile of water. We would drift helplessly. If we approached an undersea cliff I must raise us at once to prevent us being smashed against it. And if the cliff were too lofty to be cleared in time. . . .

I mentioned this to the Professor.

"That would be unfortunate," he said, with his frosty smile. "Stanley assures us this glass is unbreakable. He means commercially unbreakable. What would happen to it if it were submitted to the strain of being flung against a rock pile—in addition to the enormous stress of the water pressure—I don't know. It's your job to see that we don't have to find out!"

It had been planned to test the sphere empty first to see how it stood the strain.

We drifted to a full stop over the center of Penguin Deep where we were to gamble our lives in a game with Neptune. Sea anchors were rigged to lessen our drift and the donkey engine was geared to the first cable drum.

There was an impressive row of these drums, each holding an interminable length of three-quarter-inch cable. The bulk of a mile of steel cable has to be seen to be believed!

The glass sphere was lifted from the hold, delicately for all its enormous weight, and swung over the rail preparatory to being lowered into the depths.

Not until that moment did I notice two things: that there was no fastening of any kind to keep the thick lid in place: and that the three-quarter-inch cable looked like a pack thread in comparison to the ponderous bulk it strained to support.

"We couldn't use a heavier cable," said the Professor, "because of the strain. We're overloading the hoist as it is. As for the lid being fastened down—I think you'll find it will be pressed into place securely enough!"

There was unanimous silence as the great globe slipped into the sea—down and down until the last reflection of the morning sun ceased to shimmer from its surface. Drum after drum was played out, till the first mate held his hand up to check the engineer.

"Five thousand feet, sir," he called to Stanley.

"Haul it back up. And let us hope," Stanley added fervently, "that we'll find the gadget in one piece."

The engine began to snort rhythmically. Dripping, vibrating, the coils of cable began to crawl back in place on the drums. There was a glint under the surface again as the sunlight reflected on the nearing sphere.

The great ball flashed out of the water, and a cheer burst from the throats of all of us. It was absolutely unharmed. Only—there was a beading of fine moisture inside the thick globe. What that could mean, none of us could figure out.

"Difference in temperature?" worried the Professor. "No, it's as cold inside as out. Molecules of water driven by sheer pressure through five feet of glass to unite in drops on the inside? Possibly. Well, there's one way to find out. Stanley, Martin—are you ready?"

We nodded, and prepared to visit the bottom a mile below the *Rosa's* keel. The preparation consisted merely in donning heavy, fleece-lined jumpers to protect us from the cold of the sunless depths.

Soberly we entered the ball to undergo whatever ordeal awaited us on the distant ocean floor. How comparative distance is! A mile walk in the country—it is nothing. A mile ascent in an airplane—a trifle. But a mile descent into pitch black, bone chilling depths of water—that is an immense distance!

Copper wire, on a separate drum, was connected from the engine switch to the copper thread that curled through the glass wall to my telegraphic key. We strapped the mouthpieces of the breathing tubes over our heads, and Browne started the slow turning of the compression pump.

The Professor snapped the searchlight on and off several times to see that it was in working shape. He raised his hand, I pressed the key, and the long descent began.

That plunge into the bottomless depths remains in my memory almost as clearly as the far more fantastic adventures that came to us later.

Smoothly, rapidly, the yellow-green of the surface water dimmed to olive. This in turn grew blacker and blacker. Then we were slipping down into pitch darkness—a big bubble lit by a meagre lamp and containing three fragile human beings that dared to trust the soft pulp of their bodies to the crushing weight of the deepest ocean.

The most impressive thing was the utter soundlessness of our descent. At first there had been a pulsing throb of the donkey engine transmitted to us by the sustaining cable. This died as we slid farther from the Rosa. At length it was hushed entirely, cushioned by the springy length of steel. There was no stir, no sound of any kind. As far as our senses could tell us, we were hanging motionless in the pressing, awesome blackness.

The Professor switched off our light and turned on the searchlight which he trained downward through the wall at as steep an angle as the flooring would permit. Even then the illusion of motionlessness was preserved. There was nothing in the water to mark our progress. We might have been floating in a back void of space.

Down and down we went, for an interminable length of time—till at length we reached the abysmal level where the sun never shone and the eyes of man had never gazed till now.

Words were made to describe familiar articles. I find now when I am faced with the necessity of portraying events and objects beyond the range of normal human experience that I cannot conjure up words to fit. I despair of trying to make you see what we saw, and feel what we felt.

But try to picture yourself in the glass ball with us:

All is profound blackness save for a streak of white, dying about fifty feet away, which is the beam of our searchlight. Twenty feet below is a bare floor of flinty lava and broken shell. This is unrelieved by sea-weed of any kind, appearing like an imagined fragment of Martian or lunar landscape.

The ball sways idly to the push of some explicable submarine current. It is like being in a captive balloon, except that the connecting cable extends stiffly upward instead of downward.

There is a realization, an instinctive *feel* of awful pressure around you. Logic tells you how you are clamped about, but deeper than logic is the intuition that the glass walls are pressing in on themselves—at the point of collapse. Your ears, tingle with the feel of it: your head rings with it.

You are breathing in through your nose—thin, unsatisfying gulps of air that cause your lungs to labor at their task; and you are exhaling through, your mouth, with difficulty, into the barrel of the powerful pump. No bubbles arise from the tiny hole where the used air is forced into the water. The pressure is too enormous for that. Only a thin, milky line marks its escape from the sphere.

In a ghostly way you see Stanley turning the pump handle. With a handful of waste which he has borrowed from the *Rosa's* engine room, the Professor wipes from the section of wall through which the searchlight plays the moisture that constantly collects there. I sit with my hand near the key, peering downward and ahead like an engineer in a locomotive cab, ready to raise the shell or lower it as occasion warrants.

And always the suffocating awareness of pressure. . . .

Strange and mystic journey as the tortured glass sphere floated over the bottom, following the slow drift of the *Rosa* far above!

The finger of light played along the tilted side of a wrecked tramp steamer. There was a crumpled gash in the bow. From this ragged hole suddenly appeared a great, serpentine form. . . .

The Professor clutched at his camera, pointed it, and clenched his hands in a frenzy of disappointment. The serpent shape had disappeared back into the hull. A little later and we had drifted slowly past the wreck.

"Damn it!" the Professor snatched away his mouthpiece to exclaim: "If we could only *stop*."

The bottom changed character shortly after we had passed the hulk. We began to creep over low, gently rounded mounds.

These were so regular in form that they were puzzling. About fifty feet across and ten in altitude, they looked artificial in their symmetry—like great saucers set on the ocean floor bottom side up. They took on a dirty black hue as our light struck them, and glowed with a faint phosphorescence as they stretched away into the darkness.

A twelve-foot monstrosity, all toad-like head and eyes, swam into the light beam and bumped blindly against the glass ball. For an instant it goggled crazily at us. The Professor took its picture. It blundered away. As it reached the darkness beyond the beam it, too, showed phosphorescent. A belt of blue-white spots like the portholes of a liner extended down its ugly sides.

Along the bottom, between the curious mounds, writhed a wormlike thing. But it was too huge to be described as truly wormlike—it was eighteen or twenty feet long and a foot thick. It was blood red, almost blunt ended and patently without eyes.

I took my gaze off it for an instant. When I looked again it had disappeared. I blinked at this seeming miracle and then discovered a foot or so of its tail protruding from under the edge of one of the mounds. It was threshing furiously about.

It was at this instant that I suddenly found increased difficulty, and glanced at Stanley.

He had stopped pumping and was clutching at the Professor's arm with one hand while he pointed down with the other. The Professor motioned him toward the pump, and began to click pictures furiously with the camera pointed at the nearest mound.

Wondering at the urgency of Stanley's gesture and the frantic clicking of the camera shutter, I looked more closely at the curious, saucer-like hump.

Under closer inspection something remarkably like a huge, mud-colored eye was revealed! And as we drifted along, twenty feet away on the farther slope, another appeared!

Paralyzed, I stared at the edges of the thing. They were waving almost imperceptibly up and down, *creeping*!

The mounds were living creatures! Acres and acres of them lying lethargically on the bottom waiting for something to crawl within range of their monstrous edges!

Involuntarily I pressed the key to raise us. But we had gone only a few feet when the Professor called to me.

"Down again, Martin. I don't think these things will bother us unless we scrape against them. Anyway they can't hurt the shell."

I lowered the ball to our former twenty-foot level, and there we swung just over the monsters' backs.

* * * *

THE Professor had said that the giant inverted saucers would probably not bother us if we did not come in contact with them. It soon became apparent that, in a measure, he was right. The creatures either could not or would not lift their enormous bulks from the sea floor.

A gigantic wriggling thing, all grotesque fringe and tentacles, drifted down into the range of our light. Lower it floated until it hovered just above one of the larger mounds. The Professor got its portrait. At the same instant, as though it had heard the click of the shutter and been frightened by it, the thing dropped another foot—and touched the sloping back.

With the speed of light the inverted saucer became a cup. Like a clenching fist, the cup closed over one of the straggling tentacles.

There followed a tug of war that was all the more ghastly for its soundlessness. The hunted jerked spasmodically to get away from the hunter. So wild were its efforts that several times it raised the monster clear of the bottom for a foot or so. But the grim clutch could not be broken.

Closer and closer it was dragged. Then, after a supreme paroxysm, the tentacle parted and the prey escaped. The tentacle disappeared into the mass of the baffled hunter. It made no attempt to follow the fleeing creature. It slowly relaxed along the bottom and waited for its next meal.

The unearthly incident gave us fresh confidence, convincing us that the monsters did not move unless they were directly touched. Of course we could not foresee the fatal accident that was going to put us within reach of one of the giant saucers.

We thought for awhile that these great blobs of cold life were the largest creatures of the depths. It was soon made clear to us how mistaken that notion was!

For a time we gazed spellbound at the nightmare assortment of grotesqueries that gradually assembled around us, attracted no doubt by our light. The things were mainly sightless and of indescribable shape. Most of them were phosphorescent, and they avoided collisions in a way that suggested that they had some buried sense of light perception.

As time passed the Professor emptied his camera, refilled it several times and groaned that he had no more film. Twice as we drifted along I raised us to keep us clear of a gradual upward slope of the smooth floor.

Stanley removed his mouthpiece long enough to suggest that we go back to the surface: we had been submerged for nearly four hours now. But before we could reply a violent movement was felt.

The ball rocked and twirled so that we were forced to cling to the circular bench to avoid being thrown to the floor. It was as though a hurricane of wind had suddenly penetrated the unruffled depths.

"Earthquake?" called Stanley.

"Don't know," answered the Professor. He swung the searchlight in an arc and focussed it at length on something that appeared only as a field of blurred movement. He wiped the moisture from the wall before the lens, and there was revealed to us a sight that makes my heart pound even now when I recall it to memory.

Something vast and serpentine had ventured too near the bottom—and had been caught by the death traps there!

The creature was a writhing mass of gigantic coils. It was impossible even to guess at its length, but its girth was such that the mound-shaped monsters that had fastened to it could not entirely encircle it.

There it twined and knotted: a mighty serpent of the deepest ocean, snapping its awful length and threshing its powerful tail in an effort to dislodge the giant leeches that were flattened against it. And every time it touched the bottom in its blind frenzy, more of the teeming deathtraps attached themselves to it, crawling over their fellows in an effort to find unoccupied areas.

Soon the sea-serpent was a distorted, creeping mass. For one appalling instant its head came into our view. . . .

It resembled the head of a crocodile, only it was ten times larger and covered with scale like the armor plate of a destroyer. The jaws, wide open and slashing with enormous, needle-shaped teeth at the huge parasites, were large enough to have held our glass sphere. One eye appeared. It was at least three feet across and of a shimmering amethyst color.

One of the deadly saucers wrapped itself around the great head. The entire mass of attackers and attacked settled slowly to the bottom.

But before it completely succumbed the beaten monster gave one last, convulsive flick of its tail. . . .

"Good God!" cried Stanley, shrinking away from the pump and staring upward.

I followed his gaze with my own eyes.

In the faint reflected glow of the searchlight I could see row on row of large cups flattened against the top of the ball. As I watched these flattened still more and the big sphere quivered perceptibly.

In its death struggle the mighty serpent had flicked one of the huge leeches against us. It now clung there with blind tenacity, covering nearly two-thirds of our shell with the underside of its body.

I reached for the control key to send us to the surface.

"Don't!" snapped the Professor. "The weight—"

He needed to say no more. My hand recoiled as though the key had been red hot.

The three-quarter-inch cable above us was now sustaining, in addition to its own huge weight, our massive glass ball and the appalling tonnage of this grim blanket of flesh that encircled us. Could it further hold against the strain of lifting that combined tonnage through the press of the water? Almost certainly it could not!

There was nothing we could do but hang there and discover at first hand exactly what happened to things that were clamped in those mighty, living vises!

The Professor turned on the interior bulb. The result was ghastly. It showed every detail of the belly of the thing that gripped us.

Crowded over its entire under surface were gristly, flattened suckers. Now and then a convulsive ripple ran through its surface tissue and great ridges of flesh stood out. With each squeeze the glass shell quivered ominously as though the extreme limit of its pressure resisting power were being reached—and passed.

"A nice fix," remarked the Professor, his calm, dry voice acting like a tonic in that moment of fear. "If we try to go up, the cable would probably break. If we try to outlast the patience of this thing we might run out of air, or actually be staved in."

He paused thoughtfully.

"I suggest, though, that we follow the latter course for awhile at least. It would be just too bad if that cable broke, gentlemen!"

Stanley shuddered, and looked at the dirty white belly that pressed against the glass walls on all sides.

"I vote we stay here for a time."

"And I," was my addition.

I relieved Stanley at the pump. He and the Professor sat down on the bench. Casting frequent glances at the constricted blanket of flesh that covered us, we prepared to wait as composedly as we might for the thing to give up its effort to smash our shell.

The hour that followed was longer than any full day I have ever lived through. Had I not confirmed the passage of time by looking at my watch, I would have sworn that at least twenty hours had passed.

Every half-minute I gazed at that weaving pattern of cup-shaped suckers only five feet away, trying to see if they were relaxing in their pressure. I attempted to persuade myself that they were. But I knew I was only imagining it. Actually they were pressed as flat as ever, and the sphere still quivered at regular intervals as the heavy body squeezed in on itself. There was no sign that its blind, mindless patience was becoming exhausted.

There was little conversation during that interminable hour.

Stanley grinned wryly once and commented on the creature's disappointment if it actually succeeded in getting at us.

"We'd be scattered all over the surrounding half mile by the pressure of the water," he said. "There'd be nothing left for our pet to feed on but five-foot chunks of broken glass. Not a very satisfying meal."

"We might try to reason with the thing—point out how foolish it is to waste its time on us," I suggested, trying to appear as nonchalant as he was.

The Professor said nothing. He was coolly writing in his notebook, describing minutely the appearance of our abysmal captor.

Finally I chanced to look down through a section of wall not covered by our stubborn enemy. I wiped the moisture from the glass before the searchlight so that I could see more clearly.

The bottom seemed to be heaving up and down. I blinked my eyes and looked again. It was not an illusion. With a regular dip and rise we were approaching to within a few feet of the rocky floor and moving back up again. Also we were floating faster than at anytime previous. The bottom was bare again; we had left the crowding, ominous mounds.

I waved to the Professor. He snapped his notebook shut and stared at the uneasy ocean bottom.

"I've been hoping I was wrong," he said simply. "I thought I felt a wavy motion fifteen minutes ago, and it seemed to me to increase steadily."

The three of us stared at each other.

"You mean . . ." began Stanley with a shudder.

"I mean that the *Rosa*, one mile above us, is having difficulties. A storm. Judging from our movement it must be a hurricane: the length of cable would cushion us from any average wave, and we are rising and falling at least fifteen feet."

"My God!" groaned Stanley. "The *Rosa* is already heeled with the weight of us. She could never weather a hurricane!"

The plight of the crew above our heads was as clear to us as though we had been aboard with them.

Should they cut the cable, figuring that the lives of the three of us were certainly not to be set against the thirty on the yacht?

Should they disconnect the electric control and try to haul us up regardless?

Or should they try to ride out the storm in spite of being crippled by the drag of us?

"I think if I were up there I'd cut us adrift," said Stanley grimly. Both the Professor and myself nodded. "Though," he added hopefully, "my captain is a good gambler. . . ."

The cable quivered like a live thing under the terrific strain. At each downward swoop, before the upswing began, there was a sickening sag.

"We no longer have a decision to make," said the Professor. "Press the key, Martin, and God grant we can rise with all this dead weight."

And at that instant the crew of the *Rosa* were also relieved of the necessity for making a decision.

At the bottom of one of those long, sickening falls there was a jerk—and we continued on down to the ocean floor!

The sphere rolled over, jumbling the equipment in a tangled mess with the three of us in the center, bruised and cut. The light snapped off as the battery connections were torn loose.

There we lay at the bottom of Penguin Deep, in an inert sphere that was dead and dark in the surrounding blackness—a coffin of glass to hold us through the centuries. . . .

"MARTIN," I heard the Professor's voice after a time. "Stanley—can either of you move? I'm caught."

"I'm caught, too," came Stanley's gasping answer. "Something on my leg—feels like it's broken."

A heavy object was pressing across my body. With an effort I freed myself and fumbled in the pitch darkness for the other two.

"Lights first," commanded the Professor. "The pump, you know."

I did know! Frantically I scrambled in the dark till I located the batteries. They were right side up and still wired together.

The air grew rapidly foul with no one at the pump. Panting for breath I blundered at the task of connecting the light. After what seemed an eternity I accomplished it.

The light revealed Stanley with an air tank lying across his leg. The mouthpiece of his breathing tube had been forced back over his head, gashing his face in its journey. His face was white with pain.

The Professor was caught under the heavy bench. I freed him and together we attended to Stanley, finding that his leg wasn't broken but only badly bruised.

The mound-shaped monster, dislodged possibly by the fall, was nowhere to be seen.

I resumed work at the pump, the connections of which were so strongly contrived that they had withstood the shock of the upset.

For a moment we were content to rest while the air grew purer. Then we were forced squarely to face our fate.

The Professor summed up the facts in a few concise words.

"We're certainly doomed! Here at the bottom of Penguin Deep we're as out of reach of help as though we were stranded on the moon. We're as good as dead right now."

"If we have nothing left to hope for," whispered Stanley after a time, "we might as well close the air valves and get it over with at once. No use torturing ourselves. . . ."

The Professor moistened his lips.

"It might be wise." He turned to me. "What's your opinion, Martin?"

But I—I confess I had not the stark courage of these two.

"No! No!" I cried out. "Let's keep on living as long as the air holds out. Something might happen—"

I avoided their eyes as I said it, utterly ashamed of my cowardly quibbling with death. What in the name of God could possibly happen to help us?

The Professor shrugged dully, and nodded.

"I feel with Stanley that we ought to get it over in one short stab. But we have no right to force you. . . ." His voice trailed off.

We readjusted our mouthpieces. I turned automatically at the pump; and we silently awaited the last suffocating moment of our final doom.

As before, attracted by the light, a strange assortment of deep-sea life wriggled and darted about us, swimming lazily among the looped coils and twists of our cable which had settled down around us.

Among these were certain fish that resembled great porcupines. Spines a foot and a half long, like living knife blades, protected them from the attacks of other species.

They were the only things we saw that were not constantly writhing away from the jaws of some hostile monster—the only things that seemed able to swim about their own affairs without even deigning to watch for danger.

Fascinated, I watched the six-foot creatures. Here were we, reasoning humans, supposed lords of creation, slowly but surely perishing—while only a few feet away one of the lowest forms of life could exist in perfect safety and tranquility!

Then, as I watched them, I seemed to see a difference in some of them.

The majority of them had two fins just behind the gill slits, typical fish tails and blunt, sloping heads. But now and then I saw a spined monster that was queerly unlike its fellows.

Instead of two front fins, these unique ones had two vacant round holes. The head looked as though it had forgotten to grow; its place was taken by an eyeless, projecting, shield shaped cap. And there was no tail.

Glad to find something to distract my half crazed thoughts, I studied the nearest of these.

They moved slower than their tailed and finned brothers, I noticed. I wondered how they could move at all, lacking in any kind of motive power as they seemed to be.

Next instant the secret of their movement was made clear!

Out of the empty fin holes of the creature I was studying crept two long, powerful looking tentacles. But these were not true tentacles. There were no vacuum discs on them, and they moved as though supported by jointed bones—like arms.

The arms ended in flat paddles that resembled hands. These threshed the water in a sort of breast-stroke, propelling the body forward.

Shortly after the arms had appeared, the spiny head cap was cautiously extended a few inches forward from the main shell. Further it was extended as the head of a turtle might slowly appear from the protection of its bony case. And under it—

"Professor!" I screamed wildly. "My God! Look!"

Both the Professor and Stanley merely stared dully at me. I babbled of what I had seen.

"A man! A human looking thing, anyway! Arms and a head! A man inside a fish's spined hide—like armor!"

They looked pityingly at me. The Professor laid his hand on my shoulder.

"Now, now," he soothed, "don't go to pieces—"

"I tell you I saw it!" I shouted. Then, shrinking from the hysterical loudness of my own voice, I lowered my tone. "Something that looks human has occupied some of those prickly, six-foot shells. I saw arms—and a man's head! I swear it!"

"Nonsense! How could a human being stand the cold, the pressure—"

Here I happened to glance at the wall of the shell through which the searchlight shone.

"Look! See for yourself!"

Squarely in the rays of the light showed a head, projecting from one of the shells and capped with a wide flat helmet of horned bone.

There were eyes and nose and mouth placed on one side of that head—a face! There were even tabs of flesh or bony protuberances that resembled ears.

"Curious," muttered the Professor, staring. "It certainly looks human enough to talk. But it's only a fish, nevertheless. See—in the throat are gill slits."

"But the eyes! Look at them! They're not the eyes of a fish!"

And they were not. There was in them a light of reason, of intelligence. Those eyes were roaming brightly over us, observing the light, the equipment, seeming to note our amazement as we crowded to look at it.

The sphere rocked slightly. Behind the staring, manlike visitor there was a glimpse of enormous, crocodile jaws and huge, amethyst eyes. Instantly the head and arms receded, leaving an empty-seeming, lifeless shell. An impregnable fortress of spines, the thing drifted slowly away through the twisted loops of cable.

"It certainly looked like—" began Stanley shakily.

"The creature was just a fish," said the Professor shaking his head at the light in Stanley's eyes. "Some sort of giant parasite that inhabits the shells of other fish."

He opened the valve of the last air cylinder and seated himself resignedly on the bench.

"We have another half hour or so—"

All of us suddenly put out our hands to brace ourselves. The sphere had moved.

"Look at the cable!" called Stanley.

We did so. It was moving, writhing away from us over the bottom as though abruptly given life of its own. Coil after coil disappeared into the further gloom.

At length the cable was straight. The ball moved again—was dragged a few feet along the rocky floor.

Something—possessed of incredibly vast power—had seized the end of the steel cable and was reeling us in as a fisherman reels in a trout!

Slowly, unsteadily, we slid along the ocean floor. Ahead of us appeared a jagged black wall—a cliff. There was a gloomy hole at its base. Toward this we were being dragged by whatever it was that had caught the end of the cable.

Helpless, we watched ourselves engulfed by the murky den. In the beam of the searchlight we saw that the submarine cavern extended on and on for an unguessable depth. The cable, taut with the strain, stretched ahead out of sight.

Time had been lost track of during that mysterious, ominous journey. It was recalled to us by the state of the air we were breathing.

The Professor removed his mouthpiece and cast the tube aside.

"You might as well stop pumping, Martin," he said quietly. "We're done. There's no more air in the flask."

We stared at each other. Then we shook hands, solemnly, tremulously, taking leave of each other before we departed on that longest of all journeys. . . .

The air in that small space was rapidly exhausted. We lay on the floor, laboring for breath, and closed our eyes. . . .

The Professor, the oldest of the three of us, succumbed first. I heard his breath whistle stertorously and, glancing at him, saw that he was in a coma. In a moment Stanley had joined him in blessed unconsciousness.

I could feel myself drifting off. . . . Hammers beat at my ears. . . . Daggers pierced my heaving lungs. . . .

Hazily I could see scores of the bristly, manlike fish when I opened my eyes and glanced through the walls. It was not one monster then, but many that had brought us to their lair. Abruptly, as though a signal had been given, they all streamed back toward the mouth of the cavern. . . .

My eyesight dimmed. . . . The hammers pulsed louder. . . . A veil descended over my senses and I knew no more. . . .

A SOFT, sustained roar came to my ears. Through my closed eyelids I could sense light. A dank, fishy smell came to my nostrils.

I groaned and moved feebly, finding that I was resting on something soft and pleasant.

Dazedly I opened my eyes and sat up. An exclamation burst from me as I suddenly remembered what had gone before, and realized that somehow, incredibly, I was still living.

Feeling like a man who has waked from a nightmarish sleep to find himself in his tomb, I gazed about.

I was in a long, lofty rock chamber, the uneven floor of which was covered with shallow pools of water. The further end was of smooth-grained stone that resembled cement. The near end was rough like the walls; but in it there was a small, symmetrical arch, the mouth of a passage leading away to some other point in the bowels of the earth.

The place was flooded with clear light that had a rosy tinge. From my position on the floor I could not see what made the light. It streamed from a crevice that extended clear around the cave parallel with the floor and about twelve feet above it. From this groove, along with the light, came the soft roaring hiss.

Beside me was the glass ball, the cover off and lying a few feet away from the opening in the top. There was no trace of Stanley or the Professor.

I rose from my couch, a thick, mattresslike affair of soft, pliant hide, and walked feebly toward the small arch in the near end of the cave.

Even as I approached it I heard footsteps, and voices resounded in some slurring, musical language. Half a dozen figures suddenly came into view.

They were men, as human as myself! Indeed, as I gazed at them, I felt inclined to think they were even more human!

They were magnificent specimens. The smallest could not have been less than six feet three, and all of them were muscular and finely proportioned. Their faces were arresting in their expression of calm strength and kindliness. They looked like gods, arrayed in soft, thick, beautifully tanned hides in this rosy tinted hole a mile below the ocean's top.

They stared at me for an instant, then advanced toward me. My face must have reflected alarm, for the tallest of them held up his hand, palm outward, in a peaceful gesture.

The leader spoke to me. Of course the slurred, melodious syllable meant nothing to me. He smiled and indicated that I was to follow him. I did so, hardly aware of what I was doing, my brain reeling in an attempt to grasp the situation.

How marvelous, how utterly incredible, to find human beings here! How many were there? Where had they come from? How had they salvaged us from Penguin Deep? I gave it up, striding along with my towering guards like a man walking in his sleep.

At length the low passageway ended, and I exclaimed aloud at what I saw.

I was looking down a long avenue of buildings, all three stories in height. There were large door and window apertures, but no doors nor window panes. In front of each house was a small square with— wonder of wonders!—a lawn of whitish yellow vegetation that resembled grass. In some of the lawns were set artistic fountains of carved rock.

I might have been looking down any prosperous earthly subdivision, save for the fact that the roofs of the houses were the earth itself, which the building walls, in addition to functioning as partitions, served to support. Also earthly subdivisions aren't usually illuminated with rosy light that comes softly roaring from jets set in the walls.

We were walking toward a more brightly lighted area that showed ahead of us. On the way we passed intersections where other, similar streets branched geometrically away to right and left. These were smaller than the one we were on, indicating that ours was Main Street in this bizarre submarine city.

Faces appeared at door and window openings to peer at me as we passed. And even in that jumbled moment I had time to realize that these folk could restrain curiosity better than we can atop the earth. There was no hub-bub, no running out to tag after the queerly dressed foreigner and shout humorous remarks at him.

We approached the bright spot I had noticed from afar. It was an open square, about a city block in area, in the center of which was a royal looking building covered with blazing fragments of crystal and so brilliantly resplendent with light that it seemed to glow at the heart of a pink fire.

I was led toward this and in through a wide doorway. As courteously as though I were a visiting king, I was conducted up a great staircase, down a corridor set with more of the sparkling crystals and into a huge, low room. There my escort bowed and left me.

Still feeling that I could not possibly be awake and seeing actual things, I glanced around.

In a corner was another of the mattresslike couches made of the thick, soft hide that seemed to be the principal fabric of the place. A few feet away was a table set with dishes of food in barbaric profusion. None of the viands looked familiar but all appealed to the appetite. The floor was strewn with soft skins, and comfortable, carved benches were scattered about.

I walked to the window and looked out. Underneath was a plot of the cream colored grass through which ran a tiny stream. This widened at intervals into clear pools beside which were set stone benches. A hundred yards away was the edge of the square, where the regular, three storied houses began.

While I was staring at this unearthly vista, still unable to think with any coherence. I heard my name called. I turned to face Stanley and the Professor.

Both were pale in the rose light, and Stanley limped with the pain of his bruised leg: but both had recovered from their partial suffocation as completely as had I.

"We thought perhaps you'd decided to swim back up to the *Rosa* and leave us to our fates," said Stanley after we had stopped pumping each other's arms and had seated ourselves.

"And I thought—well, I didn't think much of anything," I replied. "I was too busy straining my eyesight over the wonders of this city. Did you ever see anything like it?"

"We haven't seen it at all, save for a view from the windows," said Stanley. "All we know of the place is that a while ago we woke up in a room like this, only much smaller and less lavish. I wonder why you rate this distinction?"

I described the streets as I had seen them. (It is impossible for me to think of them as anything but streets; it would seem as though the rock roof over all would give the appearance of a series of tunnels; but I had always the impression of airiness and openness.)

"Light and heat are furnished by natural gas," said the Professor when I remarked on the perfection of these two necessities. "That's what makes the low roaring noise—the thousands of burning jets. But the presence of gas here isn't as unusual as the presence of air. Where does that come from? Through wandering underground mazes, from some cave mouth in the Fiji Islands to the north? That would indicate that all the earth around here is honeycombed like a gigantic section of sponge. I wonder—"

"Have you any idea how we were rescued?" I interrupted, a little impatient of his abstract scientific ponderings.

"We have," said Stanley. "A woman told us. We woke up to find her nursing us—gorgeous looking thing—finest woman I've ever seen, and I've seen a good many—"

"She didn't exactly 'tell' us," remarked the Professor with his thin smile. Women were only interesting to him as biological studies. "She drew a diagram that explained it.

"That tunnel, Martin, was like the outer diving chamber of a submarine. We were hauled in on a big windlass—driven by gas turbines, I think. Once we were inside, a twenty-yard, counterbalanced wall of rock was lowered across the entrance. Then the water was drained out through a well, and into a subterranean body of water that extends under the entire city. And here we are."

We fell silent. Here we were. But what was going to happen to us among these friendly-seeming people; and how—if ever—we were going to get back to the earth's surface, were questions we could not even try to answer.

We ate of the appetizing food laid out on the long table. Shortly afterward we heard steps in the corridor outside the room.

A woman entered. She was ravishingly beautiful, tall, slender but symmetrically rounded. A soft leather robe slanted upward across her breast to a single shoulder fastening and ended just above her knees in a skirt arrangement. Around her head was a regal circlet of silvery gray metal with a flashing bit of crystal set in the center above her broad, low forehead.

She smiled at Stanley who looked dazzled and smiled eagerly back.

She pointed toward the door, signifying that we were to go with her. We did so; and were led down the great staircase and to a huge room that took up half the ground floor of the building. And here we met the nobility of the little kingdom—the upper class that governed the immaculate little city.

They were standing along the walls, leaving a lane down the center of the room—tall, finely modeled men and women dressed in the single garments of soft leather. There were people there with gray hair and wisdom wrinkled faces; but all were alike in being erect of body, firm of bearing and in splendid health.

They stopped talking as we entered the big room. Our gaze strayed ahead down the lane toward the further wall.

Here was a raised dais. On it was a gleaming crystal encrusted throne. And occupying it was the most queenly, exquisitely beautiful woman I had ever dreamed about.

Woman? She was just a girl in years in spite of her grave and royal air. Her eyes were deep violet. Her hair was black as ebony and gleaming with sudden glints of light. Her skin—

But she cannot be described. Only a great painter could give a hint of her glory. Too, I might truthfully be described as prejudiced about her perfections.

The Queen, for patently she was that, bowed graciously at us. It seemed to me—though I told myself that I was an imaginative fool—that her eyes rested longest on me, and had in them an expression not granted to the Professor or Stanley.

She spoke to us a melodious sentence or two, and waved her beautiful hand in which was a short ivory wand, evidently a scepter.

"She's probably giving us the keys to the city," whispered Stanley. He edged nearer the fair one who had conducted us. "I sincerely hope there's room here for us."

The open lane closed in on us. Men and women crowded about

us speaking to us and smiling ruefully as they realized we could not understand. I noticed that, for some curious reason, they seemed fascinated by the color of my hair. Red-haired men were evidently scarce there.

At length the beauty who had so captured Stanley's fancy, and who seemed to have been appointed a sort of mentor for us, suggested in sign language that we might want to return to our quarters.

It was a welcome suggestion. We were done in by the experiences and emotions that had gripped us since leaving the *Rosa* such an incredibly few hours ago.

We went back to the second floor. I to my luxurious big apartment and Stanley and the Professor to their smaller but equally comfortable rooms.

A PLEASANT period slid by, every waking hour of which was filled with new experiences.

The city's name, we found, was Zyobor. It was a perfect little community. There were artisans and thinkers, artists and laborers—all alike in being physically perfect beyond belief and cultured as no race on top the ground is cultured.

As we began to learn the language, more exact details of the practical methods of existence were revealed to us.

The surrounding earth furnished them with building materials, metals and unlimited gas. The sea, so near us and yet so securely walled away, gave them food. Which warrants a more detailed description.

We were informed that the manlike, two-armed fishes were the servants of these people—domesticated animals, in a sense, only of an extremely high order of intelligence. They were directed by mental telepathy (Every man, woman and child in Zyobor was skilled at thought projection. They conversed constantly, from end to end of the city, by mental telepathy.)

Protected in their spined shells, which they captured from the schools of porcupine fish that swarmed in Penguin Deep, they gathered sea vegetation from the higher levels and trapped sea creatures. These were brought into the subterranean chamber where our glass ball now reposed. Then the chamber was emptied of water and the food was borne to the city.

The vast army of mound-fish provided the bulk of the population's food, and also furnished the thick, pliant skin they used for clothing and drapes. They were cultivated as we cultivate cattle—an ominous herd, to be handled with care and approached by the fish-servants with due caution.

Thus, with all reasonable wants satisfied, with talent and brains to design beautiful surroundings, lighted and warmed by inexhaustible natural gas, these fortunate beings lived their sheltered lives in their rosy underground world.

At least I thought their lives were sheltered then. It was only later, when talking to the beautiful young Queen, that I learned of the dread menace that had begun to draw near to them just a short time before we were rescued. . . .

MY first impression, when we had entered the throne room that first day, that the Queen had regarded me more intently than she had Stanley or the Professor, had been right. It pleased her to treat me as an equal, and to give me more of her time than was granted to any other person in the city.

Every day, for a growing number of hours, we were together in her apartment. She personally instructed me in the language, and such was my desire to talk to this radiant being that I made an apt pupil.

Soon I had progressed enough to converse with her—in a stilted, incorrect way—on all but the most abstract of subjects. It was a fine language. I liked it, as I liked everything else about Zyobor. The upper earth seemed far away and well forgotten.

Her name, I found, was Aga. A beautiful name. . . .

"How did your kingdom begin?" I asked her one day, while we were sitting beside one of the small pools in the gardens. We were close together. Now and then my shoulder touched hers, and she did not draw away.

"I know not," she replied. "It is older than any of our ancient records can say. I am the three hundred and eleventh of the present reigning line."

"And we are the first to enter thy realm from the upper world?"

"Thou art the first."

"There is no other entrance but the sea-way into which we were drawn?"

"There is no other entrance."

I was silent, trying to realize the finality of my residence here.

At the moment I didn't care much if I never got home!

"In the monarchies we know above," I said finally, avoiding her violet eyes, "it is not the custom for the queen—or king—to reign alone.

A consort is chosen. Is it not so here? Has thou not, among thy nobles, some one thou hast destined—"

I stopped, feeling that if she dismissed me in anger and never spoke to me again the punishment would be just.

But she wasn't angry. A lovely tide of color stained her cheeks. Her lips parted, and she turned her head. For a long time she said nothing. Then she faced me, with a light in her eyes that sent the blood racing in my veins.

"I have not yet chosen," she murmured. "Mayhap soon I shall tell thee why."

She rose and hurried back toward the palace. But at the door she paused—and smiled at me in a way that had nothing whatever to do with queenship.

AS the time sped by the three of us settled into the routine of the city as though we had never known of anything else.

The Professor spent most of his time down by the sea chamber where the food was dragged in by the intelligent servant-fish.

He was in a zoologist's paradise. Not a creature that came in there had ever been catalogued before. He wrote reams of notes on the parchment paper used by the citizens in recording their transactions. Particularly was he interested in the vast, lowly mound-fish.

One time, when I happened to be with him, the receding waters of the chamber disclosed the body of one of the odd herdsmen of these deep sea flocks. Then the Professor's elation knew no bounds. We hurried forward to look at it.

"It is a typical fish," puzzled the Professor when we had cut the body out of its usurped armor. "Cold blooded, adapted to the chill and pressure of the deeps. There are the gills I observed before . . . yet it looks very human."

It surely did. There were the jointed arms, and the rudimentary hands. Its forehead was domed; and the brain, when dissected, proved much larger than the brain of a true fish. Also its bones were not those of a mammal, but the cartilagenous bones of a fish. It was not quite six feet long; just fitted the horny shell.

"But its intelligence!" fretted the Professor, glorying in his inability to classify this marvelous specimen. "No fish could ever attain such mental development. Evolution working backward from human to reptile and then fish—or a new freak of evolution whereby a fish on a short cut toward becoming human?" He sighed and gave it up. But more reams of notes were written.

"Why do you take them?" I asked. "No one but yourself will ever see them."

He looked at me with professorial absent-mindedness.

"I take them for the fun of it, principally. But perhaps, sometime, we may figure out a way of getting them up. My God! Wouldn't my learned brother scientists be set in an uproar!"

He bent to his observations and dissections again, cursing now and then at the distortion suffered by the specimens when they were released from the deep sea pressure and swelled and burst in the atmospheric pressure in the cave.

Stanley was engrossed in a different way. Since the moment he laid eyes on her, he had belonged to the stately woman who had first nursed him back to consciousness. Mayis was her name.

From shepherding the three of us around Zyobor and explaining its marvels to us, she had taken to exclusive tutorship of Stanley. And Stanley fairly ate it up.

"You, the notorious woman hater," I taunted him one time, "the wary bachelor—to fall at last. And for a woman of another world—almost of another planet! I'm amazed!"

"I don't know why you should be amazed," said he stiffly.

"You've been telling me ever since I was a kid that women were all useless, all alike—"

"I find I was mistaken," he interrupted. "They aren't all alike. There's only one Mayis. She is—different."

"What do you talk about all the time? You're with her constantly."

"I'm not with her any more than you're with the Queen," he shot back at me. "What do you find to talk about?"

That shut me up. He went to look for Mayis; and I wandered to the royal apartments in search of Aga.

IN the first days of our friendship I had several times surprised in Aga's eyes a curious expression, one that seemed compounded of despair, horror and resignation.

I had seen that same expression in the eyes of the nobles of late, and in the faces of all the people I encountered in the streets—who, I mustn't forget to add here, never failed to treat me with a deference that was as intoxicating as it was inexplicable.

It was as though some terrible fate hovered over the populace, some dreadful doom about which nothing could be done. No one put into words any fears that might confirm that impression; but continually I got the idea that everybody there went about in a state of attempting to live normally and happily while life was still left—before some awful, wholesale death descended on them.

At last, from Aga, I learned the fateful reason.

But first—a confession that was hastened by the knowledge of the fate of the city—I learned from her something that changed all of life for me.

We were surrounded by the luxury of her private apartment. We sat on a low divan, side by side. I wanted, more than anything I had ever wanted before, to put my arms around her. But I dared not. One does not make love easily to a queen, the three hundred and eleventh of a proud line.

And then, as maids have done often in all countries, and, perhaps, on all planets, she took the initiative herself.

"We have a curious custom in Zyobor of which I have not yet told thee," she murmured. "It concerns the kings of Zyobor. The color of their hair."

She glanced up at my own carrot-top, and then averted her gaze.

"For all of our history our kings have had—red hair. On the few occasions when the line has been reduced to a lone queen, as in my case, the red-haired men of the kingdom have striven together in public combat to determine which was most powerful and brave. The winner became the Queen's consort."

"And in this case?" I asked, my heart beginning to pound madly.

"In my case, my lord, there is to be no—no striving. When I was a child our only two red-haired males died, one by accident, one by sickness. Now there are none others but infants, none of eligible age. But— by a miracle—thou—"

She stopped; then gazed up at me from under long, gold flecked lashes.

"I was afraid . . . I was doomed to die . . . alone. . . ."

It was after I had replied impetuously to this, that she told me of the terror that was about to engulf all life in the beautiful undersea city.

"Thou hast wonder, perhaps, why I should be forward enough to tell thee this instead of waiting for thine own confession first," she faltered. "Know, then—the reason is the shortness of the time we are fated to spend together. We shall belong each to the other only a little while. Then shall we belong to death! And I—when I knew the time was to be so brief—"

And I listened with growing horror to her account of the enemy that was advancing toward us with every passing moment.

ABOUT twenty miles away, in the lowest depression of Penguin Deep, lived a race of monsters which the people of Aga's city called Quabos.

The Quabos were grim beings that were more intelligent than Aga's fish-servants—even, she thought, more intelligent than humans themselves. They had existed in their dark hole, as far as the Zyobites knew, from the beginning of time.

Through the countless centuries they had constructed for themselves a vast series of dens in the rock. There they had hidden away from the deep-sea dangers. They, too, preyed on the mound-fish; but as there was plenty of food for all, the Zyobites had never paid much attention to them.

But—just before we had appeared, there had come about a subterranean quake that changed the entire complexion of matters in Penguin Deep.

The earthquake wiped out the elaborately burrowed sea tunnels of the Quabos, killing half of them at a blow and driving the rest out into the unfriendly openness of the deep.

Now this was fatal to them. They were not used to physical self defense. During the thousands of years of residence in their sheltered burrows they had become utterly unable to exist when exposed to the primeval dangers of the sea. It was as though the civilization-softened citizens of New York should suddenly be set down in a howling wilderness with nothing but their bare hands with which to contrive all the necessities of a living.

Such was the situation at the time Stanley, the Professor and myself arrived in Zyobor.

The Quabos must find an immediate haven or perish. On the ocean bottom they were threatened by the mound-fish. In the higher levels they were in danger from almost everything that swam: few things were so defenceless as themselves after their long inertia.

Their answer was Zyobor. There, in perfect security, only to be reached by the diving chamber that could be sealed at will by the twenty-yard, counterbalanced lock, the Quabos would be even more protected than in their former runways.

So—they were working day and night to invade Aga's city!

"But Aga," I interrupted impulsively at this point. "If these monsters are fishes, how could they live here in air—"

I stopped as my objection answered itself before she could reply.

They would not have to live in air to inhabit Zyobor. They would inundate the city—flood that peaceful, beautiful place with the awful pressure of the lowest depths!

That thought, in turn, suggested to me that every building in Zyobor would be swept flat if subjected suddenly to the rush of the sea. The great low cavern, without the support of the myriad walls, would probably collapse—trapping the invading Quabos and leaving the rest without a home once more.

But Aga answered this before I could voice it.

The Quabos had foreseen that point. They were tunneling slowly but surely toward the city from a point about half a mile from the diving chamber. And as they advanced, they blocked up the passageway behind them at intervals, drilled down to the great underground sea that lay beneath all this section, and drained a little of the water away.

In this manner they lightened, bit by bit, the enormous weight of the ocean depths. When the city was finally reached, not only would it be ensured against sudden destruction but the Quabos themselves would have become accustomed to the difference in pressure. Had they gone immediately from the accustomed press of Penguin Deep into the atmosphere of Zyobor, they would have burst into bits. As it was they would be able to flood the city slowly, without injury to themselves.

"Now thou knowest our fate," concluded Aga with a shudder. "Zyobor will be a part of the great waters. We ourselves shall be food for these monsters. . . ." She faltered and stopped.

"But this cannot be!" I exclaimed, clenching my fists impotently. "There *must* be something we can do; some way—"

"There is nothing to be done. Our wisest men have set themselves sleeplessly to the task of defence. There it no defence possible."

"We can't simply sit here and wait! Your people are wonderful, but this is no time for resignation. Send for my two friends, Aga. We will have a council of war, we four, and see if we can find a way!"

She shrugged despairfully, started to speak, then sent in quest of Stanley and the Professor.

They as well as myself, had had no idea of the menace that crept nearer us with each passing hour. They were dumbfounded, horrified to learn of the peril. We sat awhile in silence, realizing our situation to the full.

Then the Professor spoke:

"If only we could see what these things look like! It might help in planning to defeat them."

"That can be done with ease," said Aga. "Come."

We went with her to the gardens and approached the nearest pool.

"My fish-men are watching the Quabos constantly. They report to me by telepathy whenever I send my thoughts their way. I will let you see, on the pool, the things they are now seeing."

She stared intently at the sheet of water. And gradually, as we watched, a picture appeared—a picture that will never fade from my memory in any smallest detail.

The Quabos had huddled for protection into a large cave at the foot of the cliff outside Zyobor. There were a great many Quabos, and the cave was relatively confining. Now we saw, through the eyes of the spine protected outpost of the Queen, these monstrous refugees crowded together like sheep.

The watery cavern was a creeping mass of viscous tentacles, enormous staring eyes and globular heads. The cave was paved three deep with the horrible things, and they were attached to the it walls and roof in solid blocks.

"My God!" whispered Stanley. "There are thousands of them!"

There were. And that they were in distress was evident.

The layers on the floor were weaving and shifting constantly as the bottom creatures struggled feebly to rise to the top of the mass and be relieved of the weight of their brothers. Also they were famished. . . .

One of the blood red, gigantic worms floated near the cave entrance. Like lightning the nearest Quabos darted after it. In a moment the prey was torn to bits by the ravenous monsters.

The other side of the story was immediately portrayed to us.

With the emerging of the reckless Quabos, a sea-serpent appeared from above and snapped up three of their number. Evidently the huge serpent considered them succulent tidbits, and made it its business to wait near the cave and avail itself of just such rash chance-taking as this.

While we watched the nightmare scene, a Quabo disengaged itself from the parent mass and floated upward into the clear, giving us a chance to see more distinctly what the creatures looked like.

There was a black, shiny head as large as a sugar barrel. In this were eyes the size of dinner plates, and gleaming with a cold, hellish intelligence. Four long, twining tentacles were attached directly to the head. Dotted along these were rudimentary sucker discs, that had evidently become atrophied by the soft living of thousands of the creature's ancestors.

As though emerging from the pool into which we were gazing, the monster darted viciously at us. At once it disappeared: the fish-servant through whose eyes we were seeing all this had evidently retreated from the approach; although, protected by its spines, it could not have been in actual danger.

"How dost thou know of the tunneling?" I asked Aga. "Thy fish-men cannot be present there, in the rear of the tunnel, to report."

"My artisans have knowledge of each forward move," she answered. "I will show thee."

We walked back to the palace and descended to a smooth-lined vault. There we saw a great stone shaft sunk down into the rock of the floor. On this was a delicate vibration recording instrument of some sort, with a needle that quivered rhythmically over several degrees of an arc.

"This tells of each move of the Quabos," said Aga. "It also tells us where they will break through the city wall. How near to us are they, Kilor?" she asked an attendant who was studying the dial, and who had bowed respectfully to Aga and myself as we approached.

"They will break into the city in four rixas at the present rate of advance, Your Majesty."

Four rixas! In a little over sixteen days, as we count time, the city of Zyobor would be delivered into the hands—or, rather, tentacles—of the slimy, starving demons that huddled in the cavern outside!

Somberly we followed Aga back to her apartment.

"AS thou seest," she murmured, "there is nothing to be done. We can only resign ourselves to the fate that nears us, and enjoy as much as may be the few remaining rixas. . . ."

She glanced at me.

The Professor's dry, cool voice cut across our wordless, engrossed communion.

"I don't think we'll give up quite as easily as all that. We can at least try to outwit our enemies. If it does nothing else for us, the effort can serve to distract our minds."

He drew from his pocket a sheet of parchment and the stub of his last remaining pencil. His fingers busied themselves apparently idly in the tracing of geometric lines.

"Looking ahead to the exact details of our destruction," he mused coolly, "we see that our most direct and ominous enemy is the sea itself. When the city is flooded, we drown—and later the Quabos can enter at will."

He drew a few more lines, and marked a cross at a point in the outer rim of the diagram.

"What will happen? The Quabos force through the last shell of the city wall. The water from their tunnel floods into Zyobor. But—and mark me well—*only* the water from the tunnel! The outer end, remember, is blocked off in their pressure-reducing process. The vast body of the sea itself cannot immediately be let in here because the Quabos must take as long a time to re-accustom themselves to its pressure as they did to work out of it."

He spread the parchment sheet before us.

"Is this a roughly accurate plan of the city?" he asked Aga.

She inclined her lovely head.

"And this," indicating the cross, "is the spot where the Quabos will break in?"

Again she nodded, shuddering.

"Then tell me what you think of this," said the Professor.

And he proceeded to sketch out a plan so simple, and yet so seemingly efficient, that the rest of us gazed at him with wordless admiration.

"My friend, my friend," whispered Aga at last, "thou hast saved us. Thou art the guardian hero of Zyobor—"

"Not too fast, Your Highness," interrupted the Professor with his frosty smile. "I shall be much surprised if this little scheme actually saves the city. We may find the rock so thick there that our task is hopeless—though I imagine the Quabos picked a thin section for help in their own plans."

A vague look came into his eyes.

"I must certainly get my hands on one of these monsters . . . superhumanly intelligent fish . . . marvelous—akin to the octopus, perhaps?"

He wandered off, changed from the resourceful schemer to the dreamy man of scientific abstractions.

The Queen gazed after him with wonder in her eyes.

"A great man," she murmured, "but is he—a little mad?"

"No, only a little absent-minded," I replied. Then, "Come on, Stanley. We'll round up every able bodied citizen in Zyobor and get to work. I suppose they have some kind of rock drilling machinery here?"

They had. And they strangely resembled our own rock drills: revolving metal shafts, driven by gas turbines, tipped with fragments of the same crystal that glittered so profusely in the palace walls. Another proof that practically every basic, badly needed tool had been invented again and again, in all lands and times, as the necessity for it arose.

With hundreds of the powerful men of Zyobor working as closely together as they could without cramping each others movements, and with the whole city resounding to the roar of the machinery, we labored at the defence that might possibly check the advance of the hideous Quabos.

And with every breath we drew, waking or sleeping, we realized that the cold blooded, inhuman invaders had crept a fraction of an inch closer in their tunneling.

The Quabos against the Zyobites! Fish against man! Two diametrically opposed species of life in a struggle to the death! Which of us would survive?

THE hour of the struggle approached. Every soul in Zyobor moved in a daze, with strained face and fear haunted eyes. Their proficiency in mental telepathy was a curse to them now: every one carried constantly, transmitted from the brains of the servant-fish outposts, a thought picture of that outer cavern in the murky depths of which writhed the thousands of crowding Quabos. Each mind in Zyobor was in continual torment.

Spared that trouble, at least, Stanley and the Professor and I walked down to the fortification we had so hastily contrived. It was finished. And none too soon: the vibration indicator in the palace vault told us that only two feet of rock separated us from the burrowing monsters!

The Professor's scheme had been to cut a long slot down through the rock floor of the city to the roof of the vast, mysterious body of water below.

This slot was placed directly in front of the spot in the city wall where the Quabos were about to emerge. As they forced through the last shell of rock, the deluge of water, instead of drowning the city, was supposed to drain down the oblong vent. Any Quabos that were too near the tunnel entrance would be swept down too.

In silence we approached the edge of the great trough and stared down.

There was a stratum of black granite, fortunately only about thirty feet thick at this point, and then—the depths! A low roar reached our ears from far, far beneath us. A steady blast of ice cold air fanned up against us.

The Professor threw down a large fragment of rock. Seconds elapsed and we heard no splash. The unseen surface was too far below for the noise of the rock's fall to carry on up to us.

"The mystery of this ball of earth on which we live!" murmured the Professor. "Here is this enormous underground body of water. We are far below sea level. Where, then, is it flowing? What does it empty into?

Can it be that our planet is honeycombed with such hollows as this we are in? And is each inhabited by some form of life?"

He sighed and shook his head.

"The thought is too big! For, if that were true, wouldn't the seas be drained from the surface of the earth should an accidental passage be formed from the ocean bed down to such a giant river as this beneath us? How little we know!"

The wild clamor of an alarm bell interrupted his musing. From all the city houses poured masses of people, to form in solid lines behind the large well.

In addition to men, there were many women in those lines, tall and strong, ready to stand by their mates as long as life was left them. There were children, too, scarcely in their teens, prepared to fight for the existence of the race. Every able-bodied Zyobite was mustered against the cold-blooded Things that pressed so near.

The arms of these desperate fighters were pitiful compared to our own war weapons. With no need in the city for fighting engines, none had ever been developed. Now the best that could be had was a sort of ax, used for dissecting the mound-fish, and various knives fashioned for peaceful purposes.

Again the bell clamored forth a warning, this time twice repeated. Every hand grasped its weapon. Every eye went hopefully to the hole in the floor on which our immediate fate depended, then valiantly to the section of wall above it.

This quivered perceptibly. A heavy, pointed instrument broke through; was withdrawn; and a hissing stream of water spurted out.

The Quabos were about to break in upon us!

With a crash that made the solid rock tremble, a section of the wall collapsed. It was the top half of the end of the Quabos' tunnel. They had so wrought that the lower half stayed in place—a thing we did not have time to recognize as significant until later.

A solid wall of water, in which writhed dozens of tentacled monsters, was upon us, and we had time for nothing but action.

The ditch had of necessity been placed directly under the Quabos' entrance. The first rush of water carried half over it. With it were borne scores of the cold-blooded invaders.

In an instant we were standing knee deep in a torrent that tore at our footing, while we hacked frantically with knives and axes at the slimy tentacles that reached up to drag us under.

A soft, horrible mass swept against my legs. I was overthrown. A tentacle slithered around my neck and constricted viciously like a length of rotten cable. I sawed at it with the long, notched blade I carried. Choking for air, I felt the pressure relax and scrambled to my knees.

Two more tentacles went around me, one winding about my legs and the other crushing my waist. Two huge eyes glared fiendishly at me.

I plunged the knife again and again into the barrel-shaped head. It did not bleed: a few drops of thin, yellowish liquid oozed from the wounds but aside from this my slashing seemed to make no impression.

In a frenzy I defended myself against the nightmare head that was winding surely toward me. Meanwhile I devoted every energy to keeping on my feet. If I ever went under again—

It seemed to me that the creature was weakening. With redoubled fury I hacked at the spidery shape. And gradually, when it seemed as though I could not withstand its weight and crushing tentacles another second, it slipped away and floated off on the shallow, roaring rapids.

For a moment I stood there, catching my breath and regaining my strength. Shifting, terrible scenes flashed before my eyes.

A tall Zyobite and an almost equally stalwart woman were both caught by one gigantic Quabo which had a tentacle around the throat of each. The man and woman were chopping at the viscous, gruesome head. One of the Thing's eyes was gashed across, giving it a fearsome, blind appearance. It heaved convulsively, and the three struggling figures toppled into the water and were swirled away.

The Professor was almost buried by a Quabo that had all four of its tentacles wound about him. As methodically as though he were in a laboratory dissecting room, he was cutting the slippery lengths away, one by one, till the fourth parted and left him free.

A giant Zyobite was struggling with two of the monsters. He had an ax in each hand, and was whirling them with such strength and rapidity that they formed flashing circles of light over his head. But he was torn down at last and borne off by the almost undiminished flood that gushed from the tunnel.

And now, without warning, a heavy soft body flung against my back, and the accident most to be dreaded in that mêlée occurred.

I was knocked off my feet! My head was pressed under the water. On my chest was a mass that was yielding but immovable, soft but terribly strong. Animated, firm jelly! I had no chance to use my knife. My arms were held powerless against my sides.

Water filled my nose and mouth. I strangled for breath, heaving at the implacable weight that pinned me helpless. Bright spots swirled before my eyes. There was a roaring in my ears. My lungs felt as though filled with molten lead. I was drowning. . . .

Vaguely I felt the pressure loosen at last. An arm—with good, solid flesh and bone in it—slipped under my shoulders and dragged me up into the air.

"Don't you know—can't drown a fish—holding it under water?" panted a voice.

I opened my eyes and saw Stanley, his face pale with the thrill of battle, his chin jutting forward in a berserk line, his eyes snapping with eager, wary fires.

I grinned up at him and he slapped me on the back—almost completing the choking process started by the salt water I'd inhaled.

"That's better. Now—at it again!"

I don't remember the rest of the tumult. The air seemed filled with loathsome tentacles and bright metal blades. It was a confused eternity until the decreased volume of water in the tunnel gave us a respite. . . .

As the tunnel slowly emptied the pressure dropped, and the incoming flood poured squarely into the trough instead of half over it. From that moment there was very little more for us to do.

Our little army—with about a fourth of its number gone—had only to guard the ditch and see that none of the Quabos caught the edges as they hurtled out of their passage.

For perhaps ten minutes longer the water poured from the break in the wall, with now and then a doomed Quabo that goggled horribly at us as it was dashed down the hole in the floor to whatever awesome depths were beneath.

Then the flow ceased. The last oleaginous corpse was pushed over the edge. And the city, save for an ankle-deep sheet of water that was rapidly draining out the vents in the streets, presented its former appearance.

The Zyobites leaned wearily against convenient walls and began telling themselves how fortunate they were to have been spared what seemed certain destruction.

The Professor didn't share in the general feeling of triumph.

"Don't be so childishly optimistic!" he snapped as I began to congratulate him on the victory his ditch had given us. "Our troubles aren't over yet!"

"But we've proved that we can stand up to them in a hand-to-tentacle fight—"

His thin, frosty smile appeared.

"One of those devils, normally, is stronger than any three men. The only reason all of us weren't destroyed at once is that they were slowly suffocating as they fought. The foot and a half of water we were in wasn't enough to let their gills function properly. Now if they were able to stand right up to us and not be handicapped by lack of water to breathe . . . I wonder. . . . Is that part of their plan? Is there any way they could manage . . . ?"

"But, Professor," I argued, "it's all over, isn't it? The tunnel is emptied, and all the Quabos are—"

"The tunnel isn't emptied. It's only *half* emptied! I'll show you."

He called Stanley; and the three of us went to the break.

"See," the Professor pointed out to us as we approached the jagged hole, "the Quabos only drilled through the top half of their tunnel ending. That means that the tunnel still has about four feet of water in it— enough to accommodate a great many of the monsters. There may be four or five hundred of them left in there; possibly more. We can expect renewed hostilities at any time!"

"But won't it be just a repetition of the first battle?" remonstrated Stanley. "In the end they'll be killed or will drown for lack of water as these first ones did."

The Professor shook his head.

"They're too clever to do that twice. The very fact that they kept half their number in reserve shows that they have some new trick to try. Otherwise they'd all have come at once in one supreme effort."

He paced back and forth.

"They're ingenious, intelligent. They're fighting for their very existence. They must have figured out some way of breathing in air, some way of attacking us on a more even basis in case that first rush went wrong. What can it be?"

"I think you're borrowing trouble before it is necessary—" I began, smiling at his elaborate, scientific pessimism. But I was interrupted by a startled shout from Stanley.

"Professor Martin," he cried, pointing to the tunnel mouth. "Look!"

Like twin snakes crawling up to sun themselves, two tentacles had appeared over the rock rim. They hooked over the edge; and leisurely, with grim surety of invulnerability, the barrel-like head of a Quabo balanced itself on the ledge and glared at us.

For a moment we stared, paralyzed, at the Thing. And, during that moment it squatted there, as undistressed as though the air were its natural element, its gills flapping slowly up and down supplying it with oxygen.

The thing that held us rooted to the spot with fearful amazement was the fantastic device that permitted it to be almost as much at home in air as in water.

Over the great, globular head was set an oval glass shell. This was filled with water. A flexible metal tube hung down from the rear. Evidently it carried a constant stream of fresh water. As we gazed we saw intermittent trickles emerging from the bottom of the crystalline case.

Point for point the creature's equipment was the same as diving equipment used by men, only it was exactly opposite in function. A helmet that enabled a fish to breathe in air, instead of a helmet to allow a man to breathe in water!

Stanley was the first of us to recover from the shock of this spectacle. He faced about and raised his voice in shouts of warning to the resting Zyobites. For other glass encased monsters had appeared beside the first, now.

One by one, in single file like a line of enormous marching insects, they crawled down the wall and humped along on their tentacles—around the ditch and toward us!

THE deadly infallibility of that second attack!

The Quabos advanced on us like armored tanks bearing down on defenceless savages. Their glass helmets, in addition to containing water for their breathing, protected them from our knives and axes. We were utterly helpless against them.

They marched in ranks about twenty yards apart, each rank helping the one in front to carry the cumbersome water-hoses which trailed back to the central water supply in the tunnel.

Their movements were slow, weighted down as they were by the great glass helmets, but they were appallingly sure.

We could not even retard their advance, let alone stop it. Here were no suffocating, faltering creatures. Here were beings possessed of their full vigor, each one equal to three of us even as the Professor had conjectured. Their only weak points were their tentacles which trailed outside the glass cases. But these they kept coiled close, so that to reach them and hack at them we had to step within range of their terrific clutches.

The Zyobites fought with the valor of despair added to their inherent noble bravery. Man after man closed with the monstrous, armored Things—only to be seized and crushed by the weaving tentacles.

Occasionally a terrific blow with an ax would crack one of the glass helmets. Then the denuded Quabo would flounder convulsively in the air till it drowned. But there were all too few of these individual victories. The main body of the Quabos, rank on rank, dragging their water-hose behind them, came on with the steadiness of a machine.

SLOWLY we were driven back down the broad street and toward the palace. As we retreated, old people and children came from the houses and went with us, leaving their dwellings to the mercy of the monsters.

A block from the palace we bunched together and, by sheer mass and ferocity, actually stopped the machinelike advance for a few moments. Miscellaneous weapons had been brought from the houses—sledges, stone benches, anything that might break the Quabos' helmets—and handed to us in silence by the noncombatants.

Somebody tugged at my sleeve. Looking down I saw a little girl. She had dragged a heavy metal bar out to the fray and was trying to get some fighter's attention and give it to him.

I seized the formidable weapon and jumped at the nearest Quabo, a ten-foot giant whose eyes were glinting gigantically at me through the distorting curve of the glass.

Disregarding the clutching tentacles entirely, I swung the bar against the helmet. It cracked. I swung again and it fell in fragments, spilling the gallons of water it had contained.

The tentacles wound vengefully around me, but in a few seconds they relaxed as the thing gasped out its life in the air.

I turned to repeat the process on another if I could, and found myself facing the Queen. Her head was held bravely high, though the violet of her eyes had gone almost black with fear and repulsion of the terrible things we fought.

"Aga!" I cried. "Why art thou here! Go back to the palace at once!"

"I came to fight beside thee," she answered composedly, though her delicate lips quivered. "All is lost, it seems. So shall I die beside thee."

I started to reply, to urge her again to seek the safety of the palace. But by now the deadly advance of the tentacled demons had begun once more.

Fighting vainly, the population of Zyobor was swept into the palace grounds, then into the building itself.

Men, women and children huddled shoulder to shoulder in the cramping quarters. An ironic picture came to me of the crowding masses of Quabos stuffed into the protection of the outer cave, waiting the outcome of the fight being waged by their warriors. Here were we in a similar circumstance, waiting for the battle to be decided. Though there was little doubt in the minds of any of us as to what the outcome would be.

Guards, the strongest men of the city, were stationed with sledges at the doors and windows. The Quabos, able only to enter one at a time, halted a moment and there was a badly needed breathing spell.

"We've got to find some drastic means of defense," said the Professor, "or we won't last another three hours."

"If you asked me, I'd say we couldn't last another three hours anyway," replied Stanley with a shrug. "These fish have out-thought us!"

"Nonsense! There may still be a way—"

"A brace of machine-guns. . . ." I murmured hopefully.

"You might as well wish for a dozen light cannon!" snapped the Professor. "Please try to concentrate, and see if any effective weapon suggests itself to you—something more available at the moment than machine-guns."

In silence the three of us racked our brains for a means of defence. Aga, leaving for a time the task of soothing her more hysterical subjects, came quietly over to us and sat on the bench beside me.

Frankly I could think of nothing. To my mind we were surely doomed. What arms could possibly be contrived at such short notice? What weapon could be called forth to be effective against the thick glass helmets?

But as I glanced at Stanley I saw his face set in a new expression as his thoughts took a turn that suggested possible salvation.

"Glass," he muttered. "Glass. What destroys it? Sharp blows . . . certain acids . . . variation in temperature . . . heat and cold. . . . That's it! *That's it!*"

He turned excitedly to the Queen.

"I think we have it! At least it's worth trying. If there is any tubing around. . . ." He stopped as he realized he was talking in English, and resumed stiltedly in Aga's own language.

"Hast thou, in the palace, any lengths of pipe like to that which the Quabos drag behind them?"

"No . . ." Aga began, her eyes round and wondering. Then she interrupted herself. "Ah, yes! There is! In a vault near that of Kilor's there is a great spool of it. He had it fashioned to carry air for one of his experiments—"

"Come along!" cried Stanley. "I'll explain what I have in mind while we dig up this coil of hose."

A SCORE of Zyobite workmen were gathered at once. The length of hose—made of some linen-like fabric of tough, shredded sea-weed and covered with a flexible metal sheath—was cut into three pieces each about fifty yards long. These were connected to three of the largest gas vents of the palace.

Stanley, the Professor and I each took an end. And we prepared to fight, with fire, the creatures of water.

"It ought to work," Stanley, repeated several times as though trying to reassure himself as well as us. "It's simple enough: the water in those helmets is ice cold: if fire is suddenly squirted against them they'll crack with the uneven expansion."

"Unless," retorted the Professor, "their glass has some special heat and cold resisting quality."

Stanley shrugged.

"It may well have some such properties. How such creatures can make glass at all is beyond me!"

Dragging our hose to the big front entrance of the palace, and warning the crowded people to keep their feet clear of it, we prepared to test out the efficiency of this, our last resource against the enemy.

For an instant we paused just inside the doorway, looking out at the ugly, glassed-in Things that were massing to attack us again.

The ranks of Quabos had closed in now, till they extended down the street for several hundred yards in close formation—a forest of great pulpy heads with huge eyes that glared unblinkingly at the glittering, pink building that was their objective.

"Light up!" ordered Stanley, setting an example by touching his hose nozzle to the nearest wall jet. A spurt of fire belched from his hose, streaming out for four or five feet in a solid red cone. The Professor and I touched off our torches; and we moved slowly out the door toward the ranks of Quabos.

"Don't try to save yourselves from their tentacles," advised Stanley. "Walk right up to them, direct the fire against their helmets, and damn the consequences. If they grip too hard you can always play the torch on their tentacles till they think better of it."

The Quabos' front line humped grimly toward us, unblinking eyes glaring, tentacles writhing warily, little spurts of used water trickling from their helmets.

"Keep together," warned Stanley, "so that if any one of us loses his light he can get it from the hose of one of the other two. And—*Here they come!*"

There was no more time for commands. The Quabos in front, supplied with slack in their hoses by those behind, leaped at us with incredible agility. We fell back a step so that none should get at our backs.

The last stand was begun.

* * * *

It was not a battle so much as a series of fierce duels. The Quabos realized their new danger instantly, and devoted all their efforts to extinguishing our torches. We parried and thrust with the flaming hoses in an equally desperate effort to prevent it.

One of them scuttled toward me like a great crab. A tentacle darted toward my right arm. Another was pressed against the nozzle. There was a sickening smell—and the tentacle was jerked spasmodically away.

I caught the hose in my left hand and turned the fiery jet against the water-filled helmet.

A shout of savage exultation broke from my lips. Hardly, had the flame touched the glass before it cracked! There was a report like a pistol shot—and a miniature Niagara of water and splintered glass poured at my feet!

The tentacle around my arm tightened, then relaxed. The monster shuddered in a convulsive heap on the ground.

I went toward the next one, swinging the flaring hose in a slow arc as I advanced. The creature lunged at me and threshed at the burning jet with all four of its feelers. But it had been exposed to the air for a long time now. The ghastly tentacles were dry; withered and soft. A touch of the fire seared them unmercifully.

Nevertheless with a swift move it slapped a tentacle squarely down over the hose nozzle. The flame was extinguished as the flame of a candle is pinched out between thumb and forefinger. I retreated.

"Catch!" came a voice behind me.

The Professor swung his four-foot jet my way. I held my hose to it, and the flame burst out again. A touch at my grisly antagonist's helmet—a sharp crack—the welcome rush of water over the cream-colored grass—and another monster was writhing in the death throes!

Keeping close together, the three of us faced the massed Quabos in the palace grounds. Again and again the fiery weapon of one or the other of us was dashed out—to be re-lighted from the nearest hose. Again and again loud detonations heralded the collapse of more of the invaders.

But it seemed as though their flailing tentacles were as myriad as the stars they had never seen. It seemed as though their numbers would never appreciably diminish. We thrust and parried till our arms grew numb. And still there appeared to be hundreds of the Quabos left.

By order of the Queen three stout Zyobites stepped up to us and relieved us of our exhausting labor. Gladly we handed the hoses to them and went to the palace for a much needed rest.

TWO more shifts of fighters took the flaming jets before the monsters began the retreat slowly back toward their tunnel. And here the Professor took command again.

"We mustn't let them get away to try some new scheme!" he snapped. "Martin, take fifty men and beat them back to the break in the wall. Go around a side street. They move so slowly that you can easily cut off their retreat."

"There isn't any more hose—" began Stanley.

"There's plenty of it. The Quabos brought it with them." The Professor turned to me again. "Take metal-saws with you. Cut sections of the Quabos water-hose and connect them to the nearest wall jets. Run!"

I ran, with fifty of the men of Zyobor close behind me. We dodged out the side of the palace grounds least guarded by the Quabos, ducking between their ranks like infantry men threading through an opposition of powerful but slow-moving tanks. Four of our number were caught, but the rest got through unscathed.

Down a side street we raced, and along a parallel avenue toward the tunnel. As we went I prayed that all the Quabos had centered their attention on the palace and left their vulnerable water-hoses unguarded.

They had! When we stole up the last block toward the break we found the nearest Quabo was a hundred yards down the street—and working further away with every move.

At once we set to work on the scores of hoses that quivered over the floor with each move of the distant monsters.

A Zyobite with the muscles of a Hercules swung his ax mightily down on a hose. The metal was soft enough to be sheered through by the stroke. The cut ends were smashed so that they could not be crammed down over the tapering jets; but we could use our metal-saws for cleaner severances at the other ends.

The giant with the ax stepped from hose to hose. Lengths were completed with the saws. A man was placed at each jet to hold the connections in position. Before the Quabos had reached us we had rigged six fire-hoses and had cut through forty or fifty more water-lines.

The end was certain and not long in coming.

We sprayed the monsters with fire as workmen spray fruit trees with insect poison. Stanley, the Professor and a Zyobite came up in the rear with their three hoses.

Caught between the two forces, the beaten fish milled in hopeless confusion and indecision.

In half an hour they were all reduced to huddles of slimy wet flesh that dotted the pavement from the break back to the palace grounds. The invaders were completely annihilated—and the city of Zyobor was saved!

"Now," said the Professor triumphantly, "we have only to knock out the bottom half of the tunnel wall, empty the tunnel and make sure there are no more Quabos lurking there. After that we can fill it in with solid cement. The Queen can order her fish-servants to guard the outer cave and see that no food gets in to the starving monsters there. The war is over, gentlemen. The Quabos are as good as exterminated at this moment. And I can get back to my zoological work. . . ."

Stanley and I looked at each other. We knew each others thoughts well enough.

He could resume his companionship with the beautiful Mayis. And I—I had Aga. . . .

WITH the menace of the Quabos banished forever, the city of Zyobor resumed its normal way.

The citizens lowered their dead into the great well we had cut, with appropriate rites performed by the Queen. The daily tasks and pleasures were picked up where they had been dropped. The haunting fear died from the eyes of the people.

Shortly afterward, with great ceremony and celebration, I was made King of Zyobor, to rule by Aga's side. Stanley took Mayis for his wife. He is second to me in power. The Professor is the official wise man of the city.

Life flows smoothly for us in this pink lighted community. We are more than content with our lot here. Our only concern has been the grief that must have been occasioned our relatives and friends when the Rosa sailed home without us.

Now we have thought of a way in which, with luck, we may communicate with the upper world. By relays of my Queen's fish-servants we believe we can send up the Professor's invaluable notes[A] and this informal account of what has happened since we left San Francisco that. . . .

Editor's note: There was no trace of any "notes." The yacht, Rosa, *was reported lost with all hands in a hurricane off New Zealand. Aboard her were a Professor George Berry and the owner, Stanley Browne. There is no record, however, of any pas-*

senger by the name of Martin Grey. To date no one has taken this document seriously enough to consider financing an expedition of investigation to Penguin Deep.

DEATH RAY

KIB NASTEN had worked this out pretty cleverly, he thought. Doctor Robert Wasey paid blackmail. A smooth con man named Ringo had hooked Wasey. Twice a year he called around and the doctor gritted his teeth and handed over two thousand in cash. Now the price was to be doubled, with Kib Nasten as Ringo's partner in the "clip."

Disguised as a decrepit old man, Nasten had pushed past the protesting office girl and gained the doctor's inner office. Doctor Wasey, who was leaning over a black slab of a table and working at a black, boxlike thing wheeled up beside it, stared impatiently at him.

"My dear sir," he said. "There is a patient ahead of you. If you will please wait your turn—"

Nasten stepped closer to Doctor Wasey, and in his right hand was a gun with the bulky cylinder of a silencer on it.

"This is a stick-up, you sap. Put your hands up and keep 'em there," he said in a low tone that was none the less deadly for being low.

Wasey's hands rose. Not a very large man, he seemed to shrivel a little under the menace of the gun.

"I haven't anything of value—" he faltered.

"Keep your voice down! One peep out of you, and you get it." Nasten jabbed the gun toward him. "This gat's silenced, so I could plug you easy and nobody'd know."

Doctor Wasey moistened his lips nervously.

"But I haven't any money here. I haven't a thing—"

"Bunk," said Nasten. "A guy named Ringo is supposed to come in here in about an hour and get two grand from you. Two thousand bucks. You'll have that around the place, now. I want it."

Doctor Wasey's face got, if possible, a little whiter.

"So you know—about that."

"Yeah."

"But I can't give you that! Ringo would ruin me if I didn't have it for him!"

Nasten shrugged. "Get another two grand for him." Ringo had coached him in this important line.

"I haven't got it! I already pay the man more than I have to live on myself."

"That's your tough luck," grated Nasten. "Come on. Hand over the two grand—"

There was a commotion in the anteroom. Shrill words penetrated the inner office door. They were in a woman's hysterical tone.

"I want to see Doctor Wasey. At once! He promised he'd telephone tonight and he hasn't. I want to see him immediately!"

"Damn it!" breathed Nasten. He was scared and showed it. Witnesses were the last things that he wanted now. But like a scared rat, he was all the more dangerous for being frightened.

He slid up on the black-topped table, just as the door started to open.

"I'm a patient, see?" he whispered tensely to Wasey. "Monkey around! Make a show of treating me for something! But remember my gat's right on you, so don't get funny!"

Doctor Wasey nodded and snapped a switch on the black box half over the table. Intense light rayed out.

"I'll be giving you a ray treatment," he said. "Lie still."

A woman of thirty-five or so burst in, wild-eyed and sobbing. Then, as she saw the man on the black slab, and Doctor Wasey staring at her, she collected herself a bit.

"Oh," she said, less hysterically. "Oh, I—I shouldn't have done this. I'm sorry. But Doctor, I had to know how my husband is. Has he—is it cancer? You said you'd telephone, and I didn't hear from you—"

Wasey moistened his lips. He glanced sideways at Nasten, saw the silenced gun bulge out of Nasten's coat a trifle as the man wordlessly ordered the doctor to watch his step.

"I didn't phone you," Wasey said to the woman, "because as yet there is nothing to phone about. I don't know yet if the growth is malignant or not. I think I'll have word by eleven. If I do, I'll call you."

The woman was still crying, but more quietly. "If you knew the agony of waiting— But of course you can't give an opinion till you've studied every feature of the case. I'm sorry—I came in this way. I hardly knew what I was doing. I'll hear from you at eleven, Doctor?"

Wasey nodded and started going eagerly to the door with her. Nasten stared at him. In the crook's eyes was a promise of death if Wasey tried to leave the office.

Wasey stopped at the door, while the woman crossed the anteroom, still talking to him. He stood with one hand on the door-jamb, and the other resting on a filing cabinet near the door. Nasten watched that hand.

Doctor Wasey closed the door, shutting Nasten and himself in together again. He whirled suddenly toward the low table.

But Nasten was ready for him. He saw the gun in Wasey's hand, furtively picked up from the filing cabinet. He saw the look of desperate courage on the doctor's thin, lined face.

Snarling, Nasten shot.

The slight cough of the silenced gun was followed by the scuffling thud of Wasey's dead body as it hit the floor, and the clatter of the gun dropping from his stark hand.

Raving curses under his breath, Nasten stooped and extracted a bulging wallet from the dead man's clothes. He leaped for the window. There was a fire-escape there. He half tripped over an electric cord going from a wall-plug to the black box next the low table, recovered, went on. From the fire-escape he heard a girl's scream above and behind him. He swung into a lower window, ran to the stairs and down them—and walked slowly and unobtrusively through the building lobby to the street, his shoulders bent as an old man's are bent, and with his iron-grey hair showing from under the back of his hat.

DETECTIVE BILL OLIVER shook his head at the anteroom girl's shaky description of the man.

"Sounds like a disguise to me," he said. "Any hood can put on a grey wig and stoop his shoulders a little. It isn't an old man's trick to pull a killing like this."

He went into the inner office again. The first look-around had been perfunctory. Now he was more thorough. On the floor, near the window, Wasey's dead body sprawled with a hole through its head. A gun, not discharged, lay near his right hand.

"The doc got too brave, tried to shoot, and the guy nailed him," Oliver mused. "Then he beat it out the window and down the fire-escape."

The cord trailing from the black box over the black slab of a table caught Oliver's eyes. He bent to look at it. It was looped where a hasty foot had caught in it, and jerked it loose from the wall-plug.

"Tripped over this on his way out," Oliver muttered to himself. Then he stared at the box, and slowly a glint showed in his cold blue eyes. He stepped to it, began to examine it. After a minute a grin touched his lips. It was colder than the chair before the current is turned on.

He went to the outer door of the suite of offices. A cop in uniform was there.

"Don't let anybody in," said Oliver. "And when the fingerprint men and other mugs get here, tell 'em to save their strength. I'll have the killer on ice in four hours or less."

KIB Nasten sat in Black Jack's tavern on Eighth Avenue. It was not the best place in the world for him to be at the moment. Black Jack's was one of a dozen places habitually visited by the police when crime had been done and they wanted a roundup. But Nasten paid little attention to that.

He was safe, he knew. No one could identify him as the man who had gone into Wasey's office. The grey wig and the rusty black suit and hat he'd worn were at the bottom of the river, with a stone to hold them down. The gun he'd had to kill the doctor lay in the watery depths beside the disguise.

A man came in the front door. Nasten looked up perfunctorily, then straightened as he recognized the newcomer. It was a dick. Detective William Oliver. Nasten knew him a lot better than he cared to!

But after a moment, Kib Nasten slumped in his chair again. They couldn't get anything on him, could they? Then, what the devil?

Detective Oliver walked up to the bar. He stared expressionlessly at Jack, owner and manager, behind a mahogany length. Jack, black-haired, black-eyed, with a. smile that was as false as a lead dime painted always on his oily fat face, stared back.

"Anything on your mind?" Jack said to Oliver. "Or did you just drop in to hoist one?"

"No drinks," said Oliver. His eyes were roaming the place, taking in the occupants of first one table and then another, studying the faces lined over the bar. As his gaze traveled, men glared back, and then avoided it.

"I've got a lot on my mind," said Oliver slowly, gaze still roaming the place. This was the fifth drinking joint he had visited so far; but his eyes were no less alert for having searched so long without finding what they sought. "Murder, Black Jack, among other things—"

His voice trailed away. His gaze stopped. He walked toward Nasten's table.

"Mr. Kib Nasten in person," he drawled. "How are you, Kib? Last time I saw you was when I picked you up on an assault charge."

Nasten felt cold as he stared at Oliver's bleak face. But he reminded himself he was as safe as if he were in church. Thirty guys willing to swear he had been here at Black Jack's all evening.

"Go roll a hoop," he snarled, with an arrogance born of his feeling of perfect safety.

"Hoops, is it?" said Oliver. "Sure, I'll roll one—toward Doctor Wasey's office! Ever hear of Doctor Wasey?" His hand closed on Nasten's left arm midway between wrist and elbow.

The cold feeling grew in Nasten's chest. But his dark, narrowed eyes did not waver as he said:

"Never heard of him. What about him?"

"He died three hours ago, that's all," Oliver said softly. "Died of a bullet from a silenced gun."

The man-hunter's glint in his cold blue eyes flared higher as his fingers explored the arm that Nasten tried to jerk free.

"Nice," Oliver said. "As airtight as anything I've ever seen. Now your left hand, Nasten. Let's have a look at that, just to refresh my memory."

Nasten's left hand was clenched and under the table. He tried to keep it there; the detective's tone was shattering to bits his feeling that everything was all right.

But Oliver jerked up on the arm he clutched, and Nasten's hand came into view above the level of the table.

"Okay," said Oliver, nodding, staring at his left hand.

Nasten's teeth showed a tendency to chatter. Something had gone wrong! He hadn't the least notion what it was, but he knew there'd been a slip.

The hysterical dame who had busted into old Wasey's office? Had she spotted his disguise and tipped the cops? No—she hadn't even looked squarely at Nasten; must have thought of him as just another patient on the black slab of a table. The girl in the anteroom?

Nasten could swear she hadn't glommed the falsity of the grey hair and the stoop. Then what—

"Nasten," said Oliver, "I'm taking you in for the murder of Doctor Robert Wasey."

Nasten cursed, and rose like an uncoiling spring. His hand shot to the wall.

Always he took this table, at the rear, near the back wall. And that was not by chance, as Oliver soon learned. There was a square tin box projecting from the wall at this point. It was the fuse box.

As Nasten's right hand tripped the master switch that turned out every light in the place, his left, with its curled little finger, clawed loose from the detective's grip and smashed the table over and up.

Oliver exclaimed in the darkness, staggering from the impact of the table against his stomach. Nasten streaked for the rear door of Jack's place.

"Get that cop!" somebody yelled in the dark tumult of the room.

There was a scuffling of many feet, a sound of chairs tipping as men got eagerly up from tables. The scuffling feet converged toward the spot where Detective Oliver had stood.

* * * *

NASTEN sped from the rear door of Jack's place like a rabbit with a hound on its trail. He jumped from the doorway into an alley as dark as Jack's place had been. He ran down the alley on silent feet.

Dimly, he was still wondering what had slipped, what had led Oliver straight from Wasey's office to him. But only the back of his mind was concerned with that. The rest was concentrating frantically on escape.

There was a bend in the alley. It led to the side street next to Jack's place. Nasten lurked in darkness for several minutes, listening, watching. Then he went toward the side street. He had to. There was no other way to go, and he knew it.

He came onto the sidewalk. No one was in sight in either direction who seemed interested in him. There was a battered old sedan at the curb and—by the luck of the devil—its keys glinted in the ignition.

With a breath like a sob coming from his lips, Nasten jumped to the car, wrenched open the door. He got behind the wheel, rasped into first gear, and tore ahead so fast that the tires squealed on the pavement.

Behind him, the dick who had somehow put the bee on him almost certainly lay dead, with his head kicked to a jelly in the darkness. Under him was a car that could not be identified in any way as his. Ahead of him was the whole United States to hide in.

Movement in the rear-view mirror caught his startled gaze. He stared, hypnotized, at the reflection of a body rising from behind the front seat. Then he turned.

Detective Oliver sat comfortably in the rear seat. His police revolver rested easily but unwaveringly on his knee, with its muzzle pointing at the back of Nasten's neck.

"Turn around and watch the road," Oliver said. "Don't go over fifteen miles an hour. Take the next turn to the left and keep on going. To Headquarters!"

Nasten turned back, white-faced, too stunned to utter a word.

"Figured it might be kind of hard to get you out of Jack's joint with all your pals around," Oliver grunted. "So I let you get yourself out. I slipped behind the bar when you started for the back door, and slid along it to the front door. Only way you could get to the street from the back door was out that alley—where I'd parked ahead of time. I got in the back of my car to nail you when you sneaked out the areaway, and you're considerate enough to get right in with me!"

Still Nasten said nothing. He couldn't. Rigid, wide-eyed with, fear, he rolled the car at the commanded fifteen miles an hour toward Headquarters.

* * * *

AT Headquarters, Kib Nasten strove desperately to regain a little of his former arrogance. There couldn't be any tie-up between him and Doctor Wasey!

"You guys can't hold me here," he mumbled. "I don't know what the rap is, but I ain't the one to pin it on. I was at Jack's all evening—"

"Sure," rumbled Oliver, staring at him out of hard blue eyes. "I know. Murphy, is that print ready yet?"

The uniformed cop addressed by Oliver nodded and handed over a large photographic print. Nasten stared at it with eyes no less fearful for being blank with ignorance of what it was all about.

He saw a large picture that looked like a cloud scene, shot through in places by dim light, studded here and there by boldly black objects.

"Nice of you to have your picture taken before you rubbed out Doctor Wasey," said Oliver.

"Picture?" faltered Nasten, heart beginning to hammer in his throat.

Oliver nodded.

"Different than any I've ever seen in a rogue's gallery, but even better. It shows the bones of a hand holding a gun with a silencer on it. And it shows a backbone and a couple of floating ribs and then another hand—a left hand—with a little finger curled up where the bone was broken and a bum job of setting done on it. Your finger, Nasten. And it shows a bulge in the bone of the left arm where that was badly set at the same time. Your arm, Nasten. It shows keys and coins and things too, but we'll skip them."

"What are you—talking about?" Nasten gasped thickly, panic in his voice.

"This print," Oliver said. "This X-ray picture of your middle. Wasey was getting ready to take a picture of a man's busted arm when you came along and were dumb enough to let him get you as a subject instead. It came out good, too. Too good for you! Only one other crook in the files has a curled little finger like yours, and he's in the big house. The re-set bone in your left arm will help before a jury, too."

Nasten's fingernails bit into his palms. The big box next to the black-topped table! Little as he knew about doctor's offices, it had seemed half familiar even then. But not familiar enough!

Discretion, the animal cleverness of saying nothing to the cops under any circumstances, was shocked clear out of his head.

"Damn him!" he screamed. "He said he was giving me a ray treatment! Ultraviolet—"

"Not violet," said Detective Oliver, "but X."

Then he corrected himself, a smile as cold as the chair before the current is turned on touching his hard lips.

"Not exactly X, either. It's the kind—for you—that the news hawks are always playing up in the Sunday hot sheets. A death ray, Nasten! And Mrs. Wasey can use the two thousand. It seems her husband told her things—"

THE RED HELL OF JUPITER

CHAPTER I
The Red Spot

COMMANDER Stone, grizzled chief of the Planetary Exploration Forces, acknowledged Captain Brand Bowen's salute and beckoned him to take a seat.

Brand, youngest officer of the division to wear the triple-V for distinguished service, sat down and stared curiously at his superior. He hadn't the remotest idea why he had been recalled from leave: but that it was on a matter of some importance he was sure. He hunched his big shoulders and awaited orders.

"Captain Bowen," said Stone. "I want you to go to Jupiter as soon as you can arrange to do so, fly low over the red area in the southern hemisphere, and come back here with some sort of report as to what's wrong with that infernal death spot."

He tapped his radio stylus thoughtfully against the edge of his desk.

"As you perhaps know, I detailed a ship to explore the red spot about a year ago. It never came back. I sent another ship, with two good men in it, to check up on the disappearance of the first. That ship, too, never came back. Almost with the second of its arrival at the edge of the red area all radio communication with it was cut off. It was never heard from again. Two weeks ago I sent Journeyman there. Now *he* has been swallowed up in a mysterious silence."

An exclamation burst from Brand's lips. Sub-Commander Journeyman! Senior officer under Stone, ablest man in the expeditionary forces, and Brand's oldest friend!

Stone nodded comprehension of the stricken look on Brand's face. "I know how friendly you two were," he said soberly. "That's why I chose you to go and find out, if you can, what happened to him and the other two ships."

Brand's chin sank to rest on the stiff high collar of his uniform.

"Journeyman!" he mused. "Why, he was like an older brother to me. And now . . . he's gone."

There was silence in Commander Stone's sanctum for a time. Then Brand raised his head.

"Did you have any radio reports at all from any of the three ships concerning the nature of the red spot?" he inquired.

"None that gave definite information," replied Stone. "From each of the three ships we received reports right up to the instant when the red area was approached. From each of the three came a vague description of the peculiarity of the ground ahead of them: it seems to glitter with a queer metallic sheen. Then, from each of the three, as they passed over the boundary—nothing! All radio communication ceased as abruptly as though they'd been stricken dead."

He stared at Brand. "That's all I can tell you, little enough, God knows. Something ominous and strange is contained in that red spot: but what its nature may be, we cannot even guess. I want you to go there and find out."

Brand's determined jaw jutted out, and his lips thinned to a purposeful line. He stood to attention.

"I'll be leaving to-night, sir. Or sooner if you like. I could go this afternoon: in an hour—"

"To-night is soon enough," said Stone with a smile. "Now, who do you want to accompany you?"

Brand thought a moment. On so long a journey as a trip to Jupiter there was only room in a space ship—what with supplies and all—for one other man. It behooved him to pick his companion carefully.

"I'd like Dex Harlow," he said at last. "He's been to Jupiter before, working with me in plotting the northern hemisphere. He's a good man."

"He is," agreed Stone, nodding approval of Brand's choice. "I'll have him report to you at once."

He rose and held out his hand. "I'm relying on you, Captain Bowen," he said. "I won't give any direct orders: use your own discretion. But I would advise you not to try to land in the red area. Simply fly low over it, and see what you can discern from the air. Good-by, and good luck."

Brand saluted, and went out, to go to his own quarters and make the few preparations necessary for his sudden emergency flight.

The work of exploring the planets that swung with Earth around the sun was still a new branch of the service. Less than ten years ago, it had been, when Ansen devised his first crude atomic motor.

At once, with the introduction of this tremendous new motive power, men had begun to build space ships and explore the sky. And, as so often happens with a new invention, the thing had grown rather beyond itself.

Everywhere amateur space flyers launched forth into the heavens to try their new celestial wings. Everywhere young and old enthusiasts set

Ansen motors into clumsily insulated shells and started for Mars or the moon or Venus.

The resultant loss of life, as might have been foreseen, was appalling. Eager but inexperienced explorers edged over onto the wrong side of Mercury and were burned to cinders. They set forth in ships that were badly insulated, and froze in the absolute zero of space. They learned the atomic motor controls too hastily, ran out of supplies or lost their courses, and wandered far out into space—stiff corpses in coffins that were to be buried only in time's infinity.

To stop the foolish waste of life, the Earth Government stepped in. It was decreed that no space ship might be owned or built privately. It was further decreed that those who felt an urge to explore must join the regular service and do so under efficient supervision. And there was created the Government bureau designated as the Planetary Exploration Control Board, which was headed by Commander Stone.

Under this Board the exploration of the planets was undertaken methodically and efficiently, with a minimum of lives sacrificed.

Mercury was charted, tested for essential minerals, and found to be a valueless rock heap too near the sun to support life.

Venus was visited and explored segment by segment; and friendly relations were established with the rather stupid but peaceable people found there.

Mars was mapped. Here the explorers had lingered a long time: and all over this planet's surface were found remnants of a vast and intricate civilization—from the canals that laced its surface, to great cities with mighty buildings still standing. But of life there was none. The atmosphere was too rare to support it; and the theory was that it had constantly thinned through thousands of years till the last Martian had gasped and died in air too attenuated to support life even in creatures that must have grown greater and greater chested in eons of adaptation.

Then Jupiter had been reached: and here the methodical planet by planet work promised to be checked for a long time to come. Jupiter, with its mighty surface area, was going to take some exploring! It would be years before it could be plotted even superficially.

BRAND had been to Jupiter on four different trips; and, as he walked toward his quarters from Stone's office, he reviewed what he had learned on those trips.

Jupiter, as he knew it, was a vast globe of vague horror and sharp contrasts.

Distant from the sun as it was, it received little solar heat. But, with so great a mass, it had cooled off much more slowly than any of the other planets known, and had immense internal heat. This meant that the air—which closely approximated Earth's air in density—was cool a few hundred yards up from the surface of the planet, and dankly hot close to the ground. The result, as the cold air constantly sank into the warm, was a thick steamy blanket of fog that covered everything perpetually.

Because of the recent cooling, life was not far advanced on Jupiter. Too short a time ago the sphere had been but a blazing mass. Tropical marshes prevailed, crisscrossed by mighty rivers at warmer than blood heat. Giant, hideous fernlike growths crowded one another in an everlasting jungle. And among the distorted trees, from the blanket of soft white fog that hid all from sight, could be heard constantly an ear-splitting chorus of screams and bellows and whistling snarls. It made the blood run cold just to listen—and to speculate on what gigantic but tiny-brained monsters made them.

Now and then, when Brand had been flying dangerously low over the surface, a wind had risen strong enough to dispel the fog banks for an instant; and he had caught a flash of Jovian life. Just a flash, for example, of a monstrous lizard-like thing too great to support its own bulk: or a creature all neck and tail, with ridges of scale on its armored hide and a small serpentine head weaving back and forth among the jungle growths.

Occasionally he had landed—always staying close to the space ship, for Jupiter's gravity made movement a slow and laborious process, and he didn't want to be caught too far from security. At such times he might hear a crashing and splashing and see a reptilian head loom gigantically at him through the fog. Then he would discharge the deadly explosive gun which was Earth's latest weapon, and the creature would crash to the ground. The chorus of hissings and bellowings would increase as he hastened slowly and laboriously back to the ship, indicating that other unseen monsters of the steamy jungle had flocked to tear the dead giant to pieces and bolt it down.

Oh, Jupiter was a nice planet! mused Brand. A sweet place—if one happened to be a two-hundred-foot snake or something!

He had always thought the entire globe was in that new, raw, marshy state. But he had worked only in one comparatively small area of the northern hemisphere; had never been within thirty thousand miles of the red spot. What might lie in that ominous crimson patch, he could not even guess. However, he reflected, he was soon to find out, though he might never live to tell about it.

Shrugging his shoulders, he turned into the fifty story building in which was his modest apartment. There he found, written by the automatic stylus on his radio pad, the message: "Be with you at seven o'clock. Best regards, and I hope you strangle. Dex Harlow."

DEX Harlow was a six-foot Senior Lieutenant who had been on many an out-of-the-way exploratory trip. Like Brand he was just under thirty and perpetually thirsting for the bizarre in life. He was a walking document of planetary activity. He was still baked a brick red from a trip to Mercury a year before: he had a scar on his forehead, the result of jumping forty feet one day on the moon when he'd meant to jump only twenty; he was minus a finger which had been irreparably frost-bitten on Mars; and he had a crumpled nose that was the outcome of a brush with a ten-foot bandit on Venus who'd tried to kill him for his explosive gun and supply of glass, dyite-containing cartridges.

He clutched Brand's fingers in a bone-mangling grip, and threw his hat into a far corner.

"You're a fine friend!" he growled cheerfully. "Here I'm having a first rate time for myself, swimming and planing along the Riviera, with two more weeks leave ahead of me—and I get a call from the Old Man to report to you. What excuse have you for your crime?"

"A junket to Jupiter," said Brand. "Would you call that a good excuse?"

"Jupiter!" exclaimed Dex. "Wouldn't you know it? Of course you'd have to pick a spot four hundred million miles away from all that grand swimming I was having!"

"Would you like to go back on leave, and have me choose someone else?" inquired Brand solemnly.

"Well, no," said Dex hastily. "Now that I'm here, I suppose I might as well go through with it."

Brand laughed. "Try and get you out of it! I know your attitude toward a real jaunt. And it's a real jaunt we've got ahead of us, too, old boy. We're going to the red spot. Immediately."

Dex's sandy eyebrows shot up. "The red spot! That's where Coblenz and Heiroy were lost!"

"And Journeyman," added Brand. "He's the latest victim of whatever's in the hell-hole."

Dex whistled. "Journeyman too! Well, all I've got to say is that whatever's there must be strong medicine. Journeyman was a damn fine man, and as brave as they come. Have you any idea what it's all about?"

"Not an idea. Nobody has. We're to go and find out—if we can. Are you all ready?"

"All ready," said Dex.

"So am I. We'll start at eleven o'clock in one of the Old Man's best cruisers. Meanwhile, we might as well go and hunt up a dinner somewhere, to fortify us against the synthetic pork chops and bread we'll be swallowing for the next fortnight."

They went out; and at ten minutes of eleven reported at the great space ship hangars north of New York, with their luggage, a conspicuous item of which was a chess board to help while away the long, long days of spacial travel. Brand then paused a little while for a final check-up on directions.

They clambered into the tiny control room and shut the hermetically sealed trap-door. Brand threw the control switch and precisely at eleven o'clock the conical shell of metal shot heavenward, gathering such speed that it was soon invisible to human eyes. He set their course toward the blazing speck that was Jupiter, four hundred million miles away; and then reported their start by radio to Commander Stone's night operator.

The investigatory expedition to the ominous red spot of the giant of the solar system was on.

CHAPTER II
The Pipe-like Men

BRAND began to slacken speed on the morning of the thirteenth day (morning, of course, being a technical term: there are no horizons in space for the sun to rise over). Jupiter was still an immense distance off; but it took a great while to slow the momentum of the space ship, which, in the frictionless emptiness of space, had been traveling faster and faster for nearly three hundred hours.

Behind them was the distant ball of sun, so far off that it looked no larger than a red-hot penny. Before them was the gigantic disk of Jupiter, given a white tinge by the perpetual fog blankets, its outlines softened by its thick layer of atmosphere and cloud banks. Two of its nine satellites were in sight at the moment, with a third edging over the western rim.

"Makes you think you're drunk and seeing triple, doesn't it?" commented Dex, who was staring out the thick glass panel beside Brand. "Nine moons! Almost enough for one planet!"

Brand nodded abstractly, and concentrated on the control board. Rapidly the ship rocketed down toward the surface. The disk became a whirling, gigantic plate; and then an endless plain, with cloud formations beginning to take on definite outline.

"About to enter Jupiter's atmosphere." Brand spoke into the radio transmitter. Over the invisible thread of radio connection between the space ship and Earth, four hundred million miles behind, flashed the message.

"All right. For God's sake, be careful," came the answer, minutes later. "Say something at least every half hour, to let us know communication is unbroken. We will sound at ten second intervals."

The sounding began: *peep*, a shrill little piping noise like the fiddle of a cricket. Ten seconds later it came again: *peep*. Thereafter, intermittently, it keened through the control room—a homely, comforting sound to let them know that there was a distant thread between them and Earth.

Lower the shell rocketed. The endless plain slowly ceased its rushing underneath them as they entered the planet's atmosphere and began to be pulled around with it in its revolution. Far to the west a faint red glow illumined the sky.

The two men looked at each other, grimly, soberly.

"We're here," said Dex, flexing the muscles of his powerful arms.

"We are," said Brand, patting the gun in his holster.

The rapid dusk of the giant planet began to close in on them. The thin sunlight darkened; and with its lowering, the red spot of Jupiter glared more luridly ahead of them. Silently the two men gazed at it, and wondered what it held.

They shot the space ship toward it, and halted a few hundred miles away. Watery white light from the satellites, "that jitter around in the sky like a bunch of damned waterbugs," as Dex put it, was now the sole illumination.

They hung motionless in their space shell, to wait through the five-hour Jovian night for the succeeding five hours of daylight to illumine a slow cruise over the red area that, in less than a year, had swallowed up three of Earth's space ships. And ever as they waited, dozing a little, speculating as to the nature of the danger they faced, the peep, peep of the radio shrilled in their ears to tell them that there was still a connection—though a very tenuous one—with their mother planet.

"Red spot ten miles away," said Brand in the transmitter. "We're approaching it slowly."

The tiny sun had leaped up over Jupiter's horizon; and with its appearance they had sent the ship planing toward their mysterious destination. Beneath them the fog banks were thinning, and ahead of them were no clouds. For some reason there was a clarity unusual to Jupiter's atmosphere in the air above the red section.

"Red spot one mile ahead, altitude forty thousand feet," reported Brand.

He and Dex peered intently through the port glass panel. Ahead and far below, their eyes caught an odd metallic sheen. It was as though the ground there were carpeted with polished steel that reflected red firelight.

Tense, filled with an excitement that set their pulses pounding wildly, they angled slowly down, nearer to the edge of the vast crimson area, closer to the ground. The radio keened its monotonous signal.

Brand crawled to the transmitter, laboriously, for his body tipped the scales here at nearly four hundred pounds.

"We can see the metallic glitter that Journeyman spoke of," he said. "No sign of life of any kind, though. The red glow seems to flicker a little."

Closer the ship floated. Closer. To right and left of them for vast distances stretched the red area. Ahead of them for hundreds of miles they knew it extended.

"We're right on it now," called Brand. "Right on it—we're going over the edge—we're—"

Next instant he was sprawling on the floor, with Dex rolling helplessly on top of him, while the space ship bounced up twenty thousand feet as though propelled by a giant sling.

The peep, peep of the radio signaling stopped. The space ship rolled helplessly for a moment, then resumed an even keel. Brand and Dex gazed at each other.

"What the hell?" said Dex.

He started to get to his feet, put all his strength into the task of moving his Jupiter-weighted body, and crashed against the top of the control room.

"Say!" he sputtered, rubbing his head. "Say, what *is* this?"

Brand, profiting by his mistake, rose more cautiously, shut off the atomic motor, and approached a glass panel again. "God knows what it is," he said with a shrug. "Somehow, with our passing into the red area, the pull of gravity has been reduced by about ten, that's all."

"Oh, so that's all, is it? Well, what's happened to old Jupe's gravity?"

Again Brand shrugged. "I haven't any idea. Your guess is as good as mine."

He peered down through the panel, and stiffened in surprise.

"Dex!" he cried. "We're moving! And the motor is shut off!"

"We're drawing down closer to the ground, too," announced Dex, pointing to their altimeter. "Our altitude has been reduced five thousand feet in the last two minutes."

Quickly Brand turned on the motor in reverse. The space ship, as the rushing, reddish ground beneath indicated, continued to glide forward as though pulled by an invisible rope. He turned on full power. The ship's progress was checked a little. A very little! And the metallic red surface under them grew nearer as they steadily lost altitude.

"Something seems to have got us by the nose," said Dex. "We're on our way to the center of the red spot, I guess—to find whatever it was that Journeyman found. And the radio communication his been broken somehow. . . ."

Wordlessly, they stared out the panel, while the shell, quivering with the strain of the atomic motor's fight against whatever unseen force it was that relentlessly drew them forward, bore them swiftly toward the heart of the vast crimson area.

"Look!" cried Brand.

For over an hour the ship had been propelled swiftly, irresistibly toward the center of the red spot. It had been up about forty thousand feet. Now, with a jerk that sent both men reeling, it had been drawn down to within fifteen thousand feet of the surface; and the sight that was now becoming more and more visible was incredible.

Beneath was a vast, orderly checkerboard. Every alternate square was covered by what seemed a jointless metal plate. The open squares, plainly land under cultivation, were surrounded by gleaming fences that hooked each metal square with every other one of its kind as batteries are wired in series. Over these open squares progressed tiny, two legged figures, for the most part following gigantic shapeless animals like figures out of a dream. Ahead suddenly appeared the spires and towers of an enormous city!

Metropolis and cultivated land! It was as unbelievable, on that raw new planet, as such a sight would have been could a traveler in time have observed it in the midst of a dim Pleistocene panorama of young Earth.

It was instantly apparent that the city was their destination. Rapidly the little ship was rushed toward it; and, realizing at last the futility of its laboring, Brand cut off the atomic motor and let the shell drift.

Over a group of squat square buildings their ship passed, decreasing speed and drifting lower with every moment. The lofty structures that were the nucleus of the strange city loomed closer. Now they were soaring slowly down a wide thoroughfare; and now, at last, they hovered above a great open square that was thronged with figures.

Lower they dropped. Lower. And then they settled with a slight jar on a surface made of reddish metal; and the figures rushed to surround them.

Looking out the glass panel at these figures, both Brand and Dex exclaimed aloud and covered their eyes for a moment to shut out the hideous sight of them. Now they examined them closely.

Manlike they were: and yet like no human being conceivable to an Earth mind. They were tremendously tall—twelve feet at least—but as thin as so many animated poles. Their two legs were scarce four inches through, taper-less, boneless, like lengths of pipe; and like two flexible pipes they were joined to a slightly larger pipe of a torso that could not have been more than a foot in diameter. There were four arms, a pair on each side of the cylindrical body, that weaved feebly about like lengths of rubber hose.

Set directly on the pipe-like body, as a pumpkin might be balanced on a pole, was a perfectly round cranium in which were glassy, staring eyes, with dull pupils like those of a sick dog. The nose was but a tab of flesh. The mouth was a minute, circular thing, soft and flabby looking, which opened and shut regularly with the creature's breathing. It resembled the snout-like mouth of a fish, of the sucker variety; and fish-like, too, was the smooth and slimy skin that covered the beanpole body.

Hundreds of the repulsive things, there were. And all of them shoved and crowded, as a disorderly mob on Earth might do, to get close to the Earthmen's ship. Their big dull eyes peered in through the glass panels, and their hands—mere round blobs of gristle in the palms of which were set single sucker disks—pattered against the metal hull of the shell.

"God!" said Brand with a shudder. "Fancy these things feeling over your body. . . ."

"They're hostile, whatever they are," said Dex. "Look out: that one's pointing something at you!"

One of the slender, tottering creatures had raised an arm and leveled at Brand something that looked rather like an elongated, old-fashioned flashlight. Brand involuntarily ducked. The clear glass panel between them and the mob outside gave him a queasy feeling of being exposed to whatever missile might lurk in the thing's tube.

"What do we do now?" demanded Dex with a shaky laugh. "You're chief of this expedition. I'm waiting for orders."

"We wait right here," replied Brand. "We're safe in the shell till we're starved out. At least they can't get in to attack us."

But it developed that, while the slimy looking things might not be able to get in, they had ways of reaching the Earthmen just the same!

The creature with the gun-like tube extended it somewhat further toward Brand.

Brand felt a sharp, unpleasant tingle shoot through his body, as though he had received an electric shock. He winced, and cried out at the sudden pain of it.

"What's the matter—" Dex began. But hardly had the words left his mouth when he, too, felt the shock. A couple of good, hearty Earth oaths exploded from his lips.

The repulsive creature outside made an authoritative gesture. He seemed to be beckoning to them, his huge dull eyes glaring threateningly at the same moment.

"Our beanpole friend is suggesting that we get out of the shell and stay awhile," said Dex with grim humor. "They seem anxious to entertain us—*ouch!*"

As the two men made no move to obey the beckoning gesture, the creature had raised the tube again; and again the sharp, unpleasant shock shot through them.

"What the devil are we going to do?" exclaimed Brand. "If we go out in that mob of nightmare things—it's going to be messy. As long as we stay in the shell we have some measure of protection."

"Not much protection when they can sting us through metal and glass at will," growled Dex. "Do you suppose they can turn the juice on harder? Or is that bee-sting their best effort?"

As though in direct answer to his words, the blob-like face of the being who seemed in authority convulsed with anger and he raised the tube again. This time the shock that came from it was sufficient to throw the two men to the floor.

"Well, we can't stay in the ship, that's certain," said Brand. "I guess there's only one thing to do."

Dex nodded. "Climb out of here and take as many of these skinny horrors with us into hell as we can," he agreed.

Once more the shock stung them, as a reminder not to keep their captors waiting. With their shoulders bunched for abrupt action, and their guns in hand, the two men walked to the trap-door of the ship. They threw the heavy bolts, drew a deep breath—and flung open the door to charge unexpectedly toward the thickest mass of creatures that surrounded the ship!

In a measure their charge was successful. Its very suddenness caught some of the tall monstrosities off guard. Half a dozen of them stopped the fragile glass bullets to writhe in horrible death on the red metal paving of the square. But that didn't last long.

In less than a minute, thin, clammy arms were winding around the Earthmen's wrists, and their guns were wrenched from them. And then started a hand-to-hand encounter that was all the more hideous for being so unlike any fighting that might have occurred on Earth.

With a furious growl Dex charged the nearest creature, whose huge round head swayed on its stalk of a body fully six feet above his own head. He gathered the long thin legs in a football grip, and sent the thing crashing full length on its back. The great head thumped resoundingly against the metal paving, and the creature lay motionless.

For an instant Dex could only stare at the thing. It had been so easy, like overcoming a child. But even as that thought crossed his mind, two of the tall thin figures closed in behind him. Four pairs of arms wound around him, feebly but tenaciously, like wet seaweed.

They began to constrict and wind tighter around him. He tore at them, dislodged all but two. His sturdy Earth leg went back to sweep the stalk-like legs of his attackers from under them. One of the things went down, to twist weakly in a laborious attempt to rise again. But the other, by sheer force of height and reach, began to bear Dex down.

Savagely he laced out with his fists, battering the pulpy face that was pressing down close to his. The big eyes blinked shut, but the four hose-like arms did not relax their clasp. Dex's hands sought fiercely for the thing's throat. But it had no throat: the head, set directly on the thin shoulders, defied all throttling attempts.

Then, just as Dex was feeling that the end had come, he felt the creature wrench from him, and saw it slide in a tangle of arms and legs over the smooth metal pavement. He got shakily to his feet, to see Brand standing over him and flailing out with his fists at an ever tightening circle of towering figures.

"Thanks," panted Dex. And he began again, tripping the twelve-foot things in order to get them down within reach, battering at the great pulpy heads, fighting blindly in that expressed craving to take as many of the creatures into hell with him as he could manage. Beside him fought Brand, steadily, coolly, grim of jaw and unblinking of eye.

Already the struggle had gone on far longer than they had dreamed it might. For some reason the grotesque creatures delayed killing them. That they could do so any time they pleased, was certain: if the monsters could reach them with their shock-tubes through the double insulated hull of the space ship, they could certainly kill them out in the open.

Yet they made no move to do so. The deadly tubes were not used. The screeching gargoyles, instead, devoted all their efforts to merely hurling their attenuated bodies on the two men as though they wished to capture them alive.

Finally, however, the nature of the battle changed. The tallest of the attackers opened his tiny mouth and piped a signal. The ring of weaving tall bodies surrounding the two opened and became a U. The creatures in the curve of the U raised their shock-tubes and, with none of their own kind behind the victims to share in its discharge, released whatever power it was that lurked in them.

The shock was terrific. Without the glass and metal of the ship to protect them, out in the open and defenceless, Brand and Dex got some indication of its real power.

Writhing and twitching, feeling as though pierced by millions of red hot needles, they went down. A swarm of pipe-like bodies smothered them, and the fight was over.

CHAPTER III
The Coming of Greca

THE numbing shock from the tubes left the Earthmen's bodies almost paralyzed for a time; but their brains were unfogged enough for them to observe only too clearly all that went on from the point of their capture.

They were bound hand and foot. At a piping cry from the leader, several of the gangling figures picked them up in reedy arms and began to walk across the square, away from the ship. Brand noticed that his bearers' arms trembled with his weight: and sensed the flabbiness of the substance that took the place in them of good solid muscle. Physically these things were soft and ineffectual indeed. They had only the ominous tubes with which to fight.

The eerie procession, with the bound Earthmen carried in the lead, wound toward a great building fringing the square. In through the high arched entrance of this building they went, and up a sloping incline to its tower-top. Here, in a huge bare room, the two were unceremoniously dumped to the floor.

While three of the things stood guard with the mysterious tubes, another unbound them. A whole shower of high pitched, piping syllables was hurled at them, speech which sounded threatening and contemptuous but was otherwise, of course, entirely unintelligible, and then the creatures withdrew. The heavy metal door was slammed shut, and they were alone.

Brand drew a long breath, and began to feel himself all over for broken bones. He found none; he was still nerve-wracked from that last terrific shock, but otherwise whole and well.

"Are you hurt, Dex?" he asked solicitously.

"I guess not," replied Dex, getting uncertainly to his feet. "And I'm wondering why. It seems to me the brutes were uncommonly considerate of us—and I'm betting the reason is one we won't like!"

Brand shrugged. "I guess we'll find out their intentions soon enough. Let's see what our surroundings look like."

They walked to the nearest window-aperture, and gazed out on a startling and marvelous scene.

Beneath their high tower window, extending as far as the eye could reach, lay the city, lit by the reddish glare of the peculiar metal with which its streets were paved. For the most part the metropolis consisted of perfectly square buildings pierced by many windows to indicate that each housed a large number of inmates. But here and there grotesque turrets lanced the sky, and symbolic domes arched above the surrounding flat metal roofs.

One building in particular they noticed. This was an enormous structure in the shape of a half-globe that reared its spherical height less than an eighth of a mile from the building they were in. It was situated off to their right at the foot of a vast, high-walled enclosure whose near end seemed to be formed by the right wall of their prison. They could only see it by leaning far out of the window; and it would not have come to their attention at all had they not heard it first—or, rather, heard the sound of something within it: for from it came a curious whining hum that never varied in intensity, something like the hum of a gigantic dynamo, only greater and of a more penetrating pitch.

"Sounds as though it might be some sort of central power station," said Brand. "But what could it supply power for?"

"Give it up," said Dex. "For their damned shock-tubes, perhaps, among other things—"

He broke off abruptly as a sound of sliding bolts came from the doorway. The two men whirled around to face the door, their fists doubling instinctively against whatever new danger might threaten them.

The door was opened and two of their ugly, towering enemies came in, their tubes held conspicuously before them. Behind came another figure; and at sight of this one, so plainly not of the race of Jupiter, the Earthmen gasped with wonder.

They saw a girl who might have come from Earth, save that she was taller than most Earth women—of a regal height that reached only an inch or two below Brand's own six foot one. She was beautifully formed, and had wavy dark hair and clear light blue eyes. A sort of sandal covered each small bare foot; and a gauzy tunic, reaching from above the knee to the shoulder, only half shielded her lovely figure.

She was bearing a metal container in which was a mess of stuff evidently intended as food. The guards halted and stepped aside to let her pass into the room. Then they backed out, constantly keeping Dex and Brand covered with the tubes, and closed and barred the door.

The girl smiled graciously at the admiration in the eyes of both the men—a message needing no inter-planetary interpretation. She advanced, and held the metal container toward them.

"Eat," she said softly. "It is good food, and life giving."

For an instant Brand was dumbfounded. For here was language he could understand—which was incredible on this far-flung globe. Then he suddenly comprehended why her sentences were so intelligible.

She was versed in mental telepathy. And versed to a high degree! He'd had some experience with telepathy on Venus; but theirs was a crude thought-speech compared to the fluency possessed by the beautiful girl before him.

"Who are you?" he asked wonderingly.

"I am Greca"—it was very hard to grasp names or abstract terms—"of the fourth satellite."

"Then you are not of these monsters of Jupiter?"

"Oh, no! I am their captive, as are all my people. We are but slaves of the tall ones."

Brand glanced at Dex. "Here's a chance to get some information, perhaps," he murmured.

Dex nodded; but meanwhile the girl had caught his thought. She smiled—a tragic, wistful smile.

"I shall be happy to tell you anything in my power to tell," she informed him. "But you must be quick. I can only remain with you a little while."

She sat down on the floor with them—the few bench-like things obviously used by the tall creatures as chairs were too high for them—

and with the informality of adversity the three captives began to talk. Swiftly Brand got a little knowledge of Greca's position on Jupiter, and of the racial history that led up to it.

FOUR of the nine satellites of Jupiter were now the home of living beings. But two only, at the dawn of history as Greca knew it, had been originally inhabited. These were the fourth and the second.

On the fourth there dwelt a race, "like me," as Greca put it—a kindly, gentle people content to live and let live.

On the second had been a race of immensely tall, but attenuated and physically feeble things with great heads and huge dull eyes and characters distinguished mainly for cold-blooded savagery.

The inhabitants of the fourth satellite had remained in ignorance of the monsters on the second till one day "many, many ages ago," a fleet of clumsy ships appeared on the fourth satellite. From the ships had poured thousands of pipe-like creatures, armed with horrible rods of metal that killed instantly and without a sound. The things, it seemed, had crowded over the limits of their own globe, and had been forced to find more territory.

They had made captive the entire population of the satellite. Then— for like all dangerous vermin they multiplied rapidly—they had overflowed to the first and fifth satellites—the others were uninhabitable— and finally to the dangerous surface of Jupiter itself. Everywhere they had gone, they had taken droves of Greca's people to be their slaves, "and the source of their food," added Greca, with a shudder; a statement that was at the moment unintelligible to the two men.

Brand stared sympathetically at her. "They treat them very badly?" he asked gently.

"Terribly! Terribly!" said Greca, shuddering again.

"But you seem quite privileged," he could not help saying.

She shook her dainty head pathetically. "I am of high rank among my people. I am a priestess of our religion, which is the religion of The Great White One who rules all the sky everywhere. The Rogans" (it was the best translation Brand could make of her mental term for the slimy tall things that held them captive) "—the Rogans hold my fate over the heads of my race. Should they rebel, I would be thrown to the monster in the pen. Of course the Rogans could crush any revolt with their terrible tubes, but they do not want to kill their slaves if they can help it. They find it more effective to hold their priestesses in hostage."

Brand turned from personal history to more vital subjects.

"Why," he asked Greca, "are the shining red squares of metal laid everywhere over this empire of the Rogans?"

"To make things light," was the reply. "When the Rogans first came to this mighty sphere, they could hardly move. Things are so heavy here, somehow. So their first thought was to drive my enslaved people to the casting and laying of the metal squares and the metal beams that connect them, in order to make things weigh less."

"But how do the plates function?"

Greca did not know this, save vaguely. She tried to express her little knowledge of the scientific achievements of the savage Rogans. After some moments Brand turned to Dex and said:

"As near as I can get it, the Rogans, by this peculiar red metal alloy, manage to trap and divert the permanent lines of force, the magnetic field, of Jupiter itself. So the whole red spot is highly magnetized, which somehow upsets natural gravitational attraction. I suppose it is responsible for the discoloration of the ground, too."

He turned to question the girl further about this, but she had got nervously to her feet already.

"I'll be taken away soon," she said. "I was brought in here only to urge you to eat the food. I must be interpreter, since the Rogans speak not with the mind, and I know their hateful tongue."

"Why are they so anxious for us to eat?" demanded Dex with an uneasy frown.

"So you will be strong, and endure for a long time the—the ordeal they have in store for you," faltered the girl at last. "They intend to force from you the secret of the power that drove your ship here, so they too may have command of space."

"But I don't understand," frowned Brand. "They must already have a means of space navigation. They came here to Jupiter from the satellites."

"Their vessels are crude, clumsy things. The journey from the nearest satellite is the limit of their flying range. They have nothing like your wonderful little ships, and they want to know how to build and power them."

She gazed sorrowfully at them and went on: "You see, yours is the fourth space ship to visit their kingdom; and that makes them fearful because it shows they are vulnerable to invasion. They want to stop that by invading your planet first. Besides their fear, there is their greed. Their looking-tubes reveal that yours is a fruitful and lovely sphere, and they are insatiable in their lust for new territories. Thus they plan to go to your planet as soon as they are able, and kill or enslave all the people there as they have killed and enslaved my race."

"They'll have a job on their hands trying to do that!" declared Dex stoutly.

But Brand paled. "They can do it!" he snapped. "Look at those death-tubes of theirs. We have no arms to compete with that." He turned to Greca. "So the Rogans plan to force the secret of our motors from us by torture?"

She nodded, and caught his hand in hers.

"Yes. They will do with you as they did with the six who came before you—and who died before surrendering the secret."

"So! We know now what happened to Journeyman and the others!" burst out Dex. "I'll see 'em in hell before I'll talk!"

"And me," nodded Brand. "But that doesn't cure the situation. As long as ships disappear in this red inferno, so long will the Old Man keep sending others to find out what's wrong. The Rogans will capture them as easily as they captured us. And eventually someone will happen along who'll weaken under torture. Then—"

He stopped. A dread vision filled his mind of Earth depopulated by the feebly ferocious Rogans, of rank on rank of Earth's vast armies falling in stricken rows at the shock of the Rogans' tubes.

Greca caught the vision. She nodded. "Yes, that is what would happen if they found ways of reaching your globe."

"But, God, Brand, we can't allow that!" cried Dex. "We've got to find a way to spike the guns of these walking gas-pipes, somehow!"

Brand sighed heavily. "We are two against hundreds of thousands. We are bare-handed, and the Rogans have those damned tubes. Anyway, we are on the verge of death at this very moment. What under heaven can we do to spike their guns?"

He was silent a moment: and in the silence the steady hum from the domed building outside came to his ears.

"What's in that big, round topped building, Greca?" he asked quietly.

"I do not know, exactly," replied the girl. "There is some sort of machinery in it, and to it go connecting beams from all the square metal plates everywhere. That is all I know."

Brand started to question her further, but her time was up. The two guards poked their loathsome pumpkin heads in the doorway and contemptuously beckoned her out. She answered resignedly, in the piping Rogan tongue, and went with them. But she turned to wave shyly, commiseratingly at the two men; and the expression in her clear blue eyes as they rested on Brand made his heart contract and then leap on with a mighty bound.

"We have in ally in her," murmured Brand. "Though God only knows if that will mean anything to us. . . ."

CHAPTER IV
In the Tower

"WHAT I can't figure out," said Dex, striding up and down the big bare room, "is why we're needed to tell them about the atomic motor. They've got our ship, and three others besides. I should think they could learn about the motor just by taking it apart and studying it."

Brand grinned mirthlessly, recalling the three years of intensive study it had taken him to learn the refinements of atomic motive power. "If you'd ever qualified as a space navigator, Dex, you'd know better. The Rogans are an advanced race; their control of polar magnetism and the marvelously high-powered telescopes Greca mentions prove that; but I doubt if they could ever analyze that atomic motor with no hint as to how it works."

Silence descended on them again, in which each was lost in his own thoughts.

How many hours had passed, the Earthmen did not know. They had spent the time in fruitless planning to escape from their tower room and go back to the ship again. Though how they could get away in the ship when the Rogans seemed able to propel it where-ever they wished against the utmost power of their motor, they did not attempt to consider.

One of Jupiter's short nights had passed, however—a night weirdly made as light as day by red glares from the plates, which seemed to store up sunlight, among their other functions—and the tiny sun had risen to slant into their window at a sharp angle.

Suddenly they heard the familiar drawing of the great bolts outside their door. It was opened, and a dozen or more of the Rogans came in, with Greca cowering piteously in their midst and attempting to communicate her distress to Brand.

At the head of the little band of Rogans was one the prisoners had not seen before. He was of great height, fully two feet taller than the others; and he carried himself with an air that proclaimed his importance.

The tall one turned to Greca and addressed a few high-pitched, squeaky words to her. She shook her head; whereupon, at a hissed command, two of the Rogans caught her by the wrists and dragged her forward.

"They have come to question you," Greca lamented to Brand. "And they want to do it through me. But I will not! I will not!"

Brand smiled at her though his lips were pale.

"You are powerless to struggle," he said. "Do as they ask. You cannot help us by refusing, and, in any case, I can promise that they won't learn anything from us."

The tall Rogan teetered up to the prisoners on his gangling legs, and stared icily at them. Crouched beside him, her lovely body all one mute appeal to the Earthmen to forgive her for the part she was forced to play, was Greca.

At length the Rogan leader spoke. He addressed his sibilant words to Greca, though his stony eyes were kept intently on the Earthmen.

"He says," exclaimed Greca telepathically, "to inform you first that he is head of all the Rogan race on this globe, and that all on this globe must do as he commands."

Brand nodded to show he understood the message.

"He says he is going to ask you a few questions, and that you are to answer truthfully if you value your lives:"

"First, he wants to know what the people of your world are like. Are they all the same as you?"

Dex started to reply to that; but Brand flung him a warning look. "Tell him we are the least of the Earth people," he answered steadily. "Tell him we are of an inferior race. Most of those on Earth are giants five times as large as we are, and many times more powerful."

Greca relayed the message in the whistling, piping Rogan tongue. The tall one stared, then hissed another sentence to the beautiful interpreter.

"He wants to know," said Greca, "if there are cities on your globe as large and complete as this one."

"There are cities on Earth that make this look like a—a—" Brand cast about for understandable similes—"like a collection of animal burrows."

"He says to describe your planet's war weapons," was the next interpretation. And here Brand let himself go.

With flights of fancy he hadn't known he was capable of, he described great airships, steered automatically and bristling with guns that discharged explosives powerful enough to kill everything within a range of a thousand miles. He told of billions of thirty-foot giants sheathed in an alloy that would make them invulnerable to any feeble rays the Rogans might have developed. He touched on the certain wholesale death that must overtake any hostile force that tried to invade the planet.

"The Rogan shock-tubes are toys compared with the ray-weapons of Earth," he concluded. "We have arms that can nullify the effects of yours and kill at the same instant. We have—"

But here the Rogan leader turned impatiently away. Greca had been translating sentence by sentence. Now the tall one barked out a few syllables in a squeaky voice.

"He says he knows you are lying," sighed Greca. "For if you on Earth have tubes more effective than theirs why weren't you equipped with them on your expedition here to the red kingdom?"

Brand bit his lips. "Check," he muttered. "The brute has a brain in that ugly head."

The Rogan leader spoke for a long time then; and at each singsong word, Greca quivered as though lashed by a whip. At length she turned to Brand.

"He has been telling what his hordes can do, answering your boasts with boasts of his own. His words are awful! I won't tell you all he said. I will only say that he is convinced his shock-tubes are superior to any Earth arms, and that he states he will now illustrate their power to you to quell your insolence. I don't know what he means by that. . . ."

But she and the Earthmen were soon to find out.

The Rogan leader stepped to the window and arrogantly beckoned Brand and Dex to join him there. They did; and the leader gazed out and down as though searching for something.

He pointed. The two Earthmen followed his leveled arm with their eyes and saw, a hundred yards or so away, a bent and dreary figure trudging down the metal paving of the street. It was a figure like those to be seen on Earth, which placed it as belonging to Greca's race.

The tall leader drew forth one of the shock-tubes. Seen near at hand, it was observed to be bafflingly simple in appearance. It seemed devoid of all mechanism—simply a tube of reddish metal with a sort of handle formed of a coil of heavy wire.

The Rogan pointed the tube at the distant figure.

Greca screamed, and screamed again. Coincident with her cry, as though the sound of it had felled him, the distant slave dropped to the pavement.

That was all. The tube had merely been pointed: as far as Brand could see, the Rogan's "hand" had not moved on the barrel of the tube, nor even constricted about the coil of wire that formed its handle. Yet that distant figure had dropped. Furthermore, fumes of greasy black smoke now began to arise from the huddled body; and in less than thirty seconds there was left no trace of it on the gleaming metal pavement.

"So that's what those things are like at full power!" breathed Dex. "My God!"

The Rogan leader spoke a few words. Greca, huddled despairingly on the floor, crushed by this brutal annihilation of one of her country-men before her very eyes, did not translate. But translation was un-necessary. The Rogan's icy, triumphant eyes, the very posture of his grotesque body, spoke for him.

"That," he was certainly saying, "is what will happen to any on your helpless planet who dare oppose the Rogan will!"

He whipped out a command to the terror-stricken girl. She rose from her crouching position on the floor; and at length formulated the Ro-gan's last order:

"You will explain the working of the engine that drove your space ship here."

Dex laughed. It was a short bark of sound, totally devoid of humor, but very full of defiance. Brand thrust his hands into the pockets of his tunic, spread his legs apart, and began to whistle.

Aquiver that might have been of anger touched the Rogan leader's repulsive little mouth. He glared balefully at the uncowed Earthmen and spoke again, evidently repeating his command. The two turned their backs to him to indicate their refusal to obey.

At that, the tall leader pointed to Dex. In an instant three of the guards had wound their double pairs of arms around his struggling body. Brand sprang to help him, but a touch of the mysterious discharge from the leader's tube sent him writhing to the floor.

"It's no use, Brand," said Dex steadily. He too had stopped strug-gling, and now stood quietly in the slimy coils of his captors' arms. "I might as well go along with them and get it over with. I probably won't see you again. Good luck!"

He was borne out of the room. The Rogan leader turned to Brand and spoke.

"He says that if your comrade does not tell him what he wants to know, your turn will come next," sobbed Greca. "Oh! Why does not The Great White One strike these monsters to the dust!"

She ran to Brand and pressed her satiny cheek to his. Then she was dragged roughly away.

The great door clanged shut. The heavy outer fastenings clicked into place. Dex had gone to experience whatever it was that Journeyman and the rest had experienced in this red hell. And Brand was left behind to reflect on what dread torments this might comprise; and to pray desperately that no matter what might be done to his shrinking body he would be strong enough to refuse to betray his planet.

CHAPTER V
The Torture Chamber

SWIFTLY Dex was carried down the long ramp to the ground floor, the arms of his captors gripping him with painful tightness. Heading the procession was the immensely tall, gangling Rogan leader, clutching Greca by the wrist and dragging her indifferently along to be his mouthpiece.

They did not stop at the street level; they continued on down another ramp, around a bend, descending an even steeper incline toward the bowels of Jupiter. Their descent ended at last before a huge metal barrier which, at a signal from the leader, drew smoothly up into the ceiling to disclose a gigantic, red-lit chamber underlying the foundations of the building.

In fear and awe, Dex gazed around that huge room.

It resembled in part a nightmare rearrangement of such a laboratory as might be found on Earth; and in part a torture chamber such as the most ferocious of savages might have devised had they been scientifically equipped to add contrivances of supercivilization to the furthering of their primitive lust for cruelty.

There were great benches—head-high to the Earthman—to accommodate the height of the Rogan workmen. There were numberless metal instruments, and glass coils, and enormous retorts; and in one corner an orange colored flame burnt steadily on a naked metal plate, seeming to have no fuel or other source of being.

There was a long rack of cruelly pointed and twisted instruments. Under this was a row of long, delicate pincers, with coils on the handles to indicate that they might be heated to fiendish precision of temperatures. There were gleaming metal racks with calibrated slide-rods and spring dials to denote just what pull was being exerted on whatever unhappy creature might be stretched taut on them. There were tiny cones of metal whose warped, baked appearance testified that they were little portable furnaces that could be placed on any desired portion of the anatomy, to slowly bake the selected disk of flesh beneath them.

Dex shuddered; and a low moan came from Greca, whose clear blue eyes had rested on the contents of this vast room before in her capacity as hostage and interpreter for the inhuman Rogans.

And now another sense of Dex's began to register perception on his brain.

A peculiar odor came to his nostrils. It was a musky, fetid odor, like that to be smelled in an animal cage; but it was sharper, more acrid than anything he had ever smelled on Earth. It smelled—ah, he had it!—*reptilian*. As though somewhere nearby a dozen titanic serpents were coiled ready to spring!

Looking about, Dex saw a six-foot square door of bars in one wall of the laboratory—like the barred entrance to a prison cell. It was from the interstices of this door that the odor seemed to emanate; but he had no chance to make sure, for now the Rogan leader approached him.

"I will first show you," he said, through his mouthpiece, Greca, "what happens to those who oppose our orders. We have a slave who tried to run away into the surrounding jungles three suns ago. . . ."

A man was dragged into the chamber. He was slightly taller and more stockily muscled than an Earthman might be; but otherwise, in facial conformation and general appearance, he might have come here straight from New York City. Dex felt a great pang of sympathy for him. He was so plainly one of humankind, despite the fact that he had been born on a sphere four hundred million miles from Dex's.

The fellow was paralyzed with horror. His eyes, wide and glazed, darted about the torture room like those of a trapped animal. And yet he made no move to break away from the clutch of the two Rogans who held him. He knew he was helpless, that wild-eyed glance told Dex. Knew it so thoroughly that not even his wildest terror could inspire him to try to make a break for freedom, or strike back at the implacable Rogan will.

At a nod from the leader, the man was stripped to the waist. Here Dex started in amazement. The man's broad chest was seamed and criss-crossed by literally hundreds of tiny lateral scars, some long healed, and some fresh incisions.

He was dragged to a metal plate set upright in the wall, and secured to it by straps of metal. Evidently the miserable being knew what this portended, for he began to scream—a monotonous, high-pitched shriek that didn't stop till he was out of breath.

The Rogan leader stared at him icily, then depressed a small lever set in the wall beside him. The plate against which the captive was bound began to shine softly with a blue light. The slave twisted in his bonds, screaming again. Rhythmic shudders jerked at his limbs. His lips turned greenish white. The shudders grew more pronounced till it seemed as though he were afflicted with a sort of horrible St. Vitus dance. Then the tall Rogan pulled back the lever. The slave hung away from his supporting shackles, limp and unconscious.

Dex moistened his lips. An electric shock? No, it was something more terrible than that. Some other manifestation of the magnetic power the Rogans had harnessed—a current, perhaps, that depolarized partly the atoms of the body structure? He could only guess. But the convulsed face of the unfortunate victim showed that the torment, whatever it was, was devilish to the last degree!

"That will be the next to the last fate reserved for you," the Rogan informed Dex, through Greca. "Death follows soon after that—but not too soon for you to see and feel what waits for you behind the barred door!" And he nodded toward the cage-entrance affair, from which came the musky, reptilian stench.

"Now that you have seen something of what will happen to you if you refuse to tell us what we want to know, we shall proceed," said the leader.

He pointed toward one of the gargantuan work benches, and two of the Rogans slid down from it a contrivance that looked familiar to Dex. An instant's scrutiny showed him why it was familiar: it was a partly dismantled atomic motor.

In spite of the ordeal that faced him, Dex felt a thrill of elation as he looked at the motor. In its scattered state, it told a mute story: a story of long and intensive study by the Rogans, which had yielded them no results! Only too obviously, the intricate secret of atomic power had not let itself be solved.

On the heels of the elation that filled his heart, came a sickening realization of his dilemma. He could not have told the Rogans what they wanted to know even if he had wished to! He himself didn't know the principles of the atomic engine. As Brand had remarked, he was no space navigator; he was simply a prosaic lieutenant, competent only at fighting, not at all versed in science.

He knew, though, that it would do no good to assert his ignorance to the Rogans. They simply wouldn't believe him.

"You will rebuild this engine for us," ordered the tall leader, "showing us the purpose of each part, and how the power is extracted from the fuel. After that you will set it running for us, and instruct us in its control."

Dex braced himself. His final moment had come.

By way of indicating his refusal he looked away from the dismantled motor and said nothing. The Rogan repeated his command. Dex made no move. Then the leader acted.

He said something to the Rogan guards who had been standing by all this while, alert against an outbreak from their prisoner. Dex was caught up, carried to one of the metal racks, and thrown down on its calibrated bed. Loops of metal, like handcuffs, were snapped around his wrists and ankles; and a metal hoop was clamped over his throat, pinning him to the torture rack. Resistance would have been useless, and Dex submitted quietly.

Yhe contrivance, with him on it, was wheeled toward the barred door. It was halted at a spot marked on the floor, about thirty feet from the bars. The Rogan leader stepped alongside the rack, with Greca trembling beside him.

Dex closed his eyes for a moment, grimly marshaling strength of will to go through the trial that was just beginning.

The Rogan leader depressed another lever in the rock wall. The barred door slid slowly up, to reveal the receding darknesses of some great cave, or room, that adjoined the laboratory. Dex rolled his eyes so that he could watch the doorway; and, in a cold perspiration, waited for whatever might appear.

It was not long in coming!

The reptilian smell suddenly grew stronger. There was a booming hiss, a savage bellowing. A clattering of vast scales rattled out as some body weighing many tons was dragged over rock flooring. Then, before Dex's staring eyes appeared a huge, wedge-shaped head, at sight of which he bit his lips to keep from crying aloud.

Often enough he had seen one of those terrific heads looming in the fog of the northern hemisphere of Jupiter. He did not know the genus of the vast monster that bore it, but he did know it for the fiercest of the lizard giants that roamed the Jovian jungles. A creature larger than a terrestrial whale, with great long neck and heavy long tail dragging yards behind it, it would find the puny bulk of a man nothing but a morsel in its jaws!

Again the gigantic thing hissed and bellowed. And then its huge head came through the six-foot door and its neck uncoiled to send the gaping jaws within a foot of Dex. There it struggled to reach him, prevented by the small doorway that restrained the bulk of its enormous body, its head only inches away from the cleverly measured spot to which the metal rack had been wheeled.

Dex stared, hypnotized, into the dull, stony eyes of the beast, gasping for breath in the stench of its exhalations. The jaws snapped shut, fanning his cheek. He fought for self-control. Steady! Steady! The slimy Rogans had no intention of feeding him to the thing yet. Not till they had made more determined efforts to wring from him the secret of the motor. They were just prefacing actual physical torture with hellish mental torture, that was all.

That he was right in his guess was proved in a few moments. He heard a louder hiss from the great lizard so near him. Opening his eyes, he saw the Rogan leader in the process of forcing the serpentine neck to withdraw foot by foot back into the doorway, using his shock-tube as a sort of distant prod.

The monster swayed its ugly flat head back and forth, hissing deafeningly at the sting of the tube, now and again lunging with its vast unseen body at the too narrow entrance that kept it from entering the laboratory. Dex could hear the foundation walls of the building creak at the onslaught of that tremendous weight.

If it would only break through! he thought savagely. But it wasn't going to. In a short while it was cowed by the deadly tube, and withdrew its head awkwardly from the chamber. The barred door slid down into place; and the Rogan leader once more turned his attention to his prisoner.

"You will be wheeled within reach of the creature as the last step of your fate," Dex was informed. "Meanwhile, we shall start with something less deadly. . . ."

A cogged wheel beside him was turning a notch. Dex felt the sliding bed of the rack crawl slightly under him. Intolerable tension was suddenly placed on his arms and legs. The leader stared at a spring dial; and moved the wheel another notch. The rack expanded again, stretching Dex's body till his joints cracked.

"You will tell us what we want to know," said the Rogan, glaring coldly down at him.

Dex compressed his lips stubbornly. He couldn't tell them if he wanted to, and, by God, he wouldn't if he could.

Another notch, the wheel was turned; and in spite of himself a groan escaped Dex's lips. One more notch, while the metal slide-rods beneath him lengthened a fraction of an inch. . . .

CHAPTER VI
The Inquisition

BLIND, animal fear caught Dex and shook him in its grip. Then rage filled his heart, driving out the fear as a gale dissipates fog. With pain-dimmed eyes he glared at the gangling, hateful figure that gazed down on him with icy eyes. If he could only blast that monstrous, physically feeble but mentally ferocious thing to bits! Annihilate it! Blow it to the four corners of Jupiter! And all the other Rogans with it!

And with this thought he suddenly saw, through the red mists of rage, the shock-tube that was dangling indifferently from the Rogan leader's hand.

Instantly the red mists began to clear away. Another change took place in the tortured lieutenant's mind. The blind hot rage faded into more deadly, cold wrath. A plan began to bud into thought. It was a futile plan, really. It could not possibly accomplish anything vital. But it *might* give him a chance for a little revenge before his life was snuffed out—might give him a chance to strike a blow for the dead Journeyman and the other gallant explorers who had perished here in this chamber before him.

He closed his eyes to hide the hate and calculation in them. The tall Rogan leaned lower over the rack.

"You are ready to do as I command?" he demanded.

"Yes," whispered Dex. "Yes."

In the beautiful Greca's eyes, as she translated his assent, was horror. But then, faintly, her mind caught the thought that lay beneath the Earth-man's apparent surrender. She veiled her own eyes with long lashes, lest they betray the captive's plan to the alert Rogan. Her lips moved silently; perhaps she was praying to her Great White One.

"Release him," the Rogan ordered, triumph in his bird-like, shrill voice. The metal hoops were unfastened. Dex stretched his outraged body, wincing with the pain of movement; then felt life and strength returning to him.

"Come with us to the motor," commanded the Rogan, his dull eyes glinting in anticipation of learning the coveted secret that should add one more planet to the Rogan's tyranny.

Dex walked to the dismantled atomic engine with him. He walked slowly, pretending more stiffness and weakness than he really owned to. No use in letting his captors know that his resilient muscles were so quickly throwing off the torment of the rack.

As he walked he kept his gaze covertly on that shock-tube that dangled in the leader's grasp. The rest of the guard had none; they had laid their weapons down on a far bench on their entrance to the chamber, depending on the one with which their leader was armed.

Eagerly the Rogans crowded around Dex and the motor that had thus far baffled them. They bent down from their twelve-foot heights to bring their staring goggle-eyes closer to the lesson in atomic motive power, till Dex was in a sort of small dome of Rogans, with their long, pipe-like legs forming the wall around him, and their thin torsos inclining forward to make a curved ceiling over him.

The Rogan leader drew Greca within the circle to interpret the Earthman's explanations.

Dex moved a trifle, to bring himself nearer the tall leader. Again he glanced covertly at the shock-tube.

"The first thing to tell about our motor," said Dex, stalling for time, "is that it utilizes the breaking up of the atom as its source of power."

He edged closer to the Rogan leader.

"You see those electrodes?" he said, pointing to two copper castings in a chamber between the fuel tank and the small but enormously powerful turbine that whirled with the released atomic energy. The Rogan leader blinked assent. His small, horrible mouth was pursed with his concentration of thought.

"The electrodes partially break down the atoms of fuel passing from the tank," explained Dex, desperately attempting scientific phraseology for a matter as far over his head as the remote stars. He raised his hand a trifle, bringing it nearer the Rogan's tube. . . .

"Is that the outlet from the tank?" inquired the Rogan, pointing with the tube, and so raising it out of Dex's reach.

"Yes," mumbled Dex, sick with disappointment: he'd been on the point of leaping for the weapon. He sidled close again. Greca bit her lips lest she cry out with suspense.

"The partially disintegrated atoms pass into the turbine chamber," he went on, "and are there completely broken down by heat, which has been generated by the explosive energy of the atoms passing in before them."

"I warn you to speak true," said the leader, suddenly removing his gaze from the specimen motor and staring icily down at Dex. Dex's hand dropped abruptly from its place near the tube. Again his fingers had come within a foot of it.

"We will get ahead faster," piped the Rogan, an edge of suspicion sounding in his shrill voice, "if I conduct the explanation. I will ask questions for you to answer. What is the fuel used?"

"Powdered zinc," Dex answered promptly. No harm in admitting that. The Rogans must already know it; zinc was common to Jupiter, as Earth spectroscopes had showed long since; and they had no doubt analyzed it by now. The chances were that the leader was merely testing him, to see if he were sincere in his ostensible surrender.

That his guess was right, he read in the fishy, dull eyes. The Rogan leader nodded at his answer, and some of the lurking suspicion in his gaze died down.

"How is it prepared?"

Now this marked the beginning of the end, Dex knew. The preparation of the powdered metal was half the secret of atomic power—and Dex hadn't the faintest idea what it was! This questions-and-answers affair was going to pin him down in short order!

"How is it prepared?" repeated the Rogan leader inexorably. "Tell us, or—"

But at that instant Dex attained his objective.

Once more his hand had crawled slowly toward the tube—till, once more, it was within reach. Then, more bold as his position grew more desperate, he straightened up—and, with a lightning move, had wrenched it from the sucker-disk that held it!

He shouted his triumph. He had it! *Now* let the devils put him back on the torture bed if they could! *Now* let them try to make him betray his planet!

There was an alarmed squeak from the Rogan leader, and in an instant the huge laboratory was in an uproar. The Rogan guards whipped their hose-like arms toward the Earthman. Dex, with a sweep of his hands, knocked the pipe-stem legs of two of the guards from under them, leaped over their bodies, and stood at bay in a corner—guarding the bench on which the guards had laid their tubes when they filed into the laboratory.

The air resounded with the shrill calls of the excited Rogans. Then they began to close in on him, all the while eyeing the tube in his hand with terror written large on their hideous faces.

Dex's eyes blazed with the light of vengeful exultation. For the death of Journeyman and the rest, for the coming inevitable death of himself and Brand, he was going to pay—at least in part—with the captured tube of death in his hand! It was a lovely thought, and for a few seconds he delayed acting in order to savor it.

Then, with a smile of pure happiness, he leveled the tube at the nearest Rogan in order to shrivel him to nothingness as he had seen the slave shriveled in the street.

The Rogan did not fall! Full in the face of the death tube he teetered forward, his arms reaching savagely toward the Earthman.

Dex stared incredulously. Cold fear crept into his heart. He pointed the tube more accurately, and squeezed harder on the coil handle. Still nothing happened. The Rogans warily drew closer.

Perspiration began to trickle down Dex's cheeks. In God's name, why didn't the tube work? He had thought all he had to do was point it and squeeze down on the handle. But evidently there was more to the trick than that!

He groaned. He had staged all this elaborate play for a weapon as useless to his untrained mind as one of Earth's explosive guns, with the safety-lock clamped on, would have been to an abysmal Venusian savage!

By now the nearest Rogan was within reaching distance of him. One of its two pairs of slimy arms uncoiled toward him. The other pair strained to reach around him and get to the weapons on the bench by his side.

With a cry, Dex dashed the useless shock-tube down on the reaching arms. As long as he didn't know how to work it anyway, he might as well use it as a club.

The Rogan squeaked with pain; the arms recoiled. Dex jerked the tube back over his shoulder for another blow. . . .

There was a shriek from the doomed wretch fastened to the metal plate. The slave that had been tortured before Dex's eyes as an object lesson! He had been returned to consciousness a short time since, and had been writhing and shuddering against the plate.

Dex flashed a glance at him over his shoulder, as he shrieked, and cried aloud himself at what he saw.

The tortured slave was rapidly disappearing! Another shriek left his lips, to be broken off halfway. In an instant nothing was left of the struggling body but a wisp of greasy black smoke!

Dex stared stupidly at the tube in his hand. Then, as a squeak of agony sounded from a Rogan in front of him, his mind grasped what had happened. Somehow its mechanism had been jarred into functioning when he dashed it against the groping arm. In some way its death dealing power had been unleashed. With a cry of exultation, Dex began to use it!

The Rogan in front of him, squealing, collapsed on the floor, dwindling swiftly into nothingness. Dex turned the mysterious death against another teetering creature. It too went up in oleaginous smoke.

The Rogan leader came next. Dex whirled the tube in his direction, and saw him go down. Then he sprang to annihilate still another grotesque monster who had almost reached the bench on which were the other tubes. He shouted and raved as this fourth Rogan crumbled. Torture him, would they! Plan to capture Earth, would they! He'd kill off the whole damned population with this tube!

The Rogan survivors, squeaking in panic, gave over their attempts to retrieve the tubes. They dove for various hiding places—under benches, behind retorts, anywhere to get away from the terror running amuck in their midst. And after them sprang Dex, mad with his sudden miraculous success, to ferret them out one by one and blow them into hell with their own horrible death-engine.

In his ecstasy of rage, Dex overlooked the Rogan leader. He had seen that attenuated monstrosity go down, and had assumed he was dead. But such was not the case. In the corner Dex had vacated when he sprang after the fleeing guard, the tall leader twisted feebly and sat up.

One of his four arms was missing, a smoking stump showing where the annihilating ray from the tube had blasted it off at the shoulder. But he was far from being dead. With cold purpose in his great staring eyes, he moved snakily toward the bench Dex had now left unguarded.

The Earthman got another Rogan; whirled to track down still another. Promptly the leader sank motionless to the floor. The Rogan leader continued his crawling. He reached the bench, fumbled up and along its surface for the nearest tube.

Dex, unconscious of the sure fate gathering behind him to strike him down, dashed past a great glass tank behind which Greca was huddling in mortal fear, and charged down on two more of the squeaking guards.

Then, suddenly, some sixth sense warned him that something was wrong. He whirled toward the corner he had left.

The Rogan leader, two of his surviving arms propping feebly against the bench, was pointing a shock-tube squarely at him!

Dex fell to the floor to escape the first discharge of the tube, and leveled his own. He felt the thing grow hot in his hand, saw a blinding blue-white fire leap into being in the space between them as the rays from the two tubes met and absorbed each other. He shifted, to get out of the line and blast the creature he had too hastily reckoned as dead. But he was not quick enough. A fraction before him, the Rogan leader shifted.

Dex felt a terrible burning sensation all over his body, as the ray from his tube met the conflicting ray less squarely, and allowed a little of it to reach him. He shrieked as the slave had shrieked when he felt the annihilating current from the plate sweeping through his body.

A black fog seemed to close in around the Earthman's senses. He crashed to the floor, with a glimpse of the leering triumph on the Rogan's face as the last picture to stamp itself in his failing consciousness.

The tall Rogan, obviously in great agony from his blasted arm, squeaked a faint command. The four guards who were left issued fear-fully from their hiding places and came to him.

He pointed his tube at Dex Harlow, lying unconscious on the floor. There he hesitated an instant, his soft little mouth slobbering in his rage and pain. Then he let the tube sink slowly off its line.

He gave another command. The four guards picked the Earthman up and carried him to the metal torture-plate on which the slave had met his death. The tall leader's eyes gleamed with vicious hatred as the limp body was fastened to the metal.

Mouthing and squealing with the pain of his seared arm-stump, he wobbled toward the lever, a mere turn of which would readily convert the plate into a bed of agony.

CHAPTER VII
In the Power-House

ALONE in the prison room, after Dex had been dragged away to be subjected to the Rogan inquisition, Brand gnawed at his fingers and paced distractedly up and down the stone flooring. For a while he had no coherent thought at all; only the realization that his turn came next, and that the Rogans would leave no refinement of torment untried in their effort to wring from him the secret of the atomic engine.

He went to the window, and absent-mindedly stared out. The whining hum from the great domed building off to the right, like the high-pitched droning of a swarm of gargantuan bees, came to his ears. He listened more intently, and leaned out of the window to look at the building.

Under that dome, it came to him again, was, in all probability, the mainspring of the Rogan mechanical power. If only he could get in there and look around! He might do some important damage; he might be able to harass the enemy materially before the time came for him to die.

He leaned farther out of the window, and examined the hundred feet or so of sheer wall beneath him. He saw, scrutinizing it intently, that the stone blocks that composed it were not smooth cut, but rough hewn, with the marks of the cutters' chisels plainly in evidence. Also there was a considerable ridge between each layer of blocks where the Rogans' mortar had squeezed out in the process of laying the wall.

Never in sanity would a man have thought of the thing Brand considered then. To attempt to clamber down that blank wall, with only the slight roughness of the protruding layers of mortar to hang on to, was palpable suicide!

Brand shrugged. He observed that to a man already condemned to death, the facing of probable suicide shouldn't mean much.

With scarcely an increase in the beating of his heart, he swung one leg out over the broad sill. If he fell, he escaped an infinitely worse death; if he didn't fall, he might somehow win his way into that domed building whence the hum came.

Cautiously, clutching at the rough stone with finger tips that in a moment or two became raw and bleeding masses, he began his slow descent. As he worked his way down, he slanted to the right, toward the near wall of the retaining yard whose end was formed by the round structure that was his goal.

Beneath him and to the left the broad street swarmed with figures: the tall ones of the Rogans and the shorter, sturdier ones of slaves. Any one of those dozens of grotesque pedestrians might glance up, see him, and pick him off with the deadly tubes. Under his fingers the mortar crumbled and left him hanging, more than once, by one hand. For fully five minutes his life hung by a thread apt to be severed at any time. But—he made it. Helped by the decreased gravity of the red spot, and released from inhibiting fear by the fact that he was already, figuratively, a dead man, he performed the incredible.

With a last slithering step downward, he landed lightly on the near wall of the enclosure, and started along its broad top toward his objective.

Now he was in plain sight of any one who might be looking out the windows of the tower building or from the dome ahead of him; but this was a chance he had to take, and at least he was concealed from the swarms in the street. Making no effort to hide himself by crawling along the top of the wall, he straightened up and began to run toward the giant dome.

Hardly had he gone a dozen steps when he suddenly understood the meaning of the high-walled enclosure to his right!

Off in a far corner rose a slate colored mound that at first glance he had taken for a great heap of inanimate dirt. The mound began to move toward him—and metamorphosed into an animal, a thing that made Brand blink his eyes to see if he were dreaming, and then stop, appalled, to look at it.

He saw a body that dwarfed the high retaining walls to comparative insignificance. It had a tree-like tail that dragged behind it; and a thirty-foot, serpentine neck at the end of which was a head like a sugar barrel that split into cavernous jaws lined with backward-pointing teeth. Two eyes were set wide apart in the enormous head, eyes that were dead and cold and dull, yet glinting with senseless ferocity. It was the sort of thing one sees in delirium.

With increasing energy the creature made for him, till finally it was approaching his sector of the wall at a lumbering run that was rapid for all its ungainliness.

It was apparent at a glance that the snaky neck, perched atop the lofty shoulder structure, would raise the head with its gaping jaws to his level on the wall! Brand ran. And after him thudded the gigantic lizard, its neck arching up and along the wall to reach him.

A scant five yards ahead of the snapping jaws, Brand reached his goal, the dome, and clambered over its curved, metal roof away from the monster's maw.

He stopped to pant for breath and wipe the sweat from his streaming face. "Thank God it didn't get me," he breathed, looking back at the bellowing terror that had pursued him. "Wonder why it's there? It's too ferocious to be tamed and used in any way: it must be kept as a threat to hold the slaves in hand. It certainly looks well fed. . . ."

He shuddered; then he began to explore the dome of the building for a means of entrance.

There was no opening in the roof. A solid sheet of reddish metal, like a titanic half-eggshell, it glittered under him in an unbroken piece.

He crept down its increasingly precipitous edge till he reached a sort of cornice that formed a jutting circle of stone around it. There he leaned far over and saw, about ten feet below him, a round opening like a big port-hole. From it were streaming waves of warm, foul air, from which he judged it to be a ventilator outlet.

He scrambled over the edge of the cornice, hung at arm's length, and swung himself down into the opening. And there, perched high up under the roof, he looked down at an enigmatic, eerie scene.

That the structure was indeed a strange sort of power-house was instantly made evident. But what curious, mysterious, and yet bewilderingly simple machinery it held!

In the center was a titanic coil of reddish metal formed by a single cable nearly a yard through. Around this, at the four corners of the compass, were set coils that were identical in structure but a trifle smaller. From the smaller coils to the larger streamed, unceasingly, blue waves of light like lightning bolts.

Along a large arc of the wall was a stone slab set with an endless array of switches and insulated control-buttons. Gauges and indicators of all kinds, whose purpose could not even be guessed at, were lined above and below, all throbbing rhythmically to the leap of the electric-blue rays between the monster coils.

Almost under Brand's perch a great square beam of metal came through the building wall from outside, to be split into multitudinous smaller beams that were hooked up with the bases of the coils. Across from him, disappearing out through the opposite wall, was an identical beam.

"The terminals for the metal plate system that extends over the whole red spot," murmured Brand. "This building *is* important. But what can I do to throw sand in the gears before I'm caught and killed . . . ?"

He surveyed the great round room below him more thoroughly. Now he saw, right in the center of the huge control board, a solitary lever, that seemed a sort of parent to all the other levers and switches. It was flanked by a perfect army of gauges and indicators; and was covered by a glass bell which was securely bolted to the rock slab.

"That looks interesting," Brand told himself. "I'd like to see that closer, if I can climb down from here without being observed. . . . Why"—he broke off—"where is everybody!"

For the first time, in the excitement and concentration of his purpose, the emptiness of the place struck him. There was no sign of light in the great building—no workmen or slaves anywhere. There was just the great coils, with the streamers of blue light bridging them and emitting the high-pitched, monotonous hum audible outside the dome, and the complicated control board with its quivering indicator needles and mysterious levers. That was all.

"Must be out to lunch," muttered Brand, his eyes going fascinatedly toward that solitary, parent lever under its glass bell. "Well, it gives me a chance to try some experiments, anyway."

It was about fifty feet from his perch to the floor; but a few feet to one side was a metal beam that extended up to help support the trussed weight of the roof. He jumped for this, and quickly slid down it.

He started on a run for the control board; but almost immediately he stopped warily to listen: it seemed to him that he had caught, faintly, the squeaking, high tones of Rogan conversation.

Miraculously, the sound seemed to come from a blank wall to his left. He crept forward to investigate. . . .

The mystery was solved before he had gone very far. There was an opening in the wall leading off to an annex of some kind outside the dome building. The opening was concealed by a set-back, so that at first glance it had seemed part of the wall itself. From this opening drifted the chatter of Rogans.

Brand stole closer, finally venturing to peer into the room beyond from an angle where he himself could not be seen. And he found that his whimsical reference to "lunch" had contained a ghastly element of fact!

In that annex were several dozen of the teetering, attenuated Rogans, and an equal number of slaves. And the relation of the slaves and the Rogans was one that made Brand's skin crawl.

Each Rogan had stripped the tunic from the chest of his slave. Now, as Brand watched, each drew a keen blade from his belt, and made a shallow gash in the shrinking flesh. There were a few stifled screams— some of the slaves were women—but for the most part the slashing was endured in stoical silence. When red drops began to ooze forth, the Rogans stooped and applied their horrible little mouths to the incisions. . . .

"The slimy devils!" Brand whispered hoarsely, at sight of that dreadful feeding. "The inhuman, monstrous vermin!"

But now one or two of the Rogans had begun to utter squeaks of satiation; and Brand hastened away from there and toward the control board again. He hadn't an idea of what he might accomplish when he reached it; he didn't know but that a touch of the significant looking parent-lever might blast him to bits; but he did know that he was going to raise absolute hell with something, somewhere, if he possibly could.

Swiftly he approached the great master-lever, protected by its bell of glass. (At least it looked like glass, for it was crystal clear and reflected gleamingly the blue light from the nearby coils). He tapped it experimentally with his knuckles. . . .

At once pandemonium reigned in the great vaulted building. There was a siren-like screaming from a device he noticed for the first time attached under the domed roof. A clanging alarm split the air from half a dozen gongs set around the upper walls.

Squealing shouts sounded behind Brand. He whirled, and saw the Rogans, interrupted in their terrible meal, pouring in from the annex and racing toward him. Rage and fear distorted their hideous faces as they pointed first to the big lever and then at the escaped Earthman. They redoubled their efforts to get at him, their long unsteady legs covering the distance in great bounds.

Brand swore. Was he to be caught again before he had accomplished a certain thing? When he had already managed to win clear to his objective?

He hammered at the glass bell with his fists, but realized with the first blow that he was only wasting time trying to crack it bare-handed. He glanced quickly about and saw a metal bar propped up against the control board near him.

He sprang for it, grasped it as a club, and returned to the glass bell. Raising his arms high, he brought the thick metal bar down on the glass with all his strength.

With a force that almost wrenched his arms from their sockets, the bar rebounded from the glass bell, leaving it uncracked.

"Unbreakable!" groaned Brand.

Desperately he tried again, whirling the bar high over his head and bringing it smashing down. The result was the same as before as far as breaking the bell was concerned. But—a little trickle of crushed rock came from around the bolts in the slab to which the bell was fastened.

A third time be brought the bar down. The glass bell sagged a bit sway from the slab. . . .

He had no chance for more assaults on it. The nearest Rogans had leaped for him. Slimy arms were coiling around him, while the loathsome sucker-disks tore at his unprotected face and throat.

Savagely Brand lashed out with the bar. It caved in a pair of the long, skinny legs, bringing a bloated round head down within reach. He smashed it with the bar, exulting grimly as the blow crumpled bone and flesh almost down to the little mouth which was yet carmine from its recent feeding.

The process seemed a sound one to Brand, unable as he was to reach the Rogans' heads that towered six feet above his own. Methodically, swinging the bar with the weight of his body behind it, he repeated the example. First a crash of the bar against a pair of legs, then the crushing in of the Rogan's head when he toppled with agonized squeals to the floor.

Again and again he crushed the life out of a Rogan with his one-two swing of the deadly bar. They were thinning down, now. They were wavering in their charges against the comparatively insignificant being from another planet who was defending himself so fiercely.

FINALLY one of their number turned and ran toward an exit, waving his four arms and adding his high-pitched alarms to the incessant ringing of the gongs and shrieks of the warning siren up under the roof. The rest rushed the Earthman in a body.

Steadily, almost joyfully, Brand fought on. He had expected to be annihilated by one of the Rogan shock-tubes long before now; but as yet there was no sign of any. Either these Rogan workmen were not privileged to carry the terrible things, or they were too occupied to think of going and getting them; anyhow, Brand was left free to wield his bar and continue crushing out the lives of the two-legged vermin that attacked him.

With almost a shock of surprise, he saw finally that he had battered their number down to three. At that he took the offensive himself. He rammed the bluntly pointed end of the bar almost through one writhing torso, broke the back of a second with a whistling blow, and tripped and exterminated the third almost in as many seconds. The creatures, without their death-tubes, were as helpless as crippled rats!

Panting, he turned again toward the loosened glass bell, and battered at it with the precious bar. Gradually the bolts that held it to the stone slab were wrenched out, till only one supported it. But at this point, from half a dozen set-back doorways, streams of infuriated Rogans began pouring into the building and toward him.

The one that had fled had come back with help.

CHAPTER VIII
Tremendous Odds

LIKE living spokes of a half-wheel, with the Earthman as the hub, the Rogans converged toward Brand, a howling roar outside indicating that there were hundreds more waiting to jam into the dome as soon as they were able. There were still no shock-tubes in evidence: evidently the worker who had gone for help had gathered the first Rogan citizens he had encountered on the streets. But the very numbers of the mob spelled defeat for Brand.

However, there was still the great lever behind him to yank away from its switch-socket. The glass bell was almost off now. With a last mad blow, he knocked loose the remaining bolt that held it. The bell clattered to the floor.

A concerted shriek came from the crowding Rogans as they saw the Earthman's hand close on the lever. Whatever effect the throwing of that master-switch could have, there was no doubt that they were extremely anxious to prevent it!

And now, in the rear of the crowding columns, appeared Rogans taller than the others, with an authoritative air, who waved before them, eager to unleash their power, batteries of the death-tubes.

Resigning himself to annihilation in the next instant, Brand pulled down hard on the lever.

The effect wrought by the throwing of that great switch was almost indescribable.

In a flash, as though all had been struck at once by a giant's hand, every Rogan in the mob shot toward the floor, long thin legs caving under him as if turned to water. Writhing feebly, they endeavored to get up, but could not; and, still weakly ferocious, began to creep toward the Earthman like huge-headed worms.

Brand himself had been thrown to the floor with the falling of that switch. He had felt as though an invisible ocean had been poured on him, weighting him down intolerably. To move arms or legs required enormous effort; and to get up on his feet again was like rising under a two-hundred-pound pack.

The movement of the switch, he saw, had cut off the gravity reducing apparatus of the Rogans—whatever that might consist of. They were now, abruptly, subjected to the full force of gravity exerted by Jupiter's great mass. They could no more stand erect on their tottering, lofty legs than they could fly.

But, though greatly handicapped by the gravity pull, they were still not entirely helpless. Like huge, long insects they continued to worm their way toward Brand, using their four arms and their boneless legs to help urge them over the flooring. And in their rear the Rogan guards struggled to lift their tubes and level them at the escaped prisoner.

Prompt to avoid that, Brand went down on his hands and knees. Thus he was shielded by the foremost crawling Rogans: the ones in the rear, with the tubes, could not raise themselves high enough to bore down over their fellows' heads at the Earthman.

Squatting on his knees, Brand awaited the first resolute crawlers. And, on his knees, whirling the now thrice weighty bar at heads that were conveniently low enough to be accessible, he began his last stand.

On the Rogans came, evidently determined, at any sacrifice of life, to get the Earthman away from that vital control board. And to right and left, crouching low to escape the tubes of the guards slowly crawling forward from the rear, Brand laid about him with the bar.

He got a little sick at the havoc he was wreaking on these slow-moving, gravity-crippled things: but remembrance of their grisly feeding habits, and the torture they must by now have inflicted on Dex, kept him flailing down on soft heads with undiminished effort.

With the gravity pull what it was, the Earthman was immeasurably stronger than any individual Rogan. For a time the contest was all in his favor. It was like killing slugs in a rose garden!

Nevertheless, these slugs were, after all, twelve feet long and possessed of intelligence, besides being hundreds in number. After a while the tide of battle began to turn in their favor.

Brand began to feel his arms ache burningly with the sustained effort of wielding a weapon that now weighed about twenty-five pounds. He knew he couldn't keep up the terrific strain much longer. And, in addition, he could see that the armed Rogans in the rear were steadily forging ahead among the unarmed attackers, till they soon must be in a position to blast him with their weapons.

Brand brought down his bar, with failing force but still deadly effect, on the loathsome face of the nearest Rogan, grunting with satisfaction as he saw it crumple into a shapeless mass. He thrust it, spear-like, into another face, and another.

Then, abruptly, he found himself weaponless.

Raising it high to bring it down on an attacker who was almost about to seize him, he felt the metal bar turn white hot, and dropped it with a cry as it seared the skin from the palms of his hands. Some Rogan guard in the rear had managed to train his tube on the bar; and in the instant of its rising had almost melted it.

Weaponless and helpless, Brand crawled slowly back before the tortuously advancing mob, keeping close enough to them to be shielded from the tubes of the rear guards. Without his club he knew the end was a matter of seconds.

He had an impulse to leap full into the mass of repulsive, crawling bodies and die fighting as his fists battered at the gruesome faces. But a second impulse, and a stronger one, was the blind instinct to preserve his life as long as possible.

Hesitantly, almost reluctantly, acting on the primitive instinct of self-preservation, he continued to back away from the advancing horde; away from the switch and toward the rear of the dome.

With the instant of his withdrawal, a Rogan turned toward the lever to push it back up into contact and release the red kingdom from the burden of Jupiter's unendurable gravity. And now ensued a curious struggle. The lever, placed for the convenience of creatures twelve feet or more tall, was about five feet from the floor. And the Rogan couldn't reach it!

Stubbornly he heaved and writhed in an effort to raise his inordinately heavy body from the floor to a point where one of the weaving arms could reach the switch. But the pipe-stem legs would not bear its weight. Each time it nearly reached the lever, only to fall feebly back again in a snarl of tangled limbs.

Meanwhile, Brand had flashed a quick look back over his shoulder to see, in the wall behind him, a metal door he hadn't noticed before. He found time for a flashing instant to wonder why there were no Rogans entering from that doorway, too; but it was a vain wonder, and it faded from his mind as the ever advancing, groping monsters before him kept crowding him back.

Instinctively he changed his course a trifle, to edge toward the metal door. Perhaps, behind it, there was sanctuary for a few moments. Perhaps he could force it open, spring out, and bar it again in the faces of the pursuing mob. It sounded improbable, but at least it offered him a slim chance where before no chance had seemed possible.

He reached the door at last, fumbled behind him and felt, high over his head, a massive sliding bolt.

IN the spot Brand had left, the struggle to throw the gravity-lever back into closed contact position went on. The Rogan who was fruitlessly trying to reach up to it paused and said something to one near him. That one halted, and began to crawl toward him.

The two of them tried to reach it, one bracing the other and helping him pry his body up from the implacable pull of Jupiter's uninsulated mass. The top Rogan reached a little higher. The flesh sucker-disk that served as a hand almost grasped the lever, but failed by only a few inches.

A third Rogan crawled up. And now, with two arching their backs to help the other, the thing was done. The hose-like, groping arm went up and pushed the lever back into place.

The blue streamer began to hum and crackle from coil to coil again. The invisible weight that pressed down was released as once more the giant planet's gravity was nullified. The Rogans got eagerly to their feet and began to race toward Brand in their normal long bounds.

Brand, just cautiously rising, when the power went back on, found himself leaping five feet into the air with the excess of his muscular effort. And in that leap he saw the Rogans in the rear straighten up and point their tubes. However, also in that leap, his fumbling hand shot back the bolt that securely shut the metal door.

With a shout of defiance he jumped out of the door and slammed it shut after him, feeling it grow searing hot an instant later under the impact of the rays from the tubes that had been trained on him.

A stinging shock reached him through the metal, flinging him to the ground. He rolled out of its range and leaped to his feet to race away from there. Then, with a gasp, he flattened his body back against the wall of the dome building.

He was in the enclosure that held the gigantic, lizard-like thing that had nearly got him on his escape from the tower room.

He wheeled frantically to go back and face the Rogan death-tubes. Anything rather than wait while that mammoth heap of tiny-brained ferocity ran him down and tore him to shreds! But even as he turned, he heard the bolt shoot home on the inside of the door; heard vengeful squeals of triumph from his pursuers.

AT the other end of the enclosure, near the foot of the tower building, the great lizard eyed him unblinkingly, its tremendous jaws gaping to reveal a cavernous mouth that was hideously lined with bright orange colored membrane. Then, squatting lower with every step it took, like a mountainous cat about to spring on its prey, it began to stalk on its tree-like legs toward the tiny creature that had leaped into its yard with it.

Brand whirled this way and that, mechanically seeking a way out. There was none. The walls of the great enclosure were not like the wall of the tower. Here were no rough hewn stones, with protruding ridges of mortar set between. These walls were as smooth as glass, and just as smooth was the curved wall of the dome building behind him.

The monstrous beast stalked nearer, almost on its belly now. As it advanced, the great tail stirred up a cloud of reddish dust, and left behind it a round deep depression in a surface already crisscrossed with a multitude of similar depressions. A bellowing hiss came from its gaping mouth, and it increased its pace to a thunderous, waddling rush.

CHAPTER IX
Into the Enclosure

IN the torture chamber Dex wavered slowly back to consciousness to get the growing impression that he was being immersed in a bath of liquid fire. Burning, intolerable pain assailed him with increasing intensity as his senses clarified.

At last he groaned and opened his eyes, for the moment not knowing where he was nor how he had come to be there. He saw strange torture instruments and tall monstrosities with pumpkin-shaped heads surrounding him closely in a semicircle, and staring at him out of great, dull eyes.

Remembrance came back with a rush, and he gathered his muscles to spring at the hateful figures. But he could not move. At waist and throat, at wrists and ankles, were hoops of metal. He closed his eyes again while the burning waves of invisible fire shot through him recurrently from head to foot.

Dully he wondered that he was still alive. His last recollection had been of the Rogan leader pointing his shock-tube full at him, his shapeless countenance working with murderous fury. However, alive he was; and most unenviably so!

His hands, circumscribed to a few inches of movement by the bonds on his wrists, felt the smooth substance at his back. And with a thrill of horror he realized his position: he was crucified against the metal slab on which the slave had writhed in agony a short half hour ago.

Again he strained and tugged, vainly, to get free. Off to one side, pressed back against a huge glass experimental tank, he saw the beautiful Greca, her eyes wide with horror; and caught her frantic pleading message to her "Great White One."

The Rogan leader, squealing and grimacing, advanced toward the victim on the metal plate. One of the long arms went out and a sucker-disk was pressed to Dex's cheek. Dex quivered at the loathsome contact of that soft and slimy substance; then set his jaws to keep from groaning as the disk was jerked away, to carry with it a fragment of skin and flesh.

Gingerly, the tall leader felt the twitching, blackened stump of his blasted arm. Dex grinned mirthlessly at that: he'd struck one or two blows in his own defense, anyhow!

At sight of the Earthman's grin, an expression of defiance and grim joy that needed no interpreting to be understandable, the Rogan leader fairly danced with rage. His long arm went out to the switch beside the plate, and pulled it down another notch—just a little, not nearly to the current that had torn at the slave.

At the increased torment resulting from that slight movement of the regulating lever, Dex yelled aloud in spite of all his will power. It seemed as though his whole body were about to burst into self-generated flame. Every cell and fiber of him seemed on the verge of flying apart. He could feel his eyes start from his head, could feel every hair on his scalp stand up as though discharging electric sparks.

A minute or two of that and he would go mad! He cried out again, and twisted helplessly in his bonds. And then the terrible torture stopped.

The Rogan had not touched the switch—yet whatever sort of current it was that charged the plate was abruptly clicked off, as though someone at a distance had cut a wire or thrown a master-switch.

Simultaneously with its ceasing, an invisible, crushing sea seemed to envelope everything. Dex felt his body sag against his metal bonds as if it had been changed to lead.

Before him the Rogans, who had been crowding closer to watch gloatingly each grimace he made, shot doorward as though their pipe-stem legs had been swept from under them. The leader fell on the stump of his seared arm and, a deafening squeal of rage and pain came from his little mouth. His tube fell from his grasp and rolled over the floor half a dozen yards away from him.

Amazed, observing the stricken creatures only dimly through a haze of pain, Dex saw them struggle vainly to get up again, and heard them chattering excitedly to themselves. For the moment, in the face of this queer phenomenon, the prisoner seemed to be forgotten. And Dex was quick to seize the momentary advantage.

"Greca!" he called. "The tube! There—on the floor!"

The girl raised her head quickly, and followed his imploring gaze. Laboriously she started for the tube. At the same instant the Rogan leader began to feel around him for his lost weapon. Not finding it, he raised his head and glanced about for it. He saw the girl making her way toward it and, with a squeak of terror, began to crawl toward it himself.

He was not quick enough. The girl, though not nearly as active under the increased pull of gravity as a person of Earth might be, was yet more agile than the Rogans. And she was the faster mover in this tortuous, snail-like race. While the Rogan leader was still several feet away, she retrieved the shock-tube.

"Kill him!" begged Dex. "And all the rest of the filthy creatures!"

With feminine horror of the thing that faced her, Greca hesitated an instant—a hesitation almost long enough to be fatal. Then, just as the Rogan leader was reaching savagely out for her, she leveled the tube at him and turned it to its full power.

One last thin squeal came from the Rogan's mouth, a squeal that cracked abruptly at its height. What had been its gangling body drifted up in inky smoke.

"The others!" called Dex. "Quick! Before they get their weapons—"

Greca swept the death-tube in a short arc in front of her, over the bodies of the remaining Rogans, as if spraying plants with a hose. One after another, toppling in swift succession like grotesque falling dominoes, the creatures sagged to the floor and melted away. That one small part of Jupiter's red spot, at least, was cleared of Rogan population.

Long shudders racked Greca's body, and her lips were a bloodless line in her pallid face. But she did not go into womanly hysterics or swoon at the slaughter it had been her lot to inflict. Moving as quickly as she could, she went to the metal slab and began, with shaking fingers, to undo the fastenings that held Dex prisoner.

"Good girl," said Dex, patting her satiny bare shoulder as he stood free again. "You're a sport and a gentleman. You don't understand the terms? They're Earth words, Greca, that carry the highest praise a man can give a woman. But let's get out of here before another gang comes and takes us again. Where can we hide?"

"I don't know any hiding places," confessed Greca despairingly. "The Rogans swarm everywhere. We will be seen the moment we try to leave here."

"Well, we'll hunt for a hole, anyway," said Dex. He essayed to walk. What with the tendency of his muscles to jerk and collapse with the aftermath of the torture he had endured, and the sudden and inexplicable increase in gravity that bore him down, he made heavy going of it. "First we'll go up and get Brand."

"Yes, yes," said Greca, a soft glow in her clear blue eyes. "Let us go quickly."

She started toward the door, panting with the effort of moving. But Dex halted an instant, to stoop and pick up another of the tubes.

"We might as well have one of these apiece," he said. "You've proved you have the grit to use one; and maybe the dirty rats will think twice about rushing us if we each have a load of death in our hands."

THEY made their way out of the torture laboratory, and up the incline to the street level. And it was just as they reached this that the burden of gravity under which they staggered was lifted from their shoulders as quickly as it had descended on them.

Dex raised his arms just in time to fend his body from a collision with the wall in front of him. "Now what!" he exclaimed.

Greca lifted her hand for silence, inclined her head, and listened intently. As she did so, Dex heard the same noise her quick ears had caught an instant before his: a distant pandemonium of ringing gongs and siren shrieks, and squealing cries of a multitude of agitated Rogans.

"What the devil—" began Dex. But again Greca raised her hand to silence him, and listened once more. As she listened, her sea-blue eyes grew wider and wider with horror. Then, frantically, she began to race down a long corridor away from the street door.

Dex hastened to follow her. "What is it?" he demanded, when he had caught up to her flying little feet. "This is not the way up to the room where Brand—"

"Your friend is not there," she interrupted. She explained swiftly, distractedly: "From the shouts of the Rogans I learn that he got into the great dome building, somehow, and then was driven into the pen of the. . . ."

Dex could not get the next term she used. But her telepathic message of the peril she mentioned formed in his mind clearly enough.

He got a flashing brain picture of a great, high-walled yard with a monster in it of the kind he had caught a close-range glimpse a short while before. Also, he saw a blurred, tiny figure, running from wall to wall, that was Greca's imagining of Brand and his efforts to escape the enormous beast.

"Good heavens!" groaned Dex. "Penned in with one of the things they showed me while I was stretched on the rack! Are you sure, Greca?"

She nodded, and tried to run faster. "This way," she gasped, turning down a passage to the left that ended in a massive metal door. "This leads to the enclosure. Oh, if only we can be in time!"

Her slim fingers tore at a massive bolt that secured the door. "Here," said Dex, wrenching it open for her. And they stepped out into thin sunlight, onto a hard surface of reddish ground that was crisscrossed with innumerable rounded furrows like the tracks old-fashioned, fifty-passenger airplane wheels used to make on soft landing fields.

Greca shrieked, and pointed to the far end of the enclosure. Down there, flattened against the wall of the dome building, was Brand. And waddling toward him with a tread that caused the ground to quiver, was a mate to the hideous creature the Rogans had used to terrify Dex in the torture chamber.

Dex leveled the tube he was carrying, swore, hit it frenziedly against his hand. "How do you work this damned thing, Greca—Oh! Like that! There—see if *that* puts a sting in your hide!"

The distant monster stopped its advance toward Brand. A raw white spot as big as a dinner plate leaped into being on one of its enormous hind legs. It whirled with an ear-splitting hiss, to see what thing was causing such pain in its rear. The frightful head whipped back at the end of the long neck, to nuzzle at the seared spot. Then the giant lizard turned toward Brand again.

A second time Dex pressed the central coil that formed the handle of the tube, as Greca had showed him how to do. A second time the ray shot down the field to flick a chunk of flesh weighing many pounds from the monster's flank. And this time it definitely abandoned the quarry behind it. With a scream like the keening of a dozen steam whistles, it charged back over its tracks toward the distant pigmies that were inflicting such exasperating punishment on it.

Dex swept the tube before him in a short half-circle. A smoking gash appeared suddenly in the vast fore-quarters of the monster. It stopped abruptly, its clawed feet plowing along the ground with the force of its momentum. An instant it stood there. Then, with its head swinging from side to side and lowered so that its looped neck dragged on the reddish, dusty ground, it began to back away from the source of its hurt, bellowing and hissing its rage and bewilderment.

"Brand!" shouted Dex. "This end! Run, while I hold the thing off!"

Brand began to race down the long enclosure, ten feet to a leap. The great lizard darted after him, like a cat after an escaping mouse; but a flick of the tube sent it bellowing and screaming back to its corner.

"Dex!" gasped Brand. "Thank God!"

For a moment he leaned, white and shaken, against the wall. Then Greca caught his hand in both of hers, and Dex put his arm supportingly around his shoulder. They retreated back through the doorway behind them, and slid the bolt across the metal door.

CHAPTER X
The "Tank Scheme"

"THANK God you came when you did," repeated Brand. Then, with a moment in which, figuratively, to get his feet back on earth, the wonder of Dex's appearance struck him.

"How did you manage to get away?" he asked. "I was sure—I thought—when they dragged you out of the tower room I wouldn't see you again—"

Rapidly Dex gave an account of his ordeal in the torture chamber, telling Brand in a few words how he had attempted to win free of the Rogans, how he had almost succeeded, only to be caught again and clamped to the death-plate on the wall.

"But just as the big fellow was about to cook me for good and all," he concluded, "something happened to the current, and to the gravity at the same time—"

"That was when I pulled the lever in the dome building!" exclaimed Brand.

He told of what had befallen him in the Rogan power-house. "That lever, Dex!" he said swiftly. "It's the keynote of the whole business. It absolutely controls the pull of gravity, and Lord knows what else besides. If we could only get at it again! Perhaps we could not only shut it off so that Jupiter's pull would function again, but also reverse the process so its gravity would be *increased*! Think what that would mean! Every Rogan in the red empire stretched out and immovable, possibly crushed in by his own weight!"

"It's a wonderful thought," sighed Dex; while Greca's eyes glowed with a sudden hope for her enslaved race, "but I don't see how we could ever—"

He stopped; and glanced in alarm down the passage behind them. Greca and Brand, hearing the same soft noise, whirled to look, too.

Far down the passage, just sneaking around the bend, was a group of Rogan guards, each armed with a death-tube.

"Back to the pen!" cried Brand.

He slid the bolt, and jerked the door open. They rushed into the walled enclosure again, the slamming of the door behind them cutting off the enraged squeals of the Rogans.

"This isn't going to mean anything but a short delay, I'm afraid," said Brand, clenching his fists in an agony of futility. "They'll be in here in a minute, and get us like trapped rats."

"Not before we get a lot of them," said Dex grimly.

"But that isn't enough, man! We don't want to die, no matter how decently we do it. We've won free, and stayed free this long; now, somehow, we've got to reach our ship and get back to Earth to warn them of the danger that hides here for our planet!"

He strode tensely up and down, smacking his fist into his palm. "The lever!" he exclaimed. "That lever! It's our only answer! If we could get to it. . . . But how can we? We couldn't break into the dome, now the Rogans are on the watch for us, with anything less than a charge of explosives. Or a tank. God, how I'd like to have an old-fashioned, fifty-ton army tank here now!"

Greca exclaimed aloud as Brand's fleeting mental picture of one of Earth's unwieldy, long-discarded war tanks registered on her brain.

"There is the great beast there," she said hesitantly, pointing a slim forefinger at the huge lizard that had backed into a far corner and was regarding them out of dull, savage eyes. Then she shook her head. "But that is impossible. Impossible!"

The men stared at her, with dawning realization in their minds. Then they gazed at each other.

"Of course," said Brand. "Of course! Greca, you're marvelous! Wish we had a tank? Why, we've got one! A four-legged mountain of meat that ought to be able to plow through the side of that dome like a battering ram through cardboard!"

"But it's not possible," replied Greca, her head dropping dejectedly. "My people, as driven slaves, till the fields with great animals that were trapped in the surrounding jungles. They harness other great animals to haul burdens. But none of the beasts are like *this* one. This kind cannot be tamed or harnessed. It is too ferocious. It is used only as a scourge of fear, to crush us into complete submission."

"Can't be tamed?" Brand said. "We'll see about that! Come on, Dex."

"Just a minute," said Dex. He flattened against the wall, motioning them to do the same. Then he leveled his tube at the door.

Slowly, cautiously, the door began to swing back; and the Rogan that Dex had heard fumbling with the bolt stuck his huge head out to locate the escaped prisoners.

Dex pressed the release coil of his tube. Without a sound, the Rogan slumped to the ground, a smoking cavity in its shoulders at the spot where its head had been set. In an instant the body, too, disappeared; an upward coiling wisp of black smoke marking its vanishing.

Another Rogan, tiptoeing out, met the same fate; and another. And then the door was banged shut again, and the bolt ground into place on the inside.

"That'll teach 'em to be careful how they try to rush us from *that* door," said Dex, through set teeth. "Now let's see if that tank scheme of ours can be worked."

He picked up a tube dropped by one of the Rogans, and handed it to Brand; showing him which coil to press to get full force, as Greca had in turn informed him.

"Down the field," commanded Brand. "We'll go about thirty yards apart, and try to herd this brute back through the walls of the dome building. Once it's inside, we'll try to rush to the lever before the Rogans can down us, and jam the thing past its terminal peg and into reverse action. I don't know that there *is* a reverse to it—but we can try.

"Greca dear,"—the girl started at the warmth of his thought, and a faint pink rose to her pale cheeks—"you'd better stay by my side. Your place as hostage-priestess of your people wouldn't save you if those devils catch you now. Besides, you can keep your tube leveled at the doorway as we go, and discourage any Rogans who might pluck up courage to try coming out again."

They started down the field toward the nightmare thing that snarled and hissed in its corner. On one side of the big enclosure walked Brand, with Greca close beside him, glancing continuously over her shoulder at the rear door, and holding her tube in readiness to check any charge the Rogans might attempt to make from the tower building. On the other side, keeping an equal pace, advanced Dex.

With tubes of death as whips, and with death for themselves set as the stake for which they gambled, they went about their attempt to drive the brainless monster before them through the solid wall of the dome building. And there followed what was probably the strangest animal act the universe has ever witnessed.

THE first thing to do was to rout the enormous lizard out of the corner where sullen fear had sent it squatting. Dex contrived to do that by standing next to the wall at its side, and sending a searing ray that just touched the scaly, tremendously thick hide. The monster bellowed deafeningly, and, with a spot smoking on its flank, waddled sideways to the center of the field. Its head and swaying long neck faced the Earthmen and its back was against the wall of the dome building. To that extent, at least, they had the creature placed; but they soon found that the struggle had only just begun.

Brand got far enough around to focus his tube on the tip of the huge tail, in an effort to swing the gigantic thing about. There was an unearthly shriek from the colossal beast, and a foot and a half of its tail disappeared.

"Careful," called Dex, his jaw set and grim as the monster lashed out in its wrath. "If you bore in too long with that tube there'll be nothing left of our tank but a cloud of smoke."

Brand nodded, wordlessly, walking on the balls of his feet like a boxer, holding himself ready to swerve the thing should it charge them. Which—next instant—it did!

With a whistling bellow it gathered its tons of weight and thundered with incredible quickness at the gnats that were stinging its flanks and tail.

Desperately Brand played the tube across the vast chest, scoring a smouldering gash in the scale-covered flesh just above the gash Dex had seared a few moments before.

"Sorry, old fellow," Brand muttered to the screaming beast. "We hate to bait you like this, but it has to be done. Come on, now, through that wall behind you, and give us a chance at the lever."

But through the wall behind it the vast creature, not unnaturally, refused to go! It darted from side to side. Backward and forward. Up to the wall, only to back bewilderedly away from it. And constantly the tubes flicked their blistering, maddening rays along its monstrous sides and tail, as the Earthmen tried to guide it into the wall.

"Hope there's enough left of it to do the trick," said Brand, white-lipped. The monster was smoking in a dozen spots now, and several of the hump-like scales on its back had been burned away till the vast spine looked like a giant saw that was missing a third of its teeth. "God, I'm thinking we'll kill it before we can drive it through that wall!"

Greca nodded soberly, keeping her eyes on the distant door to their rear. Twice that door had been opened, and twice she had directed the death rays into its opening to mow down the gangling figures behind it. But she had said nothing of this to her man. He was busy enough with his own task!

"The door to the dome—" Dex shouted suddenly.

But Brand merely nodded, even as a discharge from his tube annihilated the Rogan that had appeared in the doorway before them. He had seen that door stealthily opening even before Dex had.

"It had better be soon, Dex!" he called. "Rogans in front of us— Rogans behind us—and—look out! On your side of the fence, there!"

Dex whirled in time to pick off a grotesque, pipe-like figure that had suddenly appeared on the broad wall of the enclosure. Then he turned to the frenzied problem of driving the monster through the building wall.

"The thing's going mad, Brand!" he cried, his voice high-pitched and brittle. "Watch out!"

It was only too evident that his statement was true. The baited monster, harried blindly this way and that, hounded against the blank wall behind it by something that bit chunks of living flesh out of its legs and sides, was losing whatever instinctive mental balance it had ever had. Its dimly functioning brain, probably no larger than a walnut in that gigantic skull, ceased more and more to guide it.

With a rasping scream that set the Earthmen's teeth on edge, it charged for the wall on Dex's side. Dex just managed to swerve it with a blast from the tube so prolonged that half its great lower jaw fell away.

At this the titanic thing went wholly, colossally mad! It whirled toward Brand, jerking around again as a searing on that side jarred its dull sensory nerves, then headed at last straight toward the stone wall of the dome building.

With the rays from both tubes flicking it like monstrous spurs, it charged insanely toward the bulge of the circular wall. With all its tons and tons of weight it crashed against the stonework. There was a thunderous crackling noise, and the wall sagged in perceptibly, while the metal roof bent to accommodate the new curvature of its supporting beams.

The monstrous lizard, jerked off its huge legs by the impact, staggered up and retreated toward the two men. But again the maddening pain in its hindquarters sent it careening toward the building wall. This time it raised high up on its hind legs in a blind effort to climb over it. "God, it must be five stories tall!" ejaculated Brand. Thunderingly its forelegs came down on the edge of the roof.

There was another deafening crash of stone and shrieking of torn metal. Just under the cornice, the wall sagged away from the roof and the top rows of heavy stone blocks slithered inward.

"Again!" shouted Brand.

His tube was pointing almost continuously now at the metal door leading from the dome building. The Rogans inside, at the shocks that were battering down a section of their great building, were all trying to get out to the yard at once. In a stream they rushed for the doorway. And in loathsome heaps they fell at the impact of the ray and shriveled to nothingness on the bombarded threshold.

"Once more—" Brand repeated, his voice hoarse and tense.

And as though the monster heard and understood, it rushed again with all its vast weight and force against the wall in a mad effort to escape the things that were blasting the living flesh from its colossal framework.

This charge was the last. With a roaring crash a section of the building thirty yards across went back and down, leaving the massive roof to sag threateningly on its battered truss-work.

It was as though the side of an ant-heap had been ripped away. Inside the domed building hundreds of Rogans ran this way and that on their elongated legs, squealing in their staccato, high-pitched tongue.

With blind fury the mad monster charged in through the gaping hole it had battered for itself. In all directions the Rogans scattered. Then an authoritative tall figure with a tube in each of its four sucker-disks, whipped out a command and pointed to the great coils which lay immediately in the berserk monster's path.

The command restored some sort of order. Losing their fear of the beast in their greater fear of the damage it might do, the Rogans massed to stop it before it could demolish the Rogan heart of power.

At this point Brand saw an opening of the kind he had been praying for. The Rogans had retreated before the terrific charge of the monster in such a way that the space between its vast bulk and the control board was clear.

"After me!" he shouted to Dex. "One of us has got to reach that lever while the creature's still there to shield us!"

The two Earthmen dashed through the jagged hole in the wall and raced to the control board just as the huge lizard, a smoking mass, sank to the floor. Brand gazed almost fearfully at the lever-slot.

Was there a reverse to the gravity-control action? There was room in the slot for the lever to be pulled down below the neutral point, if that meant anything. . . .

Behind them the great bulk of the dead lizard was disappearing with incredible quickness under the rays of the tubes directed on it. Now the pumpkin-shaped heads on the opposite side were visible through a fleeting glimpse of a skeleton that was like the framework of a skyscraper. And now the colossal bones themselves were melting, while over everything hung a pall of greasy black smoke.

"Hurry, for God's sake!" gasped Dex.

Brand threw down the lever till it stuck. At once that invisible ocean poured crushingly over them, throwing them to their knees and sweeping the Rogans flat on their hideous faces just as half a hundred tubes were flashing down to point at the Earthmen.

"More—if you can!" grated Dex, whirling this way and that and spraying the massed Rogans with his death-dealing tube. Dozens went up in smoke under that discharge; but other dozens remained to raise themselves laboriously and slowly level their suddenly ponderous weapons at the Earthmen.

Brand set his jaw and threw all his weight on the lever. It bent a little, caught at the neutral point—and then jammed down an appreciable distance beyond it.

Instantly the blue streamers, that had stopped their humming progress from coil to coil with the movement of the switch to neutral, started again in reversed direction. And instantly the invisible ocean pressed down with appalling, devastating force.

Greca and Brand and Dex were flattened to the floor as if by blankets of lead. And the scattered Rogans about them ceased all movement whatever.

"Oh," sobbed Greca, fighting for breath. "Oh!"

"We can't stand this," panted Dex. "We've fixed the Rogans, all right. But we've fixed ourselves, too! That lever has to go up a bit."

Brand nodded, finding his head almost too heavy for his neck to move. Sweat beaded his forehead—sweat that trickled heavily off his face like drops of liquid metal.

With a tremendous struggle he got to his knees beneath the master-switch. There he found it impossible to raise his arms; but, leaning back against the control board and so getting a little support, he contrived to lift his body up enough to touch the down-slanting lever with his head and move it back along its slot a fraction of an inch. The giant coils hummed a note lower; and some of the smashing weight was relieved.

"That does it, I think," Brand panted, his voice husky with exhaustion and triumph.

He began to crawl laboriously toward the nearest street exit. "On our way!" he said vibrantly. "To the space ship! We leave for Earth at once!"

SLOWLY, fighting the sagging weight of their bodies, the two Earthmen inched their way to the street, helping Greca as they went. Among the sprawled forms of the Rogans they crept, with great dull eyes rolling helplessly to observe their progress, and with feeble squeals of rage and fear and malediction following their slow path.

On the street a strange and terrible sight met their eyes.

Strewn over the metal paving like wheat stalks crushed flat by a hurricane, were thousands of Rogans. Not a muscle of their pipe-like arms or legs could they move. But the gravity that crushed them rigidly to the ground did not quite hold motionless the shorter and more sturdily built slaves.

Among the thousands of squealing, panting Rogans that lay as though paralyzed on the metal paving, crawled equal thousands of Greca's enslaved people. Their eyes flamed with fanatic hate. And methodically—not knowing what had caused their loathed masters to be stricken helpless, and not caring as long as they *were* helpless—the slaves were seeking out the shock-tubes that here and there had fallen from the clutch of Rogan guards. Already many had found them; and everywhere gangling, slimy bodies were melting in oily black smoke that almost instantly vanished in thin air.

As it was in these streets and in the great square in the center of which rested the Earthmen's ship, just so, they knew, was it being repeated all over the red empire. Slowly crawling, fiercely exulting slaves were exterminating the tyrannous things that had held them so long in dreadful bondage! Before the sun should set on another flashing Jovian day there would be no Rogan left in the red spot.

"AND so it ends," said Brand with a great sigh. He moved over beside Greca, and touched her lovely bare shoulders. They were shaking convulsively, those shoulders; and she had buried her face in her hands to keep from gazing at the ghastly carnage.

Brand pressed her to him. "It's terrible—yes. But think what it means! The knell of all the Rogans been sounded to-day. As soon as the secret of these death-tubes has been analyzed by our science and provided against, my friend and I will return from Earth with a force that shall clear the universe of the slimy devils. Meanwhile, your people are safe here; with the gravity what it is, no Rogan attacking hordes can land."

They crawled tortuously over the square to the space ship. Brand turned again to Greca; and now in his eyes was a look that needed no language of mind or tongue for its complete expression.

"Will you come to Earth with me, Greca, and stay by my side till we return to set your people in power again?"

Greca shook her head, slowly, reluctantly. "My people need leaders now. I must stay and help direct them in their new freedom. But you— you'll come back with the others from Earth?"

"Try and stop him!" grinned Dex. "And try and stop me, too! From what I know now of the way they grow 'em on your satellite"—his eyes rested on Greca's beauty with an admiration that turned her to rosy confusion—"I'd say I'd found the ideal spot to settle down in!"

Brand laughed. "He's answered for me too. And now, a salute that is used on Earth to express a promise. . . ." He kissed her—to her utter astonishment and perplexity, but to her dawning pleasure. "Good-by for a little while."

The two Earthmen hoisted themselves heavily over the sill of the control room of their ship, and crawled inside.

They secured the trap-door, and turned on the air-rectifiers. Brand moved to the controls, waved to Greca, who was smiling at him through the glass panel, and pointed the ship on its triumphant, four hundred million mile journey home.

www.ingramcontent.com/pod-product-compliance
Lightning Source LLC
Chambersburg PA
CBHW031417250626
47155CB00004B/1521